Belle Signore

by Marcelo Antinori

© Copyright 2023 Marcelo Antinori

ISBN 979-8-88824-066-3

All rights reserved. No part of this publication may be reproduced, stored in a retrieval system, or transmitted in any form or by any means—electronic, mechanical, photocopy, recording, or any other—except for brief quotations in printed reviews, without the prior written permission of the author.

This is a work of fiction. All the characters in this book are fictitious, and any resemblance to actual persons, living or dead, is purely coincidental. The names, incidents, dialogue, and opinions expressed are products of the author's imagination and are not to be construed as real.

Published by

◣ köehlerbooks™

3705 Shore Drive
Virginia Beach, VA 23455
800-435-4811
www.koehlerbooks.com

BELLE SIGNORE

— A NOVEL —

MARCELO ANTINORI

VIRGINIA BEACH
CAPE CHARLES

I tell stories. Some are true, others not. Which is which? I don't know anymore.

PROLOGUE

Campo Santa Margherita is one of the few large squares in Venice not surrounded by canals, boats, and gondolas. It is a gathering point for locals, and there, occasional tourists gently blend among small tables spread before little restaurants and cafes. It is an easy walk from the Ponte Della Academia, but not so close to any of the major tourist destinations such as Ponte Rialto or Piazza San Marco. That is why Eileen and Vicenza chose to rent an apartment there. After two months of traveling by road from Sicily to Venice, switching hotels every other day, they longed for a break. Two weeks in Venice, no driving, no packing, just a place where they could cook their meals, and a ravishing hideout to wait for two old friends sailing on the Adriatic.

The two women had arrived a week before and were still fascinated by the city. They had a glimpse of the Grand Canal from their apartment terrace and had already wandered through all canals and bridges. A dreamlike place. On that morning, they felt part of the city and had planned to buy vegetables at a groccery boat docked at San Barnaba, have a lazy coffee at the square, and go back to the apartment. They would finally meet their friends that evening.

It was a regular morning walk, but nothing seemed casual when they were around; two lively women, one American from Iowa and the other born in a small coastal town in Sicily. When they got into the Campo, it was as if everyone else faded away, opening room for them to shine. Holding Vicenza's by the arm, Eileen wore loose khaki pants, a colorful, mostly yellow, T-shirt, and a large, eye-catching green Pakistani scarf. Their clothes matched in part their personalities. Vicenza, a little soberer, had favored simple jeans, a creamy cotton shirt, and a blue silk handkerchief tied around her neck.

They stopped near the old well to observe a painter and his easel. His trashed clothes and the timeworn piece of cloth spotted with mixed colors that he held seemed alluring. His wrinkled face and his toothless open mouth, as if holding his breath while waiting for the brush to finish a delicate touch, was a sight strikingly contrasting with the elegance of the colors and details seeming to float over the canvas. The women stood a few steps behind, patiently waiting while he mixed red, yellow, and black in the pallet, trying to reach the exact shaded sunset color he was looking for.

"It's a landscape, but not like others," whispered Eileen. "I bet you can display a hundred paintings around the square, and his work will be the one attracting attention," and, she added, "Nothing there is banal or tedious."

Vicenza nodded, agreeing, but chose not to comment; she knew that Eileen could hang near the painter for hours, and Vicenza's attention had already jumped elsewhere. She was eyeing a young girl talking to a group of students in one of the corners of the square. The girl appeared very young, but others listened to her. Vicenza gently pulled Eileen toward the group, where the girl was passionately speaking about the climate and the future. They listened for a while until Eileen suggested, "We must go now. Better be back at the apartment when our friends call us. We still don't know where and if we will meet them."

They resumed walking to the San Barnaba Canal. There was a oneness in their attitude and gestures; two women, stronger for being together. They had followed their instincts, reached the highest stars, and were still alive to enjoy it. There was nothing else to prove or do, and even if the morning breeze was blowing against them, making Eileen's scarf fly behind her, they simply ignored it and kept walking confidently.

Everything on that morning was so different from their first catastrophic meeting on the steps of the little Post Office in Clairsville.

1.

First, there were sparkles. "What an annoying woman," Eileen said as soon as she got inside the post office. Miss Dillan, the clerk, was surprised by the remark. The quick exchange of words between the two women on the steps at the entrance had spawned sparks of hate.

Eileen and Vicenza had seen each other, but they had never spoken. Eileen was the writer who had moved to Clairsville, and Vicenza, a headstrong Italian who was generally talkative but secretive about her private life.

Vicenza started the conversation. She was leaving the post office when Eileen arrived, and instead of a simple greeting, Vicenza confronted Eileen, asking if it was true that Eileen was planning to fire her gardener.

"Oh yes," Eileen replied curtly "Can you believe I told her to cut down an old oak, and she refused?"

Vicenza thought for a second about shutting up; it was not her style to meddle in other people's lives, but she waved her head gently, suggesting Eileen keep talking.

"Unbelievable," Eileen continued. "I heard she is good, but I own the house, the garden, and the oak, and if I want to cut it down, I believe it's my choice to do so."

It was midafternoon, the post office was about to close, and no cars could be seen on the road, just the two women on the steps. Eileen with her blond Iowan Norwegian hair, and Vicenza, a Sicilian with her dark eyes and a solid Mediterranean look. She was carrying letters she had just retrieved from the post office.

"Hum, hum," murmured Vicenza waving her empty hand, still reluctant to say something. She preferred to avoid confrontation, but she knew Miss Tsuharu was a good gardener, and her friend. She risked. "Your gardener might be a little stubborn. *Testa di Legno*, as they say in my country. I know she hates to cut down living trees. Is the old oak threatening your house?"

"Not according to her," replied Eileen. "The trunk is hollow, and Ms. Tsuharu said it could stand for twenty more years by cutting a few branches, but that's not the point. I want to have an open lawn in front of the house, and I don't like the old oak there."

Vicenza bit her tongue. She waved the letters as if they were a hand fan and tried for an instant to keep her silence but finally capitulated.

"If that's the case, you hired the wrong gardener. I know her. She also works for me, and she doesn't do lawns." And as she had already started, Vicenza didn't stop. "There are plenty of people who could do the lawn for you, but Miss Tsuharu is not a lawnmower. She is a refined gardener capable of surrounding your house with vibrant colors, exotic shades of green, and even ponds and stones or a mystic stream. That is what she does. And I encourage you to see what she did in the large house next to mine. It's breathtaking."

Eileen was taken aback by Vicenza's insistence. Her dispute with the gardener was part of a mounting frustration with the people of this small town.

In Clairsville, on her first days, she enjoyed friendly receptions and a sense of community. Everyone, the grocery cashier, the library clerk, and the hardware store attendant, quickly learned her name. She met the antique store manager, the bakery shop owner, and the lady at the fish market, and talked with them. She was delighted. Nothing was impersonal. No more of the distant and cold relations Eileen experienced in the big city.

Despite welcoming gestures, Eileen hadn't made any friends. Everyone, though nice, seemed aloof, and now Eileen felt attacked.

"What is breathtaking for you might not be for me," Eileen huffed She might be a refined gardener, good for her, but what I need is a lawnmower."

Vicenza didn't go further. She realized it was pointless and walked away, doing her best to keep smiling. *Bitch,* she thought. *Definitely an arrogant and stubborn woman!*

• • •

Eileen was fuming when she stepped into the post office, venting her anger at the clerk. "That Vicenza is annoying and nosy. What gives her the right to tell me what to do?"

Miss Dillan, the clerk, gently weighed in.

"I would say it's probably a misunderstanding. I have known Miss Vicenza for more than twenty years, and I can tell you for sure that she is a sweet and kind person. Not only here with me in the post office, but also for our whole community." And Miss Dillan added politely. "Nobody supports Clairsville more than her."

Miss Dillan was probably the person there Eileen appreciated most. From the very first day they chatted, and it was Miss Dillan who helped Eileen find everything she needed.

Clairsville was a small place, and could feel limited, especially for newcomers. It comprised of just a couple of rural roads, a few houses, and only one public building, the post office. Not even the old church was active anymore. The church building with a few cracks on the walls had been for sale for three years, and all furniture had been auctioned and sold. The nearest gas station was closed a long time ago as well as the general store next to it. People in the hamlet very seldom got together, and it seemed to Eileen that the only thing they had in common was the zip code.

Yet, Eileen loved the place and the creek. She had bought a waterfront property where she could walk, kayak, mingle with neighbors, and eventually write a new novel. She didn't know anyone when she moved, and Miss Dillan helped her find a plumber, an HVAC expert, and a contractor to fix the porch floor and the kitchen door. That is why her polite but firm defense of Vicenza rattled Eileen, causing her to reflect on her behavior.

Eileen got into her car but did not move. She wanted to think. Her car was parked at the crossroad in front of the post office building, a one-story house recently painted, with two narrow windows, a single wooden door, and an old red roof. That was it. Nothing else around. Three local roads leading to the few houses, and a fourth and wider one connecting to the highway. She had bought her house the previous summer but had only moved in the early fall. It was already almost March, and still there was nobody Eileen could call a true, loyal friend. Inside the parked car, she recalled what she wrote about one of her characters. *"Real people inspired her stories but were not welcomed in her life."* That was a perfect portrait of herself. Most of her encounters were limited to greetings and quick chitchats. Even with Miss Dillan, with whom she only talked about where to shop or whom to call when needed. *Ironic.* Being part of the community was one of her goals, but it proved elusive.

It was already two-thirty, time to close the post office. Miss Dillon was walking to her car when Eileen approached. "I want to apologize for my words. I don't know. I had a bad day. You were right, everybody here has been nice to me, and there was no reason for that obnoxious comment." Before Miss Dillan had time to reply, Eileen continued. "Let me amend it inviting you for a cup of coffee and a slice of an apple tart that I bake his morning."

Miss Dillan was surprised but accepted. She did not have much to do at home, and she also wanted to know where Eileen lived. They drove both cars along the road that led to the pier, passing a few simple houses on the right side, mostly fishers' families. On the left, were just a series of driveway entrances leading to large and more exclusively waterfront properties. One of them was Eileen's, and when they turned into her driveway and parked in front of the house, Eileen realized that Miss Dillan was the first person she invited to her home.

"Your house is beautiful," said Miss Dillan politely as they sat inside beside a fireplace.

"As you can see, I like large spaces," replied Eileen, referring to the single open space she had inside her house, including the hallway, living room, dining room, kitchen, and office. "I'm a little claustrophobic, and I hate walls, but the truth is that I spend most of my time there." She pointed to a wide table in front of the kitchen. "There is where I work, among that mess of papers, and my favorite walk in the winter is from that chair to the fridge." And Eileen continued, proud of her decoration. "If you have a waterfront property, you must take advantage of it. This whole space and my room have wide glass doors leading to the terrace and the creek. I love that view. When I saw this terrace for the first time, I decided to buy the house. All those glass doors probably make the heater bill higher in the winter, but I don't care. And I light the fireplace every day. It relaxes me. "

Miss Dillan was also surprisingly talkative.

"I love mystery novels," she said, "and I read yours."

"Thank you, but I have never seen you at the Clairsville Book Club's meetings, and I noticed your name is on the email list."

"I follow the emails, and I read the novels, but I feel embarrassed to go to meetings. To be honest, I've never been in one of them."

Eileen asked about her preferences, and Miss Dillan shyly confessed that she loved horror books.

"Why are you shy?" asked Eileen.

"I don't know. People might think that I am deranged."

"Who cares! The world is full of deranged people. Can you imagine how boring life will be without them?"

Miss Dillan laughed and, encouraged by Eileen's words, continued. "The *Haunting of Hill House* is my favorite book and Stephen King my favorite author, but I also like mystery novels like yours."

Their conversation meandered from books to the more personal.

Miss Dillan told Eileen that after she divorced, "Or better saying, after he left me for a younger woman," she was living with her mother. "And we get along well," she clarified. "When the opportunity came for a promotion, I declined. I would have to work in a larger office far from here. In Clairsville, I can lunch at home and always be close to my mom."

Eileen then asked about the gardener.

Miss Dillan didn't mince words. "Miss Tsuharu moved to Clairsville eight years ago. Her son is a senior manager at the World Bank. When her husband died, she moved to the United States and lived in her son's house. But it didn't work. His wife is lovely, a Japanese translator, and their two kids, Haru and Akari, are the sweetest kids I have ever seen. But Miss Tsuharu had always lived in a small village surrounded by woods, and she didn't like the big American city. Four years and six months later, her son bought a summer vacation property on the same road as yours. It's the last one, yellow, with a dark gray roof, next to the pier. Her son enjoys fishing with the kids there, and Miss Tsuhara decided to stay all year long here, taking care of the garden. Miss Vicenza, who always buys fish at that pier, saw the work Miss Tsuharu did in her garden and invited her to help with the landscape of the White Stone House."

"That's Miss Vicenza's house?" asked Eileen.

"No. Miss Vicenza has a small house with a little garden, not so far from the post office. Miss Tsuharu was hired to work at the White Stone House."

Eileen looked confused. "You see Eileen, Miss Vicenza and her husband, Mr. Giuseppe, are the caretakers of an enormous property, which is next door to their house. They hired Miss Tsuhara to help them with gardening and landscaping.

"Why do you admire Miss Vicenza so much?" asked Eileen.

"She has always been special to me and to others. Now and then, she brings me those Italian deserts that she cooks. Her *tiramisu* is the best I have ever tasted. My mom dies for it. And Miss Vicenza comes to the post office every single day." Miss Dillan continued. "Vicenza writes and receives more letters than anyone here. Her family and friends are from Sicily, and they always write to her. It seems that they are not into computers and emails."

"When did she move here?" asked Eileen.

"A long time ago. She lived in the gray house near the post office. The one where Miss Cynthia and her husband Peter had lived. Later, Miss Vicenza and her husband bought the house near the big White Stone House mansion. Her husband rarely comes to the post office, but Miss Vicenza never misses a day."

"She probably has many friends here," Eileen said.

"I am not sure. I know very little about their life. She and her husband always helped with our events. The *arancini* that she prepares are famous in our county, but they never joined the potlucks we organized. Some people complained, saying they were arrogant, but finally understood that they love their privacy." And after a bite of the tart, Miss Dillan added politely, "By the way, your tart is as good as those prepared by Miss Vicenza."

"Do you know why Miss Vicenza and her husband moved to Clairsville?" Eileen asked.

"I don't know, But I can tell for sure that she is a kind person, and if you meet her again, you will like her. Next week you will complete eight months here, and it is time to have new friends."

"I'm amazed at your memory," said Eileen. "You know the year Miss Tsuharu arrived from Japan, the year her son bought the property, and the exact week I moved in."

"I have a good memory, but to be honest, I rarely speak with customers," Miss Dillan said. "I often see people using what they know to harm others, and I don't want to be part of it. But you are different, you are a writer, and probably because of that, I trust you. Besides, Clairsville doesn't like talkers. It's a local people's saying, and I believe it's true. Here only a few people talk about other people's lives. It seems that those who are gossipers get into trouble."

"Explain it to me," Eileen pleaded.

"It started a long time ago. A woman, who was the main local gossiper, had a problem with the county because of her aseptic tank, and she had to move away. Later, a man who moved to Clairsville and was also an easy talker had his house burned in a fire, and then, it was Miss Vicenza's previous gardener. He started to drink and invent stories about people. Later he had a big fight with Jimmy, the electrician working for you, and then moved away. Coincidence, perhaps, but Clairsville doesn't seem to like talkers. That is why, better keep our mouth shut."

Interesting advice, thought Eileen, closing the door as Miss Dillan left. Still a question lingered. *Miss Dillan remembers all dates and facts precisely, but she doesn't know why and when Vicenza moved to Clairsville or what her husband does. Odd.*

2.

Time for amendments. The following morning Eileen woke up determined. She wanted to break her isolation and start by talking with Vicenza. There was no reason for that argument. Eileen had seen her a few times in the post office, chatting with neighbors, and once buying fish at the pier. Vicenza's confident posture, her gestures, constantly moving hands while speaking, and her thick eyebrows, somewhat intimidating, exuded confidence. Whatever happened the day before was Eileen's fault and not hers. She could hire whomever she wanted, but why not listen to neighbors' opinions. She drove early to Vicenza's house. *Why not?* Vicenza had encouraged her to visit the neighbor's garden.

Vicenza's house was on the opposite side of Eileen's property. It was a shorter road with no waterfront and among a few other modest homes. After the Civil War, a grateful landlord offered some plots to soldiers who fought for the Union, and that's how Clairsville was born.

Vicenza's house was at the end of the road, and Eileen saw her pickup truck parked in front of a two-story house. Small but very well cared for, it had a front porch and two rocking chairs. Eileen walked towards the door and rang the bell. She waited, rang again, but nobody came. Eileen looked around. Behind Vicenza's house was a wall of trees densely arranged.

Eileen walked around for a few minutes, and the neighbor's house also seemed empty. She was already walking back to the car when Vicenza appeared holding a mug of coffee. "Sorry, I was busy, and it took me a while to realize that the bell was ringing."

"It's me who has to say sorry," replied Eileen walking towards her. "First, an apology for yesterday. I was having a bad day. And second, sorry for showing up without warning, but I do not have your telephone number."

"Don't worry," said Vicenza. "I'm glad that you came. I should not have questioned your decisions. It's your property, and you should do whatever you want." Vicenza invited Eileen to come inside, but seemed awkwardly nervous as she was not used to having guests.

"I'm drinking coffee, and I would like to make one for you too," Vicenza said.

Eileen walked in relaxed, carefully examining her surroundings. She crossed the living room and got into a cozy kitchen, everything unpretentious but remarkably organized. There was not a chair out of place, a single pot open, or a spoon left inside the kitchen sink. Vicenza opened two cabinets in the kitchen looking for something. Eileen noticed that Vicenza seemed uncomfortable.

"Actually, I came to visit your neighbor's garden, and I'm willing to reconsider my decision about Miss Tsuharu. But I would like to better understand why you are so impressed with her work. If you don't mind, I would prefer to see the garden first and have the coffee later."

Vicenza hesitated for a second. The neighbor's house carried a secret. Still, she was pleased to see Eileen. Perhaps it was her apologetic attitude, or the casual but elegant clothes she wore, not the traditional wear-what-is-at-hand of Clairsville. *No harm to chat,* Vicenza thought.

When they were leaving the kitchen, Eileen said, "How can you keep your home so clean? My house is a mess compared to yours."

"My husband is away," replied Vicenza opening the back door. "And my house is easy to take care of. It is just a shack compared with my neighbor's. Follow me, and you will see."

They walked through Vicenza's backyard and crossed a wooden gate leading to the neighbor's garden. "They are never here," explained

Vicenza. "My husband and I keep an eye on the property to ensure that everything is fine. And one of the things we do is to supervise the gardener's work."

They passed through the high trees wall, and Eileen noticed many evergreen bushes planted within the trees. Someone from outside would never be able to realize that there was a garden inside.

When they crossed the wall of trees, Eileen stopped. She was shocked. The neighbor's property was staggering, larger than anything she had seen, a mansion with an outdoor patio, a large swimming pool, and two spacious guest houses, and everything surrounded by a dreamlike garden completely concealed from outside viewers.

"The main entrance to the property is through a private road that comes straight from the highway," Vicenza said. "They never cross Clairsville, and that is why nobody here knows them."

Eileen knew that Clairsville had huge waterfront mansions; she had seen a few pictures when looking for a property. But Vicenza's neighbor's home was more than a mansion. It was a compound of mansions. The main house was enormous, and the style was not classical American but rather something soberer with a Tuscan twist. Despite winter, the garden was a feast of colorful greens, with almost no lawn, only tiny spots covered by grass and paths surrounded by boxwoods. Some areas glowed under the sun, while others were discreetly arranged around stones, with moss and ferns protecting an intimate shade. Eileen started to ramble around, overwhelmed as Vicenza followed her in silence.

Eileen could see that there was an enormous greenhouse behind the house. "They imported some trees that would not stand the winter," Vicenza said. "In the spring, we bring them outside. And there is also a vegetable garden. Much of what they consume comes from there."

On the left side of the mansion, Eileen saw the creek's waters quivering between trees. She noticed the dock in the waterfront protected by a combination of loblolly pines and Japanese red maples. Eileen spotted a vintage wooden sailing yacht anchored with a glowing varnished deck.

Eileen was startled and walked towards the two cottages, both larger than her own house. She stopped in front of a giant weeping ficus, with roots hanging from its branches like a curtain of shadow. From there, she could see a third and smaller cottage, almost in the woods, and she spotted an area covered by tiny light gravel with a few bunches of grass, scattered around a dark and imponent bolder perched over soft gray stones.

"This garden is a dream," she exclaimed returning to reality.

"That's what you have to decide," insisted Vicenza. "If you want a big lawn, you just have to hire some kids to mow it once a week, but with Miss Tsuharu, your house landscaping and garden could be spectacular, like this."

They walked around the pool, which was open despite the still cold weather. It was dark blue contrasting with a massive white stone descending in steps to the water. Eileen had never seen such an ornate pool.

"The contrast between the pool waters and this huge stone is dazzling. Is it some kind of marble?" asked Eileen.

"No, it's limestone, and it's not from here. It's a white stone imported from Europe. That is why this whole place is called the *White Stone House*."

"The houses and grounds are stunning. Who lives here?"

"Nobody," replied Vicenza opening her arms. "The owners rarely come, and when they do, they only stay for two or three days. Isn't that great? My husband and I have been the caretakers for twenty years, and we barely see them. We hire professionals to keep the house clean, the garden maintained, and do the needed repairs. It's an easy job, and quite convenient from the financial point of view."

They toured the guest houses, all the same light green color as the main mansion, and Eileen noticed some classic Roman sculptures and large oak trees spread around them.

"Okay, that's enough," said Vicenza interrupting Eileen's daydream. "Let's go back to reality and have our coffee?"

Eileen hesitated, wanting to stay there indefinitely and even peek inside the houses, but she knew it was too much to ask.

Inside Vicenza's house, Eileen's first comment was, "I think I will call Miss Tsuharu back."

They kept chatting about the garden. Vicenza seemed to know all plant and flower names. "It took us years to have it that way. Most plants are native, with just a few imported, such as the ficus tree, some Italian pines, and the plumeria flowers."

"Is it the ficus that one with roots falling out of the branches?"

"Yes, and the plumerias are the white and yellow little flowers. Those that here they call Frangipani," Vicenza added proudly. "But those you saw were imported from Italy."

"Can you import flower seeds," asked Eileen, surprised.

"It's not easy, but when you want, there is always a way to do it," replied Vicenza with a cocky smile.

"Why did you move to Clairsville?" asked Eileen.

"Long story. Pippo and I lived in Sicily, and we were wild when young. Actually, too wild. And we decided that it was time to move to a calmer place."

"When was that?"

"More than twenty years ago," said Vicenza. "When we moved here, many people thought we would give up in a few months, but they were wrong. We survived with no complaints. And what about you? Why did you come to Clairsville? Are you searching for peace?"

"Not exactly. My life has always been peaceful. Perhaps too much. But I was tired of the big city loneliness."

"Are you married?" probed Vicenza.

"I was, long ago, and I have two sons living in California. The oldest one studies journalism in LA, and the youngest started college in San Luis Obispo. He wants to be an engineer. My ex-husband currently lives in Florence," she added with an ironic expression, "with his *male* partner, an internationally known fashion designer."

"Life is full of surprises," Vicenza said, smiling. "But there is a silver lining. Without a husband, you probably have more time to write."

"True, but I don't know if I want to write anymore." Eileen was surprised by her bluntness and honesty. She was usually very guarded, but Vicenza seemed trustworthy, so she continued. "I already wrote enough, and I believe that I don't have anything else to say."

"Writer's block?" asked Vicenza.

"Kind of, but it's not that. If I want to create a plot, I'm sure I can do it, but why? I published a few books, one of them was even adapted into a movie. My ego is served, and I have enough money to pay my bills."

"But don't you miss writing?"

"I miss it, and I'm always thinking or researching for something, but I would only write a new novel if I'm passionate about it, and I'm not. After I divorced, I went to Santa Barbara with my kids. A lovely place where I wrote a few stories but barely made friends. Then my kids were grown, so I came to Washington. Nothing changed, a thrilling city, good restaurants, nice places to go, but that was all. No friends or social life. Now I am here in Clairsville in search of people. I want to feel like part of a real community. I know there are no stories here, and few things happen, but at least I know that Jimmy is my grumpy electrician, Miss Tsuharu is stubborn, and Miss Dillan is an enchanting woman. I know the names and lives of those around me, and in a certain sense, I care for them. And even if it's illogical, I feel they care for me."

"And why don't you write a story about them? Do you know that your grumpy Jimmy sings, is an excellent chef, and is the sweetest man in town when he is drunk? Miss Dillan, our post office clerk, has a photographic memory and can tell you how many letters each one of us received last year. I'm surprised that she talked to you. She is known as a woman of few words. And there is more. You haven't met

La Vero. She is the most unique person around, a Mexican woman who used to clean my neighbor's house and now paints colorful church benches. You must visit her. The work she does is baffling."

"I know that they all have their stories," replied Eileen, "but I already read so many novels that I would only be satisfied by something yet untold. Something powerful and mysterious. Who knows? But let me tell you that you convinced me to ask Miss Tsuharu's help with the garden." She paused. "But now it's getting late, I have to go back home."

Vicenza just nodded. She was probably thinking about an incredible story she knew had never been told, but she could not reveal it. Not if she wanted to stay alive.

3.

Meeting the neighbors. Talking with Vicenza was refreshing. The Italian woman was intense yet pleasant, different from all the women she met in Clairsville. Still, Eileen was intrigued. *How could a woman like Vicenza be fulfilled living at the bottom of a rural road?*

As the cold weather was fading, Eileen walked to the pier and past Miss Tsuharu's house. Her garden was less exuberant and didn't have the privacy of Vicenza's wealthy neighbors, but it was alluring. Japanese red maples, boxwoods, hydrangeas, grew next to shaded areas with moss and stones. Miss Tsuharu was kneeling next to the peonies.

Eileen approached her and mentioned how much she had loved the garden she saw.

"It took many years to get there," Miss Tsuharu replied humbly. "Miss Vicenza is mainly responsible. She designed it with another gardener. I only got the job when he moved away," Miss Tsuharu said. "She is the one who chose every plant you saw."

"I didn't know she was an expert," said Eileen.

"She was not. She told me that she could barely recognize daffodils in the spring when she got here, but she learned. Please tell me which plants you love the most."

Eileen thought for a moment. "Hydrangeas, I love their abundance, and lilies, particularly the oriental lilies, white and pink."

"I have a few of them here, but they will only bloom in the summer. First, we have the snowdrops and the daffodils that, as you can see, are ready to bloom. Later will be the turn of these peonies that I'm pruning, and in June, the lilies. But I planted them on the other side of the house. In the summer, when my grandkids are here, we spend most of the time near the dock, and that is why I prefer the lilies there. I have them in all colors, white, yellow, pink, orange and red. My granddaughter loves them."

"Could you help me with my garden?" said Eileen. "Now I understand what you were trying to tell me, and I will follow your advice."

"It would be an honor for me. Next week, I'll be at your house with some assistants to cut a few branches of the old oak. The lighter it is, the longer it will live, and I will also take a few hydrangeas, and let's hope we still have time to plant the lilies. I planted mine in the fall, but I believe the lilies will still have time to settle, but only if we are lucky and the rains do not come early. Next fall we will plant more."

Eileen returned to her house feeling lighter, but she had to hurry. She expected Jimmy, the electrician, before lunch. He was redoing her house's wiring. She saw his van turning into her driveway.

Jimmy was recommended by Miss Dillan. He was a grumpy man, and Eileen tried to soothe him with a cup of coffee. "I just made it," she said. Jimmy took it with a chilly expression. "You have an Italian last name, Palumbo. Are you Italian?"

"Not exactly, I'm Sicilian," he huffed turning back to his wires.

Eileen persisted. "I've never been to Sicily, but I read *Lampedusa* and most of Andrea Camillieri's books. I've heard that you are a great chef. Do you think you can teach me to prepare *pasta ncasciata*?"

"How do you know that dish?" Jimmy replied, turning and looking into Eileen's eyes for the first time.

"I ate it once in New York, and it's the favorite dish of Commissario Montalbano, the main character of Camillieri's novels."

"It's an easy dish to do it," Jimmy answered with a slight smile. "You just need eggplant and caciocavallo cheese."

"And do you know how to cook the arancini?" she continued.

"Of course," he answered proudly. "I'm Sicilian, and my arancini are the best on this side of the Atlantic."

Jimmy explained how to prepare and fry the stuffed rice balls. The more he talked, the more comfortable he seemed, until Eileen mentioned Vicenza.

"Yesterday, I met her, and she also cooks arancini. Do you know her?"

Jimmy frowned and his demeanor turned chilly. "Listen, you asked me to do the wiring as soon as possible. Please, let me do my work." He opened his toolbox showing that the conversation was over.

He was a proud chef, concluded Eileen, but seemingly not Vicenza's friend. Anyhow, it was a successful first step.

・・・

While walking to the post office, Eileen thought that her problem was not that she disliked meeting people but that she loved her private daily routine. She liked to plan her day, work at the computer in the early morning, read in the afternoon. Meeting people was a disruption, but she was willing to change.

As she approached the post office, she met Klaus, a retired fisherman who still wore his yellow fishing raincoat. She had chatted with him before, and to be friendly, she mentioned that the weather was improving.

"Be careful with sunny days at the end of the winter," Klaus said. "The water is still freezing. On a day like this I felt from the boat." He told her about the day he almost died of hypothermia and was saved by other watermen.

When he finished his story, Eileen mentioned the boat she saw at Vicenza's neighbor's dock. "A beautiful wooden boat."

"*Marinella* is the most exquisite boat in the Chesapeake Bay," Klaus smiled.

"Who owns it?" asked Eileen.

"I don't know. They own the boat, the dock, and the property, but nobody knows who they are. Only Mr. Giuseppe and Miss Vicenza. From time to time, you can see *Marinella* sailing with guests, but it's Mr. Giuseppe and Miss Vicenza who sail it most of the time. It's a Norwegian yawl built seventy years ago. Old things like me can still be handsome when preciously maintained," Klaus quipped. "Every winter, they take the boat out of the water to paint the bottom and entirely varnish it. It's a work of art that only millionaires can afford. Mr. Giuseppe is a lucky man. He has the boat, practically for himself."

"And do you know him?"

"Every waterman knows him. Mr. Giuseppe always stops for a word when crossing fishermen's boats, and he helped many people, including my son, to get loans in moments of need. The first time I met him, I was at one of the southern creeks, and my engine quit. I signaled to him, and he helped me. He pulled my boat to a safe cove where I anchored it, and then took me back to the pier. And I know that he helped other watermen too. When Gary, my cousin's boat caught fire, Mr. Giuseppe helped him buy a new one. My son also got help from him. I can tell you for sure that he is a nice man and a skilled seaman. I often see him sailing alone, and you need to be an experienced sailor to handle those large sails on a windy day. His boat is a forty-eight foot and not an easy to navigate."

Klaus continued on his way home, and Eileen walked into the post office, where she had to wait while Miss Dillan helped a young woman who had a box full of mail to post. When she finished and the woman left, Miss Dillan explained. "Her name is Susan, and she is not from here. She and her husband met when he worked for a commercial fishing company on the West Coast. He was born here and wanted to know how they fished crabs in the Pacific, but he surprised his family, bringing a wife when he returned. His family initially rejected her, but now that the couple has a successful crab business, they praise her, and the truth is that she is the one that runs everything. That is why she always has letters to post. The husband only fishes."

Eileen told Miss Dillan that she had met Vicenza and talked with

Miss Tsuharu. Miss Dillan approved with a smile, and Eileen added, "Vicenza suggested that I meet someone you should know, Miss La Vero. Do you know where she lives?"

Miss Dillan seemed dazed. "Are you sure she suggested you meet Miss La Vero?"

"Yes," replied Eileen. "She told me that she does colorful benches, and I might need one for my terrace."

Miss Dillan shrugged and reluctantly told Eileen how to get there.

• • •

Eileen assumed the directions were wrong when she entered a narrow gravel path practically hidden in the woods. There were no houses around, but she hesitantly drove a little farther and reached a log cabin near a pond that immediately reminded her of Henry Thoreau's *Walden*.

As soon as she parked, La Vero came to the door. Eileen got the impression that she was meeting Frida Kahlo's reincarnation. La Vero wore a colorful dress, with yellow embroidery, red drawings, and shining green contrasts, like a Mexican painting. She was tall and had a braid tied around her head with a large yellow flower tucked on the left side. Stunning. And despite her exuberant clothes, she seemed reserved.

Her house was crowded with benches, chairs, and mirrors painted with Mexican motifs. Everything was chaotically placed, but colorful as her clothes.

Eileen examined La Vero's artwork and chose two pieces, a red and yellow church bench for the mudroom, and a colorful wooden mirror frame for the main entrance. She was so distracted by the liveness of La Vero's art that she barely looked at her.

When she sat to sign the check, Eileen stared at her and realized La Vero's strong hands and the prominent Adam's apple. Despite her femininity, La Vero was not born a woman.

Eileen was so intrigued that she could not resist asking. "You are a beautiful woman, but you also have manly attributes. Is there a secret there?"

"Yes, but I won't call it a secret. Better to say it's an unspoken truth. I'm a *muxe*. That is how my people call those born on a man's body and a woman's heart. For us, the Zapotecas people, the third gender is as common as the other two, and I know that it may seem strange, but I never had a problem. Either people don't notice, or they're too shy to ask. The truth is that you are one of the first persons in Clairsville to ask me this question directly."

"And how did a muxe from Oaxaca became La Vero, the Clairsville artist?" asked Eileen.

"My name is Veronica. I chose La Vero to give it an artistic touch," she said, her words and expressions sounding naturally feminine. "As a child, my dream was to visit Mexico City, the capital, and I went there, but I realized that it was not for me. Unfortunately, large cities are a problem for me. From Mexico City, I crossed the border to San Diego, where I found nothing but trouble. People seem to think that muxes are doomed to be prostitutes. I also tried Los Angeles, and later I came to Richmond, invited by a cousin from Oaxaca who lives there. Through him, I found a job at a cleaning company on the Eastern Shore, and for many years I cleaned mansions in this area. That's how I met Mr. Giuseppe and Vicenza."

"Did you clean the big house next to Vicenza's?" asked Eileen.

"Yes, for almost three years."

"And who owns that mansion?"

"I don't know, but Mr. Giuseppe and Vicenza are the ones that take care of it. We became friends, and Vicenza saw my artwork. She liked it, and I painted a chair for her. It was Vicenza who came up with the idea of the benches. They knew an Italian priest who was refurbishing a church and who wanted to get rid of the old benches. They bought them, asked me to paint them, and we quickly sold them for a lot of money. Since then, I moved to this house where I can dedicate all my time to painting."

"And you never went back to Oaxaca?"

"Oh, yes. I go there as often as I can. Last year, I went there twice. My parents still live there, and I am helping them build a new house."

Eileen wished to probe deeper, but La Vero's movements signaled that it was time to go. "Sorry, but I need to deliver some benches on the weekend, and I didn't finish them, but feel free to come back whenever you want. Next time, if you call me before, I promise to prepare a *capirotada*, which is a bread pudding that my mother used to do in Oaxaca." And she added with a contagious smile, "Vicenza loves it."

Eileen was amazed, La Vero was certainly a remarkable woman, and before going home, Eileen passed by the supermarket to buy some groceries. While paying, she spoke to the cashier, who always liked to chitchat. "I met an interesting woman, La Vero. Do you know her?"

"I know who she is, but I never saw her. She doesn't come here. I know that she paints colorful benches and that she is a close friend of Miss Vicenza."

"And you know, Miss Vicenza well?"

"Oh yes, she is very nice, and she comes here a lot, especially when there are guests in her neighbor's house. She is an excellent chef. Sometimes, she brings the desserts she makes."

"I know," said Eileen, "the famous *tiramisu*."

"It's delicious," confirmed the cashier.

"And I heard that Jimmy the electrician is a great chef too," added Eileen.

"He is. Last year we invited him to our Thanksgiving potluck, and he roasted a piglet, which you wouldn't believe. The tastiest meat I have ever eaten. Of all the Italians, he is known as the best in the kitchen."

"More than Miss Vicenza?"

"From what I heard, she is good with cakes and desserts, but he is the real chef. Many restaurants offered him a job, but he never accepted. He used to say that he only cooks for friends, and his friends are all Italians."

"Are there many Italians here?" asked Eileen.

"A few. There was a time after they arrived when some people started wondering if they were part of the Italian Mafia. The rumor was that the Department of Justice was buying houses in our county for the witness protection program."

"Was it true?" asked Eileen, surprised.

"No, it was more a joke than a rumor. How could people think that Miss Vicenza was involved with Mafia, but you know, people like to talk," the cashier added, laughing. "All Italians who came to our area are very nice. The only grumpy one is Jimmy, but a few drinks smooth his crankiness."

. . .

When Eileen got home, she Googled the FBI Witness Protection Program, and even tried to look for Mafia mentions from news articles from the mid-nineties when Vicenza moved to Clairsville. She didn't find anything that gave her a hint. Vicenza and her husband were Italians, and in Vicenza's own words, they had a wild youth. *Was it possible,* Eileen wondered, *that Vicenza and her spouse were hidden in Clairsville by the US government? Perhaps, people's suspicions are not entirely crazy.*

4.

She was curious. The pieces she bought from La Vero refreshed her house, and Eileen felt happy. The days were still cold but sunny, and Jimmy had finally finished the rewiring. Miss Tsuharu cut the old oak branches, pruned some trees, and agreed with Eileen on the overall garden structure, and the place to plant the hydrangeas. Her garden was bound to be eye-catching, very soon.

Eileen also changed her routine, visiting the post office daily to check the mail, which she rarely had, to meet neighbors, and to talk to Miss Dillan. But she never saw Vicenza there. "She comes very early," explained Miss Dillan. "Always the first, and she seems to be swamped these days."

Eileen did not have Vicenza's telephone number, but with the warmer afternoons, she started to bike and casually pass in front of Vicenza's house.

The first time, she stopped and rang the bell on the porch, no one came. Eileen went around the house. The pickup was there, and she looked through the kitchen window. The place looked empty, and the kitchen was again perfectly organized. It seemed as if nobody had touched it. In the backyard, the passage to the neighbor's property was open, and Eileen could hear people talking. She crossed through the gate to have a peek inside.

Eileen saw a few men walking towards the main house, and she left.

The next day she returned; the pickup was parked in the same place, the house was again empty, the kitchen was pristine, and the backyard gate was open. Eileen walked inside the neighbor's garden, carefully hiding behind the trees. Nobody was outside, but she saw a few people, mostly men, gathered inside some sort of sunroom with large glass windows next to the pool. Again, she fled, but this time she left a note on Vicenza's front porch with her telephone number and a message. *Would you like to come to my house for a coffee?*

The afternoon was sunny and pleasant, so Eileen continued to bike towards the pier where she encountered Klaus near his son's boat. His son was unloading bushels of oysters. Eileen's thoughts were still at Vicenza's neighbor's house, and while looking at the boat she recalled the line of Longfellow's poem. *"One if by land and two if by sea."* Perhaps she could find some answers by watching the mysterious White Stone House from the creek.

"Would it be possible for you to take me for a ride on your boat?" she asked Klaus's son. "I'm willing to pay for it. I moved here last fall, and it was too cold to kayak during winter. Now I feel that I know all roads, but I never saw the creek."

Klaus encouraged his son to accept. "Just a quick ride," he said. And after they unloaded the oysters, Eileen got into the boat, and Klaus went with them.

They slowly navigated near the shore, and Eileen saw the large waterfront houses and their docks. They passed her property and continued to the small creek where Vicenza's neighbor yacht, *Marinella*, was placidly docked. Even knowing that the mansion and the guesthouses were there, she could not see them.

"Ravishing boat," said Eileen, and father and son agreed with her.

"You should see her inside," said Klaus. "*Marinella* is beautiful. Walls, galleys, table, all in varnished teak, and a spacious cabin with a large couch and a dining table. The main bedroom has a private bathroom at the stern with a glass shower box and a sink. And there are two guest bedrooms with another bathroom on the bow. I could live there with my whole family," said Klaus, laughing.

"I know that he helped you to get a loan," said Eileen, looking at the son.

"A loan with no interest. And I'm paying it back as I can."

"Wow. With what bank did he get this deal? I also want one for me," teased Eileen.

"It was not with a bank. I would never be able to repay them. It's a man he knows with money who uses it to finance fishermen like us."

"Great," said Eileen, as the son continued. "Yesterday, he was sailing *Marinella* with other people, probably guests, and Miss Vicenza was with them." Eileen didn't ask any more questions, and they returned to the pier. She was puzzled. Since when do caretakers and guests sail together? *Intriguing.*

A cloudy past, an intriguing house, a gate in the backyard to a mansion, and a vintage yacht. And not only that, an almost exotic, somewhat Arab look, and self-confidence that certainly didn't fit in that little house at the end of the road.

• • •

The next day Eileen got a pleasant surprise. Vicenza called and came to her house. "I heard that you were asking about my *tiramisu*, and I made one just for you," said Vicenza at the door.

Before having coffee, Eileen walked with her through the garden.

"Sorry to say that I agree with Miss Tsuharu," Vicenza said. "The old oak brings personality to your property."

"Now I understand it," agreed Eileen. "Miss Tsuharu cut two branches leaning toward the house, and the treetop is lighter and safer."

Eileen showed her the place around the driveway where they planned to plant the hydrangeas as Vicenza commented. "I believe you can intercalate them with forsythias and rose knockouts. Your driveway will be as colorful as one of La Vero's benches."

"You know what I hear about you?" said Eileen, changing the

subject. "Your life is so mysterious that some people in Clairsville believe that you were part of the witness protection program," she said with a giggle.

"Who said that?" replied Vicenza.

"I don't remember," prudently responded Eileen.

Vicenza wasn't amused. Raising her right hand with the palm forward she said, "Stop. Our life is a mystery, okay, but we never bother anyone. Pippo and I love our stuff, that's all."

"You don't need to feel hurt. I was merely teasing you," replied Eileen. "I'm not a gossiper. But I'm curious, perhaps because I am a writer."

"I don't want you writing about me," said Vicenza, looking earnest.

"I promise I won't. I just want to enjoy your company, but I must confess I was intrigued when you said you had a wild youth. I'm sure that we have more interesting things to talk about than small-town gossip." Eileen continued. "Do you want to know how I discovered that my husband was gay?"

"Well, it might be fun. Go ahead," replied Vicenza, smiling.

"Actually, he told me. We had an absolutely normal life. Boring, perhaps, but not unbearable. At least for me. I was so focused on my teenage boys that I didn't realize what was happening with him. One day, he told me he wanted to take the kids to New York. We were living in Philadelphia. I'm from Iowa, my husband is from Illinois, and we both went to college in Pennsylvania. The trip was supposed to be boys' only. They spent two days there, and he opened up to the kids. When they returned, he announced to me at the kitchen table, 'I'm gay, and I do not want to live a gay's life behind your back.' He also said that he had a job offer to move to New York, but by himself. He was as straightforward and as honest.

A week later, he left the house and only took what he could fit in his car. The divorce was amicable, and I kept the house. I was so shocked and hurt, that the kids suggested a change of scenery. So, during the summer, the kids and I moved to Santa Barbara. My ex-husband and I are still friends, but I never saw him again. He lived a few years in New York and later moved with his boyfriend to Italy. The kids met him a few times in New York and once in Florence, but I believe they struggled to accept the whole thing." Eileen paused and then asked, "And what about you, Vicenza? Do you have kids?"

"No. Pippo and I were always too selfish, and thanks be to God, I never got pregnant."

"How long are you together?" Eileen asked.

"Pippo and I were best friends since we were kids. We used to play together, and when I was fifteen, we ran away from our families. My only man ever. First in Sicily and after, here in Clairsville. He is a great companion. Funny, and the smartest person I ever met. He is ambitious, always looking ahead. No matter how much we accomplish, he always wants more. Sometimes I think that it is a man thing. They are always wishing for what they don't have."

Eileen agreed. "Ernest Hemingway, an author that I particularly love, opened *The Snows of Kilimanjaro* by describing a brave leopard that died while trying to reach the top of the mountain. Some people don't understand that the higher you reach, the higher the mountain becomes."

"What are you suggesting? That we should accept what we have, and that's it?" Vicenza asked.

"No, of course not. If we stay in the valley, we are vulnerable and cannot control our life. We need to move up, but there is a point where we can stop and enjoy what we have, don't you think?"

"Maybe, but tell me now about your books," Vicenza said

"No, you tell me about your letters. Miss Dillan told me that you are her best customer. It's amazing. You receive letters every day, and I received just two or three since I got here. The rest was just bills and donation requests."

"Since I left Sicily, I never returned, and I keep writing to my friends. That's the only way I could know what is going on in my country. Newspapers never write about my friends."

"It's so surprising," said Eileen. "After more than twenty years abroad, you still have friends there."

"Many, and all women," proudly declared Vicenza, opening her arms as if she were on the stage. "And not only from my village. I have friends in Palermo, Trapani, Caltanissetta, Agrigento," and she kept waving her left hand while telling the other city's names. "Caltabellota, Salemi, Santa Ninfa, Roccamena, and Chiusa Sclafani. Little villages that you never heard about. My friends like to write me."

"And what do you tell them about? Breaking news from Clairsville," replied Eileen sarcastically.

"No. Of course not. We only talk about Sicily. My friends' lives are mostly limited to their houses and their families. None of them read newspapers, and they all hate TV news. They don't care what the politicians do or don't, but they like to write about their kids, husbands, and parents. That's what matters to them, and that is what we write about it."

"But how do you keep these exchanges if you don't have much to tell?"

"I'm not a writer like you who creates stories. I'm more of a gossiper. They all like to write me about what they heard, and when I write, I tell back to the others what I read. I'm a focal point that spreads information," Vicenza teased.

"Do you handwrite your letters?" asked Eileen.

"All of them. You should see my table. Many open letters are waiting for replies, and hundreds of notes reminding me of things that I should write about."

"And where do you write?" Eileen asked.

"At my office," responded Vicenza without thinking.

"I didn't see your office when I was at your house."

Vicenza immediately tried to clarify. "I call it my office, but it's also the second bedroom," she said and then changed the subject. "I'm worried about Pippo. He is acting weird, and I think he is depressed. His moods are affecting our work."

"From what I know, your work is to take care of your neighbor's house, which doesn't look stressful to me," Eileen said.

"We do other stuff too," replied Vicenza. "Pippo is taking some medication, and everything seems to be fine, but there are days that he is weird."

"Some people get depressed with age," Eileen said.

"But not my husband," countered Vicenza "Contrary to what you might think, our life has always been intense. We never have a dull moment. And now I'm worried. I can't do everything by myself. The last days were a nightmare. I need him . . . and I have no idea why I'm telling you that."

"I wish I could meet him," said Eileen. "From what I hear, he is a nice man."

"And what did you hear, my curious friend? Have you been going around asking about us?"

"Don't be paranoid. I'm not going around asking questions. Yesterday I talked with some fishermen, and they mentioned your husband and his boat."

"It's not his boat. He wishes. It's our neighbor's boat, and Pippo takes care of it. I'm sure that you will hear people saying that Pippo sometimes takes the boat for sailing by himself. It's true. As it's also true that sometimes he drives our neighbor's Corvettes. They have a collection, five to be precise, including a 1960 classic convertible and a brand-new Stingray that looks like a spacecraft. *Marinella*, the yacht also belongs to our neighbors, but they don't use it. We are supposed to take care of all the property, including the cars and *Marinella*, and there are days that I want to walk in the garden, others that Pippo wants to drive the Corvettes or sail in the bay, and we do it. No harm. Everything is insured, and the owners are pleased that we take excellent care of everything they have. But you know something, you are a sorceress. Miss Dillan, who doesn't talk to anybody else, is now your confidant, and look at me. You made me tell you secrets on our second meeting,"

Their conversation was interrupted when Vicenza received a phone call from La Vero. Vicenza didn't say anything, but her look was troubled, and she immediately left. Eileen was even more intrigued. What had La Vero said that made Vicenza so worried?

5.

Sailing troubled waters. When Eileen picked up her mail that evening, she waited until nobody else was inside the post office and asked Miss Dillan, "What do you know about La Vero?"

"Not too much. She moved to Clairsville when she bought James Clarence's house. Old James didn't like people and lived secluded in the woods. Everyone was surprised that La Vero chose such an isolated place, and I can assure you that it was not for the price since what she paid for the property would be enough to buy a non-waterfront house on any Clairsville road. People thought that nobody would want that property. It is completely isolated. But for the luck of Old James' sons, La Vero made an offer. It seems she needs a peaceful and silent environment to do her artwork."

"And she lives alone?" asked Eileen.

"From what I know, yes. No family and no friends other than Miss Vicenza and Mr. Giuseppe, but she always receives letters from her parents in Mexico. They write her every other week, and she replies to the letters."

"Interesting. A beautiful woman and no boyfriends?" Eileen probed.

"Not that I know," answered Miss Dillan, who stopped for a moment. Eileen knew her enough to know that she had something else to tell and waited. Miss Dillan then added, "Unless you pay attention to rumors."

"And what are the gossiping people saying about her?" asked

Eileen with a mischievous look.

"They say that Mr. Giuseppe visits her. That is why I was surprised that Miss Vicenza suggested you go there."

"And do you think it is true?" questioned Eileen.

"I don't know Mr. Giuseppe enough to say anything. I saw him a few times when he helped Miss Vicenza pick up larger packages. He is a handsome man with an imposing presence, but that's all, and he never said a word to me."

"How come?" pressed Eileen. "They have lived in Clairsville for more than twenty years, and that is all you know about him."

"That's true," Miss Dillan admitted. "He doesn't come to the post office, and he never did anything special that I heard of. They bought their house without a mortgage. And I know it because the bank clerk where they have their account is my cousin. Miss Vicenza is the one that does all the shopping and runs all errands. Mr. Giuseppe rarely leaves his home except to take care of the White Stone House. "

"Not even to drive a Corvette?" asked Eileen.

"Okay. You know about that. It seems that sometimes he rides around, driving the neighbors' Corvette."

"I'm intrigued by those neighbors. They don't use the house, the boat, or the Corvettes, but they pay Miss Vicenza and her husband to keep everything in place. Who are they?"

"Nobody knows," replied Miss Dillan, coyly. "I believe it's someone from Washington who doesn't want to be known. The property is in the name of a Panamanian holding company. All payments, including the wages of Mr. Giuseppe and Miss Vicenza, are made by the Panamanian company through an account they have at the same bank where my cousin works . . . a well-kept secret."

• • •

Eileen traveled to New York the next day. Once a year, she had a meeting with her agent to discuss her books. Eileen had not written anything new, but she liked her agent, and brainstorming ideas with him. She stayed for three days, saw two plays, and, alone in New York, she thought about Vicenza, more than she was expecting.

As soon as she returned, Eileen asked Miss Dillan about Vicenza. "She seems a little tense," said Miss Dillan. "And she is not writing as many letters as she used to. This morning, for instance, she got two, but she posted none."

Eileen decided to pass by Vicenza's house, but she called before.

"I will prefer it if I come to yours," answered Vicenza. "My house is a little messy today."

Thirty minutes later, Vicenza was at her door. "Sorry about last week, but I had to leave when I received a phone call from La Vero."

"Is everything fine?" asked Eileen.

"Now, it is. Pippo is having some problems with a new medication, but let's take another look at your garden. I need fresh air. We can walk and have new ideas for plants."

Vicenza was visibly tense, and Eileen was intrigued.

"I like how your neighbors assure their privacy," commented Eileen. "I don't need to do that, but I want to choose some bushes for the edges. I'm too exposed to my neighbors."

"I have plenty of bushes, mountain laurels, English hollies, and my favorites, the Russian olives in my . . ." Vicenza immediately corrected herself. " . . . in my neighbor's garden," she said, embarrassed. "I choose most plants for it, and sometimes I consider it mine."

Eileen also wanted to plant some pines, and they discussed where they would fit best. Vicenza seemed to be relaxing, and they continued to talk.

"Why are you so worried? Is something else going on with Pippo?" asked Eileen.

"*Mannaggia*, you are so nosy," replied Vicenza. "You will not rest until you know everything about my life."

Eileen started to justify, but Vicenza interrupted her. "It's okay. I don't mind. Go ahead." She waved her hand, encouraging Eileen to speak. "Ask me what you want to know. Neither Pippo nor myself have anything to hide from you." Vicenza's cellphone buzzed.

"Is he fine?" Vicenza said on the phone. "*Io ho detto, cazzo.* I told him not to drive with this new medication." Vicenza hung up and told Eileen, "Sorry, I have to go."

Eileen walked Vicenza inside the house and helped her to sit.

Vicenza was shivering. "He is out of his mind. I told him a hundred times that we must be careful, but he doesn't listen." She abruptly stood. "I have to go."

"Okay, you can go, but you cannot drive like this. Your hands are shaking. Let me take you home," Eileen offered.

"He is not at home," admonished Vicenza.

"It doesn't matter. I will take you wherever you want to go."

Vicenza was reluctant to accept, but she was feeling dizzy. She mumbled something that sounded like, "This will not end well. Our lives are in danger."

Eileen was unsure of what she heard, but she helped Vicenza go back to her pickup truck, and she insisted, "I will drive it."

"Okay," replied Vicenza, resigned. "Let's go to La Vero's."

Eileen looked surprised but chose to stay silent and drive. When they got to La Vero's, Eileen saw a metallic blue Corvette. Vicenza was right, it looked like a science fiction spacecraft, bizarrely contrasting with La Vero's rustic log cabin.

Vicenza, who didn't seem surprised by the Corvette, asked Eileen, "Please stay here. Let me go inside by myself."

Eileen waited inside the pickup, trying to make sense of what she was seeing. La Vero's place was sheltered amid dense woods, pines mostly, and in front of it, a futuristic Corvette. Was Vicenza's husband having an affair with a *muxe*?

Veronica came out of the house, walking with her head down and wearing a dark blue silk nightgown; her hair was loose. Even so, her beauty was impressive. *Sumptuous like a queen* came to Eileen's mind.

"Vicenza asked me to tell you to go," Veronica said, sounding distressed. "Vicenza feels better and will drive her husband back home."

Eileen was startled, said nothing, and drove off.

Later that evening, Vicenza showed up to retrieve her truck. "Okay, if you give me a good shot of whisky, I will tell you the whole thing," started Vicenza, still speaking nervously. "I need to talk, and I know you are not stupid. I can see the curiosity sparkling in your eyes.

"Pippo and I have been together for more than thirty years, and we get along perfectly, but sex has never been a priority for me." She stopped for a sip of whisky. "At the beginning it was fine, but after, I wanted it less and less, and with Pippo it was different, he wanted more and more. I was happy with whatever we had, while he needed to seduce other women, maybe it was to prove to himself that he was still charming and young. I closed my eyes, and as he traveled a lot, I am sure he had all the whores he wanted. But we were happy, as crazy as that sounds. Later Veronica came to work on our neighbor's house. She was fun, and I loved to talk with her. You saw her, she is beautiful."

"But La Vero is a—"

"You don't have to tell me. I know everything about La Vero. And when Pippo started to sleep with her, I even encouraged him. She was someone I knew, and all that anxiety Pippo had, traveling and looking for other women, disappeared. With La Vero, he was safer, and of course, I was surprised to learn that Veronica has a dick, a *minchia*, between her legs, but if Pippo was happy, I was happy too."

"Weren't you worried?" asked Eileen, shocked.

"Worried about what. There are many years that we do not make love. I knew he had to find a way to release his energy."

"How come, Vicenza? You live in the same house. He has a lover, and you don't make love. Does it look normal to you?" Eileen asked curtly.

"No. As I said, we have been doing unimaginable things together. Sorry, I cannot tell you. Our life is full of secrets," and after pausing, she continued. "Do you think that after a wild Bonnie and Clyde youth, we spent our time in Clairsville, watching birds and watering the garden? Of course not. Pippo and I are best friends and great partners, but I do not want to sleep with him, and he likes to be with Veronica. She was not a problem but the solution. We helped her buy a house in the woods where Pippo could go unnoticed whenever he wanted."

"But if it's all so fine, why are you tense and worried now? Is he threatening to leave you?"

"Don't be silly. Pippo cannot leave me. Not for a woman, and even more for a muxe. That is not the problem. What worries me is that he is getting cranky, and nothing amuses him anymore. He entirely lost interest in our work, and that is our life. We had critical guests at our neighbor's house, and he acted completely absent. That's why I suggested sailing. Please understand, Veronica, Corvettes, and *Marinella* seem to be the only stuff that satisfies him. But now it's getting worse. This morning Veronica called me because he was non-stop crying. It's not the first time. His doctor suggested a stronger medication for depression, but it doesn't seem to be working."

Vicenza became tearful, and Eileen tried to calm her.

"If you want to cry, go ahead, and if you prefer to be quiet, I will stay here with you. I don't know what you and your husband do, and I don't need to know. It might be crazy since I barely know you, but I trust that whatever it is happening, you will be capable of handling it."

"Thanks," replied Vicenza. "And sorry if I cannot tell you details of our life or even what we do together, but I cannot keep doing what we do by myself. Either Pippo and I work together, or we both die. And trust me, that's not just a figure of speech."

6.

A breeze becomes a hurricane. Eileen was worried about Vicenza and called her a few times, but they barely talked. "Give me some time," Vicenza said. Eileen started to feel bad, not emotionally, but physically. Initially she thought she had a cold, but each day she felt worse, first dizziness, then nausea, and finally, a continuous cough. She called her doctor in Washington, DC.

"Could be the COVID virus." He insisted that she should be tested. Eileen hesitated. She was not feeling good enough to drive, but at night the fever spiked and she panicked. She wanted to call Vicenza, but she felt embarrassed, and so he called Miss Dillan. "Once you mentioned that your neighbor is a nurse. Can you give me her phone number?"

A half an hour later. Miss Dillan was at her house bringing Claire with her.

Claire scared Eileen even more, donning a face mask and telling Miss Dillan not to get too close "Have you been in contact with someone who came from China or Italy?" the nurse asked.

Eileen said no, but added, "I recently spent a few days in New York."

"Then, quite probably, you have the virus. I have seen other cases at the hospital, and they have similar symptoms. New York is becoming a COVID hot spot, but there is not too much that we can do now. We will have to control your fever, and I will inform the doctors. I'm sure that they will tell you to stay home in quarantine and to avoid any contact. Do you have someone who can prepare your meals?"

Eileen didn't know what to say. "Do not worry," continued Claire, "I will ask Miss Dillan to bring you something, and I will pass here tomorrow to see how you are. But let me be honest, you might feel terrible, and I think you should tell your family and ask someone to accompany you, but make sure you and they wear a face mask."

Eileen adamantly refused. "I can take care of myself."

The next morning, it was not Miss Dillan who came with the food. The bell rang, and when Eileen opened the door, Vicenza was there, wearing a face mask.

"Miss Dillan told me. I talked with Claire, and I made a few phone calls. You must be quarantined, and, even myself, should not get closer to you. I brought you some food, but you can't stay here."

Eileen didn't have time to answer, and Vicenza continued. "You must come with me. This virus is dangerous and can kill people, or severally damage your lungs."

Eileen refused, and Vicenza insisted. "It will get worse, particularly during the night. I talked to Claire about hiring a nurse to stay with you, but it's impossible. There are just a few around here, and the hospitals need them."

"It doesn't make sense," said Eileen. "I will stay in my house."

"You don't understand. You are weak and need help, but the number of cases is growing, and you need to be isolated."

"And how can I be isolated in your house. You have a husband and enough stuff to take care of."

"You will not stay in my house. I spoke with my neighbors, and they will let you use one of the cottages. With the virus, nobody is expected to come to their property. You will be comfortable there, and I can take care of you and be around whenever you need."

Eileen relented.

"You will have to drive your car," Vicenza explained. "Claire insisted that I should not get any time near you. Please, prepare a bag with everything you will need. And do not worry because I could always come back to grab anything you forget."

Eileen was feeling dizzy and could hardly drive. She vomited before getting into her car, and she finally met Vicenza's husband. Pippo was waiting at the porch wearing a mask and welcomed her warmly. "Vicenza and I are happy that you are here."

He and Vicenza followed her from a safe distance while she walked into the neighbor's property. Although tired, Eileen meticulously examined him. She couldn't see his face, but his eyes were powerful, almost intimidating. He was tall with broad shoulders, thick chest, wearing shorts and a T-shirt.

They took Eileen to one of the smaller cottages near the woods. "It has only one bedroom," explained Vicenza. "They built this one for special guests who require privacy."

Maybe smaller but luxurious, thought Eileen when entering. The furniture was exquisite antique, and the paintings on the walls were outstanding. "All Italian painters," Vicenza said proudly.

The bedroom was spacious and had a king-sized bed and two comfortable armchairs. Vicenza walked to one of the windows and told Eileen, "From here, you can see my house, and I can see when you have the lights on."

Eileen was tired and slept right after. Later in the evening, Pippo and Vicenza came to see her; Vicenza had cooked a light zucchini risotto. They kept a good distance but chatted, and Pippo was charming. He talked about Lampedusa and his life in Palermo before writing *The Leopard*, and Eileen was impressed. They discussed European politics, the ever-present attraction to the right, and the dangers to democracy in America. Pippo took off his mask to eat, and Eileen could see that he was a self-confident and handsome man. And it was almost impossible not to stare at him. His presence was commanding, his comments thoughtful, and his jokes humorous. Whatever he did in his life, this was a man who knew what he was doing.

"I believe you might have a bad impression after that hectic day at Veronica's house," Pippo said. "Sorry, I was depressed," adding, "I know how important your friendship is to Vicenza, and we feel comfortable that you are here, safe and close to us. I'm sure that you will soon feel better."

Unfortunately, he was wrong. On the same night, Eileen's fever increased, and she started hallucinating. She got scared and called Vicenza, who stayed with her until dawn.

The next morning, Claire came bringing oxygen equipment. "Let's hope you will feel better," she said, but she was honest. "The next few nights and days will probably be tough."

The fever continued, and Eileen could barely leave the bed. Vicenza stayed almost full-time in the cottage for three days, and her husband often checked in, too. They considered taking Eileen to the hospital and talked with a doctor, but her oxygen levels remained reasonable, and the doctor recommended keeping Eileen isolated at home.

Vicenza used masks and tried to maintain her distance, but there were moments when Eileen started to hallucinate, and she got closer and even embraced her.

After a couple of nights, Eileen started to feel better as the fever subsided.

"Do you want me to call your sons?" Vicenza had repeatedly asked, and Eileen's answer was the same. "Wait until I get fully recovered. If I call, they will be worried and might even come. I don't want that. My oldest son has a new job and the youngest planned to travel with his girlfriend this summer. I'm feeling fine, don't worry. By the way, you still didn't tell me how wild you and Pippo were, and I remind you that you should never deny a sick person's request."

Her nosiness was back, making Vicenza relieved.

"Okay. You have been a lovely patient, following all my recommendations, and you deserve some answers." Vicenza sat in one of the armchairs. "Pippo and I were wild, and I mean, *really* wild. Did you watch that movie, *Bonnie and Clyde*? Well, our life was more or less like theirs. We were teenagers, and we left our houses to go to Sicily's east coast. We lived in a land of farmers with no tourists, and we grew up listening to stories about the city of Taormina. My grandfather considered it an evil place, full of foreigners and artists, even gays, as he used to say. I was fifteen, and Pippo was seventeen when we ran away. We both had a decent living in our villages, my father and my mother were teachers and had good jobs, and Pippo was the son of a powerful landowner, but we wanted to live our lives with our own rules."

Eileen perked up, listening attentively, no longer seeming ill.

"My father was a Sicilian nationalist," continued Vicenza. "He hated foreigners, and for a period, he got involved with the communists and even joined their party. That is why he and my mother lost their jobs. He attended political meetings, but soon my father realized that foreigners were making all decisions and that local communists had to follow directions from Rome or even from Russia. As a nationalist, that was unacceptable. I was a baby at that time, but I know that he and my mother lived through a rough period. My mother washed clothes, and my father worked under the sun in olive harvesting. Nobody wanted to hire them as teachers. It was Pippo's father who rescued our family. He and his family were, and still are, the most important olive oil producers in the region. When Pippo's father realized that my father renounced the communist, he helped my parents get back to teaching, and they both succeeded, first because they were competent and second because they had Pippo's father's blessing. In Sicily at that time, you were nothing if you were not part of a powerful family, and we became part of Pippo's family. Don Giacomo, Pippo's father, became my godfather."

Vicenza stopped to give Eileen a glass of orange juice. Eileen was surprised by Vicenza's candor.

"As his goddaughter," Vicenza continued, "I was invited to the family celebrations in honor of San Giacomo and at Christmas. When I got to *secondaria*, the middle school, we became buddies. Pippo was the only man I had in my life. My best friend. It was his idea to run away. Living with our parents, we always had to ask permission for everything, and we hated that.

"One day, a man we knew was taking some pigs to Ragusa, and rode in his truck. Our honeymoon started on an old truck full of pigs. Not a great beginning," she said laughing. "We had some money, but we couldn't go to hotels. They would ask for our IDs, and we were minors. The man who drove the truck helped us find a room where we stayed for a few days. It was amazing. Ragusa is a baroque city on the top of a mountain. We enjoyed the place, but we missed the sea, so we took a bus to Siracusa. A fisherman we knew was living there, and for a few weeks we worked and lived on his boat, but our dream was to be in Taormina, and we finally went there. Do you know that city, Eileen?"

"I've never been to Sicily."

"Oh, what a pity. One day I will take you there."

Eileen nodded agreeing, and Vicenza continued. "Taormina is on the Strait of Messina, where Scylla and Charybdis, the two monsters who threatened Ulysses in the Odyssey live. From there, you can see Calabria and the continent. All houses and streets of Taormina are on the mountainside with an open view of the sea, and famous writers like D.H. Lawrence and Oscar Wilde lived there. But to enjoy the place, you needed money. In less than a month we were broke. The only jobs available were cleaning hotels and restaurants. Like Ulysses in front of Scylla and Charybdis, we were forced to choose between the lesser of two evils. Either leave the city or find a job that we didn't want. But we choose a third and more pleasant alternative, stealing money from rich tourists, particularly Germans and Americans who always loved the Sicilian east coast."

Vicenza was smiling, proud of her crazy days, and Eileen was surprised but fascinated.

"Pippo has always been a handsome man," explained Vicenza, "attracting the attention of any widow or divorced woman, and I looked like a child, arousing naughty ideas among older men. It was so simple. Easy to attract them, easy to rob, and easy to get away, since our victims were in town only for a few days and couldn't explain to the police why they were hanging with Sicilian minors like us. We became masters. We rented a little apartment near Taormina, in a small village called Castelmola, and as our only problem was transportation, we solved it by stealing a white scooter. *Stellina*, as we called it."

"Keep going," Eileen pleaded. "You are in the mood to talk, and all of this is so fascinating and unexpected."

"Those were the best times." Vicenza continued, broadly smiling "Living in Castelmola and driving around with Stellina to empty tourists' pockets in Taormina."

"And weren't you afraid of the police?"

"No. We knew that if something happened, Don Giacomo would rescue us. Our big fear was that he would find us. And we had to be very careful. Sometimes the tourists didn't have cash with them, and we had to steal jewels or cameras. We knew that Don Giacomo's people would discover us if we tried to resell stolen goods it to any pawnshop, because he controlled them. But Pippo knew where his father didn't have friends, and he traveled to Naples to sell our stuff. For a year, we lived like royals. We had so much money that we didn't know how to spend it. We expanded our action area, staying in fancy hotels from Milazzo in the north to Ortigia in the south. We went wherever there were tourists, but always avoiding Catania, since Don Giacomo knew so many people there. I believe that for Pippo, part of the fun was proving that he could escape from his father's control and manage our lives without help."

"And you, what did you enjoy the most?"

"I enjoyed the freedom of waking up and doing whatever we wanted. There were no limits. With the money we got, we even rented a little yacht with a small cabin, and we spent a few weeks sailing between Milazzo and Taormina. You can't imagine what we felt crossing Capo Peloro in the Messina Strait. Pippo and I were sailing the same route as Ulysses in the Odyssey. We were not only masters of our world, but we were also navigating in history and time, with nobody to tell us when and where to stop."

"And how did all this end?"

"We decided to go back to Castelvetrano. We loved our family, friends, and places, and we missed them. We sold everything we had and hid the money in a safe place. The only thing we took back home was Stellina the scooter. We crossed Sicily from Taormina to our village, and we arrived at Pippo's parents' home with two helmets, a small bag pack, and the white scooter."

"How did your families receive you?"

"We didn't tell them what we had done, and their great worry was that we were unmarried. We insisted that we would continue to live together, and they conditioned their consent to a wedding announcement. My parents loved Pippo and Don Giacomo, and his wife, Signora Paola, liked me. It was comic. They were mad with Pippo for running away, but not with me. Traditional Sicilian families always think that only men make decisions, and because of that, women are always forgiven. Of course, the only exception is betrayal. In that case, women deserve to die, if possible, on the spot. Anyway, we got married, it was a luxurious wedding with many guests. My mom and Signora Paola planned everything together.

"And what did you do after that? Were you still wild? I remember when you told me that you came to the US looking for peace."

"After we got married, Pippo's father got sick and died. Pippo had to take care of his family's businesses. It wasn't easy. We had to do tough things, and we got in a lot of trouble. We had to disappear, and it was not simple. People were always trying to find us, and we didn't want to live on the run. We had to die and be reborn with different names, which is why we entered the American witness protection program. Who better than the FBI to conceal us? They helped us to move to the US and to buy our house. Since then, we have lived here. And now it's over. It's time for you to rest."

"Only one more question," insisted Eileen. "What exactly do you and Pippo do today?" she asked.

"Now you are asking too much," replied Vicenza with a friendly smile. "There are things that you better ignore," she teased. "Life is too short to know everything. And now tell me, don't you want to talk with your kids?

"No. I don't want to be a burden," Eileen said. "And, besides, I'm comfortable here with you."

At that moment, Vicenza did something completely unplanned, a small friendly gesture that forever changed their lives. She got closer to Eileen and kissed her lips. COVID be damned!

7.

Nothing would be the same. Vicenza left the cottage in a hurry and walked to the dock. She was confused but not surprised. Since Eileen was sick, she wanted to embrace her, and the good-night kiss came naturally after a friendly conversation. But her sexual feeling was unexpected. Eileen's lips were softer than anything she had touched before, and a wave of energy spread through her body, squeezing her most intimate parts.

Eileen, in her bed, was astonished too. She liked to be with Vicenza, but she thought it was out of curiosity. Vicenza was a unique personality, but the kiss was totally unexpected. A strange feeling penetrated Eileen, making her want more. She tried to walk to the window to look at Vicenza's house but couldn't muster the strength. She stayed awake in bed, feeling a fever returning.

They barely talked on the next day. Early in the morning, Eileen had difficulty breathing, and Vicenza called nurse Claire. After examining her, Claire was not worried. "We need to be patient," she said. "Nobody understands this virus yet, and I don't think she would be better at the hospital. From what I see, she has here everything she needs. Let's keep her at home."

Eileen had moments of extremely high fever for the next two days, and Vicenza stayed by her side in an armchair. They spoke, but never mentioned the kiss.

"How is Pippo?" Eileen asked.

"He is fine, but I haven't seen him. He is spending most of the time with La Vero. By the way, she calls every day to know how you are. I think it's good for Pippo to spend more time with her."

"Aren't you jealous?"

"No. What I want is for him to be fine again. And La Vero has a theory. Let's see if she is right. She believes that their relationship is the cause of Pippo's emotional crisis."

"What?" Eileen grimaced, confused.

Vicenza explained. "Pippo lives here, but he is still a Sicilian, and from where we came from there is no such thing as an honorable gay man."

"But you told me that Oscar Wilde loved there," teased Eileen.

"He loved Taormina," Vicenza clarified. "That is why my grandfather used to say that Taormina was an evil city. There were no open gays, especially among the older and more traditional men with whom Pippo used to deal. And here we are with Pippo, a *maschio* Sicilian, proud of his Latin lover record, flirting with La Vero's *minchia*," Vicenza laughed. "La Vero's theory is that he struggles to accept that he prefers to make love with her instead of other women."

"She could be right," said Eileen.

"I think she is, which is why I want him to be with her. Once he admits that to himself, perhaps he will be happier. And do not worry. He will not abandon me. If he leaves me for a muxe, his Sicilian friends would never forgive him.

"You are exaggerating," said Eileen.

"No, I'm not. You don't know our people. And I'm talking about our generation since I have no idea what young Sicilians think. But the people we know are conservative. No exceptions. We were all raised under Sicilian values, which are very strict by American standards. For example, when we got home and Don Giacomo discovered that our scooter was stolen. He was furious. Not because we ran away, but because his son had stolen a scooter from another Sicilian. He asked us to return the scooter, but we didn't know who the owner was, and to appease Don Giacomo, we lied, telling him that we took it from a rich *polentone* from Rome, and, after hearing that, he settled down."

"What is a *polentone*?

"That is what we call the Italians from the continent. They like *polenta*, which Sicilians only use to feed the pigs. But the point is, to steal a scooter from a Sicilian was unacceptable, but from a rich *polentone* was okay. Do you understand?"

"Let me tell you something I learned about Sicilians," said Eileen, feeling spunky. "When I woke up in the middle of the night, I did a Google search and learned about the *pentiti*, those who left the Mafia and helped authorities in exchange for witness protection. I read about Tommaso Buscetta and others. Is Pippo a *pentito*?"

"*Sei pazza*! Your writer's imagination is going too far. The pentiti helped prosecutors in Italy, and we made our deal here in the US with the FBI. And by the way, that idea that all Sicilians are Mafiosi is bullshit." Vicenza gestured.

"Don't be mad with me. The way you described your father-in-law was not so far from Mario Puzo's *Godfather*.

"Neither all Sicilians are Mafiosi, nor are all Sicilian families in criminal organizations. But for us, a family is more than parents, kids, and brothers. Here, you don't need to be worried about your house or your business, and you don't lose your job because of your opinions. In Sicily, it was different. Before the war, we were looted by the fascists and later by the Americans who thought they could do whatever they wanted after Mussolini's death. Now it is still the same. Italian politicians treat us as the bottom of their backyard. In Sicily, family was all you had to protect you, and still is. Don Giacomo protected my family. He was powerful and had land full of olive trees, and he chose to use his wealth to help people. Every day, you could see many peasants going to his house, asking for something, and he received all of them, one by one. Some were looking for jobs, others for protection against thieves or looters, and others just asking him to mediate their conflicts. That is what a good Sicilian *Padrino* does. He finds ways to help his family."

"I like when you get emotional," said Eileen. "Most people try to hide their feelings behind a smile even if they are upset, but not you. Your face and gestures reveal precisely what you are feeling, which makes you special."

・・・

Later at night, when Eileen was eating a light pasta prepared by Vicenza, she asked, "You already told me that you were part of the witness protection, but I am sure that there is something else that you are hiding. Can you tell me?"

"*Madonna*. You are really a pain in the neck," replied Vicenza, "But I agree with you, I'm tired of secrets. I will tell you everything. After Pippo and I got back to our village, many things happened, and we got into serious problems."

"With the police?" asked Eileen.

"With many people, including the police. We had to move from hideout to hideout. Our life was hell, and it was unclear what else we could do, until Pippo heard that the FBI was investigating an Italian crime boss in the US who had betrayed some Sicilian families. We came to New York and contacted the FBI, offering to provide the information they needed to put that bastard traitor in jail in exchange for a new identity."

"But didn't they know you were wanted in Italy?" asked Eileen.

"They didn't know who we were. They checked our fingerprints, but they didn't find anything," Vicenza smiled. "We had perfectly legitimate fake Italian identities. I know that this might sound a little odd to you, but trust me, it's nothing uncommon in Sicily. In Sicily we had fake documents and fingerprints. We showed the FBI our passports, and they felt for it. We helped them to arrest the traitor, and they gave us an American identity."

"Okay, but there is a piece missing in your story. How did you get in trouble with the police? Was it because of the Taormina robberies?"

"No, and that is a long story, maybe one day I will tell you, but now you must sleep. You will still stay here for a good time, and we will have plenty of time to talk."

That night, Vicenza didn't kiss her. Neither were ready to cross that line.

• • •

The following day, Vicenza arrived with unexpected news. "Our neighbors called us. They need the house for some guests, and you must move temporarily to my house."

"And what about the COVID? Aren't they scared?"

"They don't care," said Vicenza.

Eileen proposed to go to her house, but Vicenza insisted. "No, you're still too weak. Stay with me. It's just for the weekend. Monday, they will leave, and you will be back to this cottage."

Eileen was reluctant. The whole thing was crazy, but he could not deny that she enjoyed the cottage and Vicenza's care.

Eileen arrived the next morning and was escorted to a second-floor bedroom where everything seemed untouched. Vicenza explained that Pippo was still with La Vero. Eileen chose not to ask any questions as she was exhausted from the walking.

Vicenza got Eileen settled into the guest room and then hurried to go back to the mansion.

After a nap, Eileen walked to the window and saw a crew arriving to clean the main house and the guest cottages, probably the same company La Vero worked for.

Eileen put a chair next to the window and sat. She could see the neighbors' entrance driveway and the vans arriving with flowers and, later, the catering. Jimmy the electrician was there. *Maybe he's going to cook,* she thought.

She stayed at the window and followed when the guests arrived. There were six fancily dressed men who arrived in two groups. Three other vans arrived half an hour later, bringing eight young beauties. Vicenza received all of them in the driveway. Six older men and eight young models; a wild party was undoubtedly about to begin.

Later, when it was getting dark, Eileen saw Jimmy again walking in the driveway, he and two other men wearing ties and dark suits. Eileen was puzzled. It didn't look like Jimmy was there to cook.

At night, she could see that all the mansion lights were on, and the pool was illuminated. She could even hear voices, and, feeling better and more curious, walked through the backyard into the neighbor's house. She carefully crossed the gate, which was open, and hid behind bushes from where she could see the pool. A couple of waiters stood by two tables on the terrace, ready to serve food and drinks, but nobody else was there. A few minutes later, male guests walked to the pool, where, to Eileen's surprise, they were welcomed by Vicenza and Pippo, both elegantly dressed. Pippo wore a dark double-breasted suit with no tie, which gave him an even more prominent presence, and Vicenza, as an entirely different woman, was exhibiting an elegant and sober black and white Chanel. None of them or the guests wore face masks.

The guests seemed reverential to Pippo, surprising Eileen. The young escorts were not there, only the men, and one after another, they all hugged Pippo respectfully as if he were Marlon Brando's godfather.

Suddenly, Eileen saw Jimmy and another man walking around the garden and she quickly returned to Vicenza's place.

Pippo was not just a caretaker; nor was Vicenza.

8.

Time to be tender. Vicenza spent the weekend attending to her guests, while periodically checking on Eileen for a few minutes at a time.

On Monday, Vicenza woke up Eileen with another surprise. "We will have an unplanned visit this afternoon, and this one to our house. A friend called us saying that he would pass by, and I need a favor from you. Pippo and I will receive him, it will be a quick visit, but I need you to stay in your room. He is from the FBI, and I don't know what he wants. He will ask questions if he sees you here, and we don't want that. We learned that the less FBI guys know, the better."

"And what about your guests in the neighbors' house? asked Eileen.

"There is no need for major concerns. The FBI agent doesn't know about them. From time to time, they like to check in on us."

A senior FBI agent arrived with a young assistant, and Pippo and Vicenza spoke with them in the living room. The conversation was friendly, but Eileen could not resist eavesdropping from the top of the stairs.

"You are doing great, and we are thankful and proud of you," said the senior agent, "We would like your help with an internal seminar that the Department of Justice is organizing."

"No problems," answered Pippo. "What do we have to do?"

"You just have to tell about your experience with the program and eventually answer a few questions from participants, but nothing deep. Everything will be done by teleconference because of this crazy virus, and you will not be identified," he added. "You are one of our most successful cases."

"May I suggest something?" proposed Pippo. "What if Vicenza does it? She knows better than me how we overcame all the hurdles, and I will feel more comfortable keeping my privacy. I understand that any video circulation will be restricted, but you never know when there is a leak."

The FBI agent agreed and even offered to send an agent to help Vicenza write her presentation, which Vicenza politely declined. "I can do it by myself, and it will be more authentic than what a stranger could write."

Weird and ironic, thought Eileen. *They host people secretively next door, and consort with the FBI at home. Not a boring life!*

• • •

The following day, the neighbor's house guests left – first, the women, and later the men. Eileen moved back to the guest cottage.

Eileen was feeling stronger and even walked in the garden towards the dock. It was dusk, and she saw Pippo driving the Corvette to La Vero's house. Vicenza joined her. The creek was peaceful with no boats, just birds flying around. Eileen broke the silence.

"Won't you feel more comfortable telling me the whole truth? I don't think it's fair to leave me in the dark. We are friends now, and we must trust each other."

"I already told you that we got into the FBI program to obtain a new identity," replied Vicenza.

"But you didn't tell me what you are doing since then. And please don't tell me that you and Pippo are just caretakers. I saw you with your guests. By the way, you were very charming and looked beautiful."

Vicenza stayed quiet for a moment.

"If I tell you, I'll put your life in danger. It's as simple as that."

Eileen didn't reply immediately. They kept staring at each other until Eileen spoke.

"You should have thought about that when you invited me to come here. Now it's too late. We are friends, and I want to know who you really are. I like to see myself as a smart and experienced woman, and your silence, and secrets, make me feel foolish and naive."

"Okay," Vicenza relented. "We had friends in Italy, and we help them."

"Are you part of the Mafia?" Eileen blurted.

"*Cazzo*! You and your Mafia. I already told you that there is no such thing. Journalists and writers invented that name. In Sicily, what we have are *families*. They are independent, have their own activities, and sometimes manage their businesses together." Vicenza then stopped, not sure of how far she should go.

"Are you sure that you want me to talk about it?"

"I'm all yours," answered Eileen. "Pippo is playing with La Vero's dick, and we have the whole mansion for ourselves."

They watched the sunset on the creek, and Vicenza tried to choose her words carefully.

"In Sicily, families have always been the driving force, defending us, resisting, and keeping our land in peace. Sicily is a *Cosa Nostra* as we like to say. And it was not easy."

"What do you mean?" Eileen pressed.

"Sicilians are stubborn. We don't bow to anyone. Our families fought constantly because Sicilian men are stupid. They fight even when they don't need to and are in a permanent war when we lived there. A lot of good people died. And we did not want our family's businesses to collapse."

"Businesses or criminal activities?" Eileen asked.

Vicenza groaned. "It depends on what side of the table you are. Many Sicilian families operate in marginals areas, it's true. But there is no Mafia per se. Each family decides what to do. Some are more conservative, and others engage in more dangerous actions. Some don't have boundaries at all. Family bosses might temporarily agree on some actions, but each family is independent."

"And what you and Pippo do, for this Sicilian patriotic families?" teased Eileen.

"We help them with their meetings in the US. Many Sicilians have businesses in this country, most of them in partnership with Sicilian-American families, and from time to time they need to get together. That's why they use our neighbor's house, and why we take care of it."

"You are lying," replied Eileen. "I saw the deference and respect the visitors showed to you and Pippo. You are not just hostesses. You are part of it, and an important part."

Vicenza didn't reply immediately, and Eileen continued. "You and Pippo cheated, pretending to be repentant, *pentiti*, or whatever you want to call. You got a fake identity blessed by the FBI. It was an ingenious move. Do you want me to believe that all you did after that was to supervise cleaning crews and host guests for weekends with booze and whores?"

Vicenza realized that it was pointless to keep hiding.

"Okay. Do you want to know? I will tell you. When we got here, we were running away, and we just wanted a safe place where we didn't have to change hideouts every night. The plan was to stay here for a few years, waiting for things to cool down in Sicily, and after that, go back. Pippo and I wanted peace, but, obviously, we started to think about what else we could do. Here, we didn't have problems to worry about, and Pippo kept in contact with some of his Sicilian friends, and I continued to follow through my letters what was going on there."

Vicenza stood, collecting her thoughts and trying not to get agitated with her curious friend.

"Like I said, every Sicilian family has a core business. In the case of Pippo's family, it has always been olive oil, but some families used to make an extra income came from what they got for protecting people. Protection cost money, and they charged for it. It was the *pizzo*, as they called it. But this was before the world changed."

"People no longer needed help to protect their houses or businesses, but families continued to need money to remain powerful and control their own fate. Modern and profitable businesses were all in hands of foreigners, and the income provided by olives and oranges was not enough to keep a family strong. Without money, family members became vulnerable and worse. Our best people left Sicily, going to the north, or abroad. The only alternative was to get into risky businesses like drug trafficking, prostitution chains, and even arms dealings. You have seen it in many movies. We did it and it was very profitable. When we moved here, the main problem was how to launder profits and invest them in legitimate financial institutions. That is what Pippo and I started to do. It wasn't stealing or selling drugs or prostitution. It was just a financial activity. Initially we didn't have great expectations. It was just a side business to keep us in the loop with our friends, but it grew. It took years, and we learned a lot. We started to move money for our family and later for other families. We became masters," and Vicenza smiled.

"Things kept changing," she continued, "and Pippo was always looking for something else. We realized that we could never go back to Sicily, and we tried to do our best from here. Today, many violent organizations from several countries work in those marginal areas. The Russians, Albanians, Chinese, Lithuanians, Mexicans, Colombians, are all wild and uncontrolled. We needed to be aggressive to stay on top, and Pippo conceived a new version of the old pizzo. He realized that all these wild organizations were permanently confronting governments and international agencies, and they also needed protection. In Sicily, the families have built a reliable network of politicians to protect them. Here in the US, they haven't. And that's what we did. Many Sicilian families supported us, and we established a solid and reliable network. Now every family that has problems in this country knows that we can help to solve them. We charge them a pizzo for it."

"But what exactly do you do?"

"We don't do anything illegal. We just introduce people, put them together, and help them solve their disagreements. This weekend, for instance, we had Albanians and Italian Americans from Nevada discussing a partnership to bring Siberian women to Las Vegas. Pippo knew both groups and thought they could work together. We had invited them a long time ago, but they could never agree on a date. Last Thursday, the Albanians called saying that they were ready to talk, and the Americans too. They spent three days in the property enjoying young models, and now they are reaching a deal."

"So, you act like a business adviser," Eileen said.

"Yes, and sometimes as a conciliation center."

"And what exactly does Jimmy the electrician do?" asked Eileen. "I saw him among the guests."

Vicenza hesitated. "Nothing special. He helps us when we have guests. He doesn't know what we do. Pippo likes him because he never asks questions."

Eileen pressed. "He is Sicilian, isn't he?"

"Yes, and he cooks very well. Probably that is why Pippo likes him."

"Okay. For the time being, I will pretend that I believe everything you said and that there is nothing else that you are hiding," said Eileen.

"You can be sure," Vicenza replied with a mischievous look. "And now I will need your help to write my life story to the FBI."

"And what do you want me to say?"

"Whatever you want, "replied Vicenza laughing. "Let's invent something that they will love."

● ● ●

The nights of early spring were still cold, and they got inside the cottage and lit the fireplace. Maybe the flames made the night magic. All those days of seeing each other had made Eileen and Vicenza more than friends, accomplices perhaps.

Eileen took a shower, and for the first time in weeks, she dressed in a cozy gown before sitting near Vicenza. Words were not necessary; they both knew they were heading to uncharted waters.

They leaned into the couch, and without words, kissed again. The magic was even more intense. The first kiss led to touches feeding tenderness. Neither had been with a woman before. They hadn't even fantasized about it, but it happened, and it was sweet.

After her husband went to New York, Eileen never had a lover, and Vicenza didn't even know she needed one. Neither had craved sex. That night, however, everything was different. They kept kissing each other for hours, and when Vicenza touched Eileen's nipple, they both shivered. No hurries, no tension. Just a desire, getting stronger inside. Their bodies were not following planned movements, they were tenderly exploring each other with eyes closed to feel better the fingertips touching their skins. Their vaginas opened smooth and wet to caresses, and when the orgasm came, it didn't come as a peak or an end. It came as an endless beginning. They came and came again until dawn, wetting the couch in front of the fire. And the more they did, the smoother and responsive their bodies were. That night there was no thinking, just love.

9.

Working together. Eileen knew that she could go back to her home, but it was far more pleasant to be confined with Vicenza. Living together, they enjoyed a feeling of peace and pleasure. They even used the main table at the cottage as their workplace; on one side Eileen with her computer, and on the other for Vicenza handwriting letters to her Sicilian friends.

Eileen started to work on Vicenza's presentation to the FBI, and they were talking about it.

"Can you imagine how boring your life would be without your parallel activities?" asked Eileen.

"Scary," replied Vicenza.

"But we need to be careful with your fake story since it might be a trap. Whatever you say needs to be credible, otherwise, it may raise suspicions and trigger an investigation."

"Okay, tell them we continue to rob banks. They will surely believe it," Vicenza teased.

They laughed. "Is it true that you were a bank robber?"

"No way! Bank robberies were part of the fake story we told when we joined the witness protection program. We never did it"

"But you told me that you were wild," replied Eileen. "Or did you calm down when you got married?"

"Not so much. We got married, and Don Giacomo offered us a honeymoon trip to Rome, Florence, and Venice, but we didn't want to go. Pippo's older brothers were working with their father, and there was nothing for him or me to do. So, we decided to live on the boat his father had, the *Chiaro di Luna*, and let me tell you something that you would like, our love story had started there, long before we ran away, and it started with a book.

"Pippo had to read a novel during summer called *Conversazione in Sicilia*, and prepare a report for his school. At that time, he was fourteen and I was just the little goddaughter of his father who lived near the beach in Selinunte where *Chiaro di Luna* was docked. I admired Pippo. He was cool and older and had many girlfriends. Pippo told me one day about the book he had to read for school. I offered to prepare the report for him, and he agreed. Until then, I had never been inside the boat. Imagine me, the girl from Marinella de Selinunte, walking into the harbor to board Don Giacomo's yacht. I was in heaven. Thanks to that book, I became his girlfriend. I believe it is the only novel Pippo ever had in his hands, but he knows each character and every detail of the story. That is why we adopted Vittorini, the author's name, as ours when we joined the witness program. Miss Vicenza and Mr. Giuseppe Vittorini."

"And what was your real name?" asked Eileen.

"It doesn't matter," replied Vicenza, waving her left hand and changing the subject back to the honeymoon. "His father gave us the boat as a wedding gift, and we decided to use the honeymoon money to live on the boat, just the two of us, sailing around the island. We did it for more than a year, but we never left Sicily. Taormina was my favorite spot, and Pippo started to appreciate Ortigia."

After a pause, Vicenza peered into Eileen's eyes with a naughty smile. "We sailed, and to entertain ourselves, we continued to steal from wealthy tourists. Pippo kept seducing lonely women, and I enticing perverted men, but the truth is that most of the stealing was done by him with the ladies.

"We had a great time until Don Giacomo had a heart attack. Signora Paola called us, and we immediately returned. Pippo was the third male son, and his older brothers were trained to manage the family businesses, but Don Giacomo, still in the hospital, surprised us. He whispered to Pippo that he should be ready to succeed him. Don Giacomo was wise. He already knew, what became obvious later, that Pippo was the only one that could be the family *capo*."

"Wow," said Eileen, "Like Michael Corleone?"

"In a certain sense, yes. Pippo's older brothers were very nice, but they didn't have the guts and brains for the position. The family became vulnerable, and Pippo had a lot to learn. At that time, most local businesses were in trouble, and the only source of big money on the island was government contracts to build infrastructure. Most families, including Don Giacomo's, had gotten into the construction business to access those funds. However, politicians from Roma and Milano were taking the big chunk of the work, leaving just small *briciole*, or crumbs as you say, to us."

"I'm not following, said Eileen. "Why, the politicians."

"Eileen, you are naive. "Politicians always divert part of public construction funds to their own pockets, and in Sicily the biggest share was going to politicians from the north who controlled appropriations. That money was crucial for us, and they were squeezing us. *Capice?*" she said waving her hand. "To survive, some families opted for greater involvement in drug trafficking Sicily is in a good geographical position to become the gateway for drugs in Europe. Some families went heavy into that, which completely unbalanced the power. Those dealing with drugs became more powerful and threatened others."

"So, was Don Giacomo alive when this was going on?" asked Eileen.

"For more than two years, Don Giacomo was in and out of hospitals with a fragile heart. Doctors even considered a heart transplant, but they were afraid that Don Giacomo was too old. Signora Paola was the guardian of his health and didn't let the brothers or anyone else bother him. Pippo became the one making family decisions, which turned into a nightmare."

"Was Don Giacomo's family violent?" asked Eileen.

"Don Giacomo always used to say that violence does not measure the power of a family. It's the money and their choices that matter. But yes, he knew how to respond when attacked. When violence was needed, he never hesitated. Neither Don Giacomo nor Pippo. In a violent world, you cannot be a diplomat. You should also be able to bite, and bite hard."

Eileen grimaced.

"You wanted the truth. I'm telling you the truth. Violence exists, but it doesn't get you ahead. What makes you move forward are good ideas, and Pippo had them. He started to push the family more aggressively into the housing business, which transformed Pippo into a respected boss. At that time, all families' attention was on the roads. Sicily is a hilly island. Roads, tunnels, and bridges were big business, but like I said, much of that work was awarded to companies from the north. Pippo came up with the idea of building houses in Palermo while everyone else fought over infrastructure projects. There was government money available to build houses, and it was all managed in Sicily. Homes, like roads, could be sold at a premium, bringing profit to the family. But the problem was the protection of the historic sites. Everything was historic in Palermo, and to build new houses it was necessary to tear down old ones."

"But you could restore them, right?"

"No. Funds were available for new middle-income houses, not to recover old mansions. The political opposition was enormous, and other families abandoned the idea. Pippo came up with a unique strategy—form an alliance with the communists. Everybody thought he was crazy, because the communists were always hassling Sicilian families, but Pippo was a master. He convinced the communist that tearing down old mansions and replacing them with apartments benefited the poor and harmed the rich ruling class. The apartments are ugly, but they brough in a lot of income to our family. When Don Giacomo finally died, Pippo officially became the family *capo* with the blessing of Signora Paola and his brothers."

"And you were the first lady?" teased Eileen.

"Well, not precisely. Our success attracted a lot of jealousy, especially from those families from Corleone controlling the drug traffic. Pippo tried to convince them that our business would not interfere with theirs, but men are irrational. Other families feared that Pippo, with all of his money and connections to the communist, might try to take over their businesses. So, a war started, and you don't want to be the first lady in war times. They started to accuse Pippo of crimes that others had committed, and the politicians from Roma took advantage of that to prosecute him. We were permanently moving from one hideout to another. Pippo became one of the most wanted people on the entire island. Our family was strong, and our people were happy, but our life was hell. That is why we came here."

"Is Pippo still the capo?"

"No. The capo is now Carlo, Pippo's oldest brother. You cannot be the *capo* of a family being away. The boss needs to be close to know what is going on. People change, and sometimes they rethink their loyalties. A *capo* needs to be closer to anticipate movements, avoid problems, and keep everyone under control. Carlo leads the family, and when he needs to he asks Pippo's advice."

"Doesn't it bother you that they are involved in those *marginal activities*, as you called them?"

"It's true that families are involved with gambling, drug trafficking, prostitution, smuggling, and even illegal arms sales. Money is needed, and Sicilians are not afraid to take risks. We do what others refuse. When it was illegal to produce the booze in this country, we, the Sicilian families, did it. Many people like to gamble, hire prostitutes, and do coke. We took charge of delivering them. Now that pot is legal, everybody wants to produce it, but before, it was a cursed activity, and we were the ones doing it. And let me tell you something, as Pippo use to say, legal marijuana is now a business as dull as an insurance company or a bank. Before, that was much funnier. Trash collection is also a dirty and undesirable business, not so boring as legal pot, and we're involved in that, too. Today, most of our activities are in partnership with corrupt government officials who appear in the news on promoting noble causes and fundraising dinners. We pay them to show their faces while keeping the families away from the cameras. They are honorable citizens, and we are considered criminals. But who cares? Our families are safe and wealthy."

Their conversation ended when Pippo barged into the cottage raging in Italian. *"Quel maledetto arruso, vuole venire."*

"Un'altra volta?" replied Vicenza surprised and angry, adding an expression that Eileen was becoming familiar. *"Figlio di una puttana."*

As soon as Pippo left, banging the door, Vicenza explained Pippo was upset because a US senator who they disliked was coming with friends to the White Stone House for a visit.

"Why you let him?" asked Eileen.

"He's very influential in the Foreign Affairs Committee He's a closeted gay and comes here for his parties with his gay friends for the weekend. Pippo hates them because they always want to use the sailing boat, but the truth is that as an old Sicilian, he doesn't like gays."

"Interesting," replied Eileen sarcastically. "He doesn't like gays but enjoys La Vero's dick."

Vicenza didn't comment. She just looked at Eileen as if saying. *"Sei una figlia di puttana* too," and after thinking a little bit, she elaborated. "Yes, we Sicilians are weird. My oldest sister wanted to be an actress, and my father didn't like it. It was an endless nightmare at home, and my father asked Don Giacomo to interfere. My father was worried that her behavior of kissing a man in a play was dishonoring him. Don Giacomo ruled that if she wanted to be an actress, she should leave Sicily, and to offset his rudeness, he paid her moving expenditures to Rome. She went, became a TV hostess."

"Amazing, your father accepted your husband's illegal and violent activities, and could not accept your sister's kisses."

"Don't try to compare those things," scoffed Vicenza. "Sicilia is a conservative place, and people do not like to expose intimacies. Whatever couples do, they should do it inside their houses. I have kissed every single inch of your body, but I would never touch you in front of others. That is how we are."

10.

Unveiling more secrets. The guests were expected Friday evening, and Eileen left the cottage in the morning. "I think the worst is over," she told Vicenza while gathering her things. "I haven't had a fever for three days, and I feel stronger. My house is close, so I'm going to move back there. But we can keep seeing each other every day."

The virus was spreading, and most people were confining their movements, but Eileen needed groceries and she felt well enough to drive. She bought what she needed, but while going back home, she felt dizzy and realized that she would not be able to unload the car. She passed by Vicenza asking for help.

"I can go with you, but I need a few minutes," said Vicenza. "Our guests arrived, and I want to be sure that they are all well accommodated." And she added with a mischievous expression, "If you want, you can come with me and see them."

Curiosity overpowered weakness, and Eileen walked into the neighbor's garden and sat on a bench hidden by bushes. From there, she saw the guests; four of them were older, and the others, six or seven, younger and stunning. They split themselves into two guest houses.

"I can't believe it," said Eileen when Vicenza returned. "Those young guys are so cute. I never saw such pretty faces."

"And this is nothing," said Vicenza. "If you come back tomorrow when they go to the pool, you would see their bodies. Spectacular!"

"There is something I'm curious about," prodded Eileen. "Why do you and Pippo have to sleep there? Are you part of the party they have at night?"

"No, my dear," answered Vicenza. "We are not part of their gathering, but they believe we are the house owners."

"Vicenza, enough of this bullshit. You own the property, and your small house is just a front to fool the FBI."

"Okay, let's talk about this later."

"No. Answer me right now. Do you own the whole property or not? And I do not want more lies."

Vicenza stared at Eileen for a moment.

"Yes, and no. We don't *own* the house. Officially, it belongs to a Panamanian company. But there are no actual owners, and all decisions are made by us and solely by us. Pippo and I planned the house and hired architects, contractors, and all people required for maintenance. Nobody but us decides who the guests are and when they visit. And yes, the little house is just a façade. Pippo and I live in an apartment on the second floor of the mansion that I will show you when our guests leave. And now, no more questions, let's take the groceries to your house that I must return to host their dinner."

• • •

Eileen went to Vicenza's little house the following day. From there, she could see the pool from the bedroom. and Vicenza met her there. "That older one with a light green Speedo and tanned skin is US ambassador to a Scandinavian country. He is funny and charming but unbearable when there are young males around. That other one wearing that ridiculous Hawaiian shirt is a federal judge, and the fourth older man next to the senator is a congressman from North Dakota."

"You can take the four older ones for you, and I will be happy to take all the young ones for me," said Eileen teasing. "They are gorgeous."

The weekend was uneventful. The guests lingered by the pool, kayaked in the creek, and partied inside the guest houses. Pippo only joined them when they wanted to sail.

"He will never let a bunch of men, gay or not, take the boat," explained Vicenza.

Eileen sat on her terrace with binoculars watching *Marianella* sailing out of the creek with colorful guests and Pippo at the helm.

• • •

Sunday evening, they were all gone, and life was supposed to get back to normal, but on Monday, Vicenza called Eileen asking for help. Pippo didn't want to leave his bed, and not even La Vero could convince him to dress.

Eileen went to Vicenza's, and for the first time, she got inside the main mansion. Vicenza started talking about Pippo, but Eileen was distracted by the house. She walked through the pool terrace door into a large sunroom decorated in three separate arrangements. In one, an oversized couch for four people and two smaller ones with two seats; in the middle, a round table with nine chairs, and on the other side, three loveseat sofas. A vast and pleasant place for multiple gatherings and conversations.

The room had large glasses doors, allowing a view of the pool and the large white stone beyond it. Vicenza took Eileen to a hallway where a grand staircase led to the second floor. While crossing it, Eileen peaked at the dining room on the right and the living room on the left, both sumptuously decorated with antique furniture and classic paintings. In the dining room, a tapestry on the wall caught her attention. It was a bucolic image with some peasants and olive trees. Everything was astonishing.

They climbed the stairs to the second floor where there were only two carved wood double doors, one on each side. "The right one leads to a VIP guest room," explained Vicenza, "and the one to the left is our apartment."

"Here is where we live," said Vicenza opening the door. "The first floor, we only use for guests."

Eileen entered a small lobby. "We don't want guests to see inside if the doors are open," clarified Vicenza.

As Eileen crossed it, she got into a spacious but extremely cozy room with a modern kitchen, a dining table with four chairs, a living room with comfortable couches, and two large-screen TVs.

"Pippo likes to watch multiple soccer games at the same time," explained Vicenza.

Nothing there was as ostentatious as the first floor.

"I have the feeling that I wanted to stay here all day," said Eileen, walking to the terrace where she had a view of the pool, the imponent white stone, and the garden around it.

Vicenza pointed to the two doors behind a large couch, "There, we have two apartments with bedroom, closet, bathroom, and office. One for me on the right with a view to the pool, and one for Pippo on the left, but let's not bother them. La Vero is with him., and he is crying."

"Oh my God!" said Eileen.

"Don't worry," replied Vicenza, "it's not the first time. When he gets depressed, Pippo wants to stay inside his bedroom, and last time he stayed for three days. We must be patient."

Eileen saw Vicenza's office with the table that she used to handwrite letters. On the wall was a map of Sicily and plenty of photos. "As I cannot see my friends, at least I can look at their city on the map or picture of their region. It inspires me to write them. I feel that I'm not far away."

Inside the bedroom, a queen bed, and Vicenza justified. "I didn't buy a big bed since I never thought I would have someone sleeping with me. Now I think I will switch it for a king size."

They made love. More than once.

· · ·

Pippo remained for four more days confined to his bedroom. Eileen stayed at her house and Vicenza at hers, but they always slept together in one of their houses, both insisting that their room was cozier.

Eileen was feeling better each day, but Vicenza was getting anxious. Eileen often asked why, but Vicenza refused to say until she exploded one evening.

"I can handle the calls for a few days, but I can't manage all conversations by myself any longer."

"What are those conversations?" asked Eileen, trying to help.

"Conversations. That's what we do," answered Vicenza harshly.

"Look," said Eileen, "I understand that you are stressed, and I want to help. You spent all your day coming and going between our houses trying to take care of Pippo, and I see that your telephone is always ringing. I want to do something to ease your life, but I can't if you insist on keeping secrets."

They were in Vicenza's apartment sitting on the terrace. Peonies were blossoming in the garden, and the summer sun was shining.

"Okay, no more secrets. Now, I will tell you the full story, not the one you are writing to the FBI, but the real one, but first I need to explain why we had to leave Sicily. And it wasn't only because we were successful and worked with communists. She stood and began pacing.

"At the time Pippo was *capo*, violent guys from Corleone dictated most of the families' actions. If you Google, you will find names such as Toto Riina and Provenzano, or the *Corleonesi* as they were called. Many bosses followed their ideas triggering a violent and unnecessary war with the government. It was a nightmare for everyone. Some prosecutors were killed, and as Pippo was a capo, he was accused of the murders. That is why our lives became hell. The Corleonesi went to jail, and we decided to come to the US."

"So, you are saying that Pippo was involved in the deaths of Falcone and Borselino?"

"*Mannaggia?* Now you even know their names. Are you becoming an expert on Sicilian history?" asked Vicenza sarcastically.

"No, I'm not, but I'm also not dumb. I read that Sicilian families ordered the death of those prosecutors. Was Pippo part of the Commissione?"

"What are you saying? What Commissione is this?" roared Vicenza.

"Vicenza, you fooled the FBI. But you don't have to keep repeating those lies to me. I know what happened in the nineties, and I read about the Commissione who was leading the Sicilian families. Could you please confirm whether Pippo was part of it?"

Vicenza didn't answer immediately. She walked around the apartment and sat back in the armchair in front of Eileen. "Yes, but he didn't want to."

Eileen stayed in silence and kept looking into Vicenza's eyes. She knew that Vicenza had more to explain.

"I told you before that each family has its own boss. But sometimes bosses disagree and step on each other's feet. That's when coordination is necessary. That's what the Commissione does."

Eileen noticed that Vicenza mentioned the Commissione in the present tense.

Vicenza paused for a few seconds and then continued. "Yes, Pippo was part of the Commissione, but at that time, the priority was to stop the war between families. The Corleonesi wanted to be tough with the prosecutors, and the other bosses chose to compromise. It was a mistake, now we all know, but Pippo and others were concerned with the internal war that was destroying the families. The Commissione didn't direct the killings, but they could indeed have stopped it, and they didn't. Pippo was one of the capos, and because of this we had to leave Sicily. The reaction was huge and deeply hurt all families."

"Pippo is still a *capo*?" asked Eileen

"No, our family capo is his brother. Pippo is just a consigliere."

"And what are those conversations that you mentioned? You said that they are many. It could not be only with his brother.

"You are such a pain in the neck," replied Vicenza. "When will you stop with your questioning?"

"When you tell me the truth."

"The truth is that many people were impressed with the work we did here. Some families in Sicily were already cooperating with American families on drug smuggling, but that was all. After Pippo came to the US, he helped them to expand their coordination to other areas, and they started to make big money. After the whole mess with the Italian prosecutors' killings, nobody knew what to do, and families were adrift. They were looking for new voices to lead them, and Pippo, here, from the US, turned out to be what they were looking for. From here, we helped them to expand their business, and with the Corleonesi out of the picture, Pippo helped to bring peace to the families and brought them all back to work."

"Still working on those noble areas, such as prostitution, smuggling, and gambling," added Eileen sarcastically.

"All of them, noble areas," repeated Vicenza, accepting the sarcasm. "That's what our families do, and so what? That's where the money is, and those are the deals that nice people like you don't want to touch. But listen. Pippo and I don't do any of that any longer. What we do is to help the families' businesses, as I explained before. We smooth out conflicts and help legitimize businesses.

"We had spent tons of money when we first arrived here bribing FBI and DEA agents, but they were never reliable. As Don Giacomo used to say, 'If you betray once, you will betray twice.' All we had were a bunch of second-class Judas until Pippo decided to go a step further, reaching judges, high level politicians and managers of financial organizations. We knew that those people would not accept bribes, but Pippo had a theory. Power and sexual desire go hand and hand. The more power a man has, the more sex he wants. Some of them are perverted, others are gays, and some need a bunch of whores to satisfy them. Different attitudes, but one common reality—there is no such thing as a powerful monogamous man who could be happy with a once-a-week fuck with his wife. And that led us to a second and more important conclusion—every powerful man has a sexual secret. We started to hunt for them. Pippo put together a team of whores in Washington DC. According to him, they were the best, and I believe since nobody knows whores as he does. It was a group of women paid with gold, helping us identify vulnerable judges and politicians. And it worked perfectly. Later, we expanded our troops to include some gay guys. Two of them were part of the young crew you saw at the pool. Thanks to those women and men, we unveiled secrets and created a network of honorable people who we call upon when we need help or a favor.

"Now, they all trust Pippo, and practically don't do anything without consulting with him. That is why my telephone keeps ringing. And it's why Pippo is depressed, crying in his pajamas because he loves La Vero's *minchia*. Did you get it now? Can you understand why I'm stressed?"

"Interesting," said Eileen. "I respect your problem, and how ironic it is. After living a nun's life, I'm having an affair with the wife of a top Mafia consigliere."

"*Vaffanculo*," was Vicenza's reply, and Eileen understood.

11.

A treacherous puzzle. The next day, Eileen went back to the post office and Miss Dillan was happy to see her back.

"Everybody is scared about the virus," remarked Miss Dillan. "Other than you, we had two more cases in Clairsville. Vivian, who visited her mother in California, is still in the hospital, and Mr. Olsson, a retired college teacher who owns a waterfront house not so far from yours, is sick. He denies it, saying that he has the flu, but his wife told me that he couldn't taste or smell anything. That's a telltale symptom of COVID."

Eileen listened as Miss Dillan rambled on about others' illnesses. The postal clerk was unusually anxious, as if something was bothering her. "Are you sure everything is fine with you and your family?" Eileen asked.

Miss Dillan hesitated for an instant but chose to be forthright.

"My family is fine, but I am troubled by some things I heard about Vicenza, who I know is your friend. She picked up your mail while you were sick."

"That's true. Vicenza and I are friends. So, what is troubling you about her?"

"It's about Franz, who used to work at the US Marshall Office in Baltimore, and from what I heard, he was a respected agent, but something happened with his career. and Franz doesn't like Miss Vicenza and her husband."

Miss Dillan spewed a litany of rumors about the Vicenza and her husband, their connection to the mansion and fancy cars, the boat, and mysterious visitors. Franz has been in town asking around about Pietro, the former gardener of Miss Vicenza's neighbor, insinuating that Mr. Giuseppe may have had something to do with his sudden departure to Italy."

Eileen grew suspicious. She had asked Vicenza about the former gardener, and Vicenza never gave a clear answer, surprising for someone who had worked with him for fifteen years.

"Was he a nice man?" Eileen asked.

"Pietro was a hard worker. Miss Vicenza helped him with his business, and everything seemed to be going fine, but Pietro changed after his wife left him. Pietro started to drink, curse, and badmouth everyone. Miss Vicenza was patient and kept him working, but he left to go back to Italy, and we never heard from him again."

Later that evening, Eileen repeated to Vicenza what Miss Dillan had told her, and Vicenza reacted with rage.

"*Questo Frank é un strunzu.* He is a pain in the neck, always suspecting us and creating problems. He worked at the US Marshall Office, which was, in theory, the office responsible for the witness protection program, but we always dealt directly with the FBI. When his name was proposed to lead the Baltimore office, we reached our friends to discredit him. He was suspicious of us, and we didn't want him in charge. He found out and has tried to screw us since. Pippo used our contacts to force him to retire, but he still has friends in the Department of Justice, and he may be dangerous. Do not worry, though, we will do something."

"Now I'm worried," replied Eileen. "What do you mean by *do something*?"

"I won't do anything fishy, I promise. I will just ask a friend to keep an eye on him."

"Jimmy perhaps?" asked Eileen.

"Could you please take care of your own business," replied Vicenza. "You are my lover, not a detective. I'm still waiting to read the story that I'm going to tell the FBI, and by the way, now that we know that Franz is around, better be very careful in what we write."

"How much does Franz know?" asked Eileen.

"A lot. He had access to all FBI information, but he never knew about our parallel businesses. He spent years trying to prove that we were involved in illegal activities, but he never could. He even took pictures of Pippo driving the Corvette falsely alleging that the Corvette was ours, suggesting that caretakers couldn't afford such luxuries as sports cars and boats."

"Wait, the Corvette does belong to Pippo."

"I know," Vicenza said, "but nobody else knows, and he couldn't prove it. It's registered to the Panamanian company that owns the house. Anyway, we must be careful."

"Do you think that he will have access to your presentation?"

"Probably. Franz still has many friends."

"Then we better be consistent. He might also have access to your tax income information, and it's important to make your story match with the lies that you probably told to IRS."

"We don't tell lies," Vicenza teased. "It's just that we have our own interpretation of facts."

• • •

Eileen worked for two days at Vicenza's apartment, writing the presentation to the FBI. Meanwhile, Pippo was still depressed, spending his days inside his bedroom with the AC on, only going outside late at night to walk to the dock and stay near *Marinella*. The only visitors were La Vero and Jimmy.

Eileen was astonished by the complexity of Vicenza and Pippo's tax documents.

"I have no idea what they say," Vicenza said. "Our accountant prepares them."

"According to documents," said Eileen, "you and Pippo own

four limited liability companies—The Palumbo Electricity, created twenty-three years before with Giacomo Palumbo, Jimmy's full name, and you still deny that Jimmy works for you. The Trapani house sitters, established eighteen years back, is wholly owned by you and your husband, Giuseppe Vittorini. A third one, Il Giardiniere, was created one year later with Pietro Badalucco, and a fourth was established two years ago in association with Carlo Pezzini under the name Palermo Transports.

"Those companies are fake and never had offices. The accountant created them to justify some money transferring," Vicenza said.

"It doesn't matter if they were real or not. You told the IRS that they exist, and you can't deny it now. And here I see that Il Giardinieri, according to your information, was a partnership with the same guy that Franz is asking questions about. All this must be explained, otherwise, you will be in trouble.

"*Maledetta!*" cursed Vicenza.

"Don't worry, we have enough to please them." Eileen showed her the page with her notes. "But before we write the final version, I want to listen to it from you. You already read my notes, and I want you to talk pretending that you were speaking to the FBI in a large auditorium."

Vicenza laughed and stood. She then walked a few steps to the terrace door and started by waving her hands and bowing her body as if receiving applause.

"I will tell you about our life," she started, "and I will try not to be boring. I hate boring presentations. But let me be clear, it was not my idea. I was invited, and when the FBI invites you, you had better do what they want. So here goes. My husband and I lived for more than twenty years as a protected witness. The beginning was tough. We didn't know what to do. We were alone in a foreign country, and as we used to say in Sicilia, *'E' megghiu 'n curnutu o su paisi. ca un minchiune unn'ègghiè,'* which means, Better be a cuckold in your own country than an idiot abroad." Vicenza paused as if listening to imaginary laughs from the audience. "First, we tried to learn English by watching TV and reading newspapers, and thanks to the money we got from the program, we could survive, but we wanted more. You are all from the Department of Justice, and you know very well that equal justice for all, or as we say *A liggi è uguali pi tutti*, but you also know that *'ma cu avi i picciuli si nni futti'.* Those who have the dough couldn't care less. We needed *picciuli*, and where the program sent us there were three kinds of people. The rich who have waterfront houses with a dock for their yachts, those who had a lot of land to plant corn and soybeans, and the others who had to provide services wealthy people need. We wanted a job, we didn't have any skills, except robbing banks and stealing.

"We got lucky when a friend who was an electrician arrived from Italy, got a loan and established a business with us. We even tried to help with the work, but neither my husband nor I were good with wires. But as we say, *Camina chi pantofuli finu a quannu non hai i scarpi.* Walk with your slippers until you can buy your own shoes, and that's what we did. Later our neighbors asked us to housesit their property during the winter, a perfect job. We just have to pretend we own the place. We hired people to take care of it and would send all bills to the owner. We loved it, and we realized that there was no caretaking company in the area. That is when we created our own, which has been our main business since then. We worked hard, but that's the price *Nun si po' aviri la carni senz' ossu*, which means, 'You can't have meat without the bone.' We even tried other businesses, first a gardening company with another Sicilian who decided to go back to Italy, and another one, more recently, to help a Sicilian who came to the US. With him, we bought a van and opened a transport company. With all those businesses, we are doing fine. We have already fully paid our mortgage, and we have enough money to retire soon. That's been our life, and the lesson we learned is that you can do it if you try, and *Cu e fissa sta a so casa*, which means, 'If you are stupid, better stay home.'"

"That's perfect," said Eileen, applauding. "I wish we had taped it. Now you can call your FBI friends and tell them that you are ready."

Vicenza was so happy that she kissed Eileen, and they went to bed to celebrate.

They were already half naked when Vicenza's cell phone rang, and Vicenza answered it with the speakerphone. It was a man speaking English with an Italian accent. The man wanted to speak with Don Giuseppe, but he could not reach him, which was understandable since Pippo was still in his pajamas locked up in his bedroom. They used a few Italian words, but Eileen understood that the man managed a prostitution ring in London and had problems with some Albanians in charge of smuggling women from Eastern European countries. Vicenza listened and said she would convey the message to Don Giuseppe as soon as possible.

When she hung up, Eileen immediately asked, "Vicenza, are you nuts? You can't be involved with that. It is human trafficking,"

"*Dio, quanto sei ingenua.* It's not. Those women live like they're in hell in their countries and want to live as princesses in beautiful cities. This New York family's operation is not cheap prostitution in vans. They run excellent clubs, mainly in London, where those women can make a lot of money, but the girls need documents. And the beauty is that one of my friends belongs to a Sicilian family who are experts in forging immigration papers, and partner with the Albanians he mentioned. All we have to do is to put all parties in contact with one another."

"And if they don't?" asked Eileen.

"If they don't, someone will have to show their muscle, but I'm sure that it will not be necessary. The operations the Albanians have with my Sicilian-American friends provides them more profit than they could squeeze from any similar business in London."

"Could you please be more specific? What muscle are you talking about?" insisted Eileen.

"Strong muscles, and now I will show you," and while saying that,

Vicenza pressed her hand in Eileen's crotch. "I will torture them." She fingered on Eileen's vagina. Do you understand now? They will not bear the pain we will inflict them." Eileen closed her eyes in ecstasy.

12.

They were partners. Eileen and Vicenza stayed inside the bedroom late at night. They were both hungry. Vicenza proposed to cook a garlic and oil pasta, and Eileen, who couldn't conceive a meal without vegetables, washed some lettuce, tomatoes, and onions for a salad. They thought Pippo was sleeping, and they were just wearing camisoles and silk shorts, but suddenly, Pippo's apartment door opened; it was La Vero.

"Is Pippo with you?" asked Vicenza.

"No. He left to walk to *Marinella*. I was waiting for him when I heard you. I'm hungry too. Is there something that I can do to help you?"

"Yes," said Eileen pointing to a high stool near her. "Sit here and tell us how Pippo is today?"

"He seems to be in a better mood. It was not yet dark when he left, saying that he had something to do in the boat."

"I believe that you already realized that none of us is more important to him than *Marinella*, his only true love," teased Vicenza.

Eileen was staring at Veronica, fascinated with her natural beauty and elegance. She was wearing one of Pippo's T-shirts and looked ready for a photo session with her hair loose and no makeup.

"But I'm worried," said Veronica changing her expression." Sometimes he is better, probably because of the medication, but I feel that he—" She paused.

"Go ahead," said Vicenza. "There is no one else with whom you can talk about Pippo."

"I feel that he is sinking and sinking, and I don't know if we will ever have him back." Veronica got teary.

"Why are you saying that?" Vicenza asked.

"Because that is what it is. It doesn't matter if we like it or not. Pippo is going deep and deep into his destructive thoughts, and I don't see how we could get him out of it."

Eileen and Vicenza looked at each other; it was not going to be a light dinner.

"I can see that you girls are living a honeymoon moment, and I'm happy for that," said Veronica, "but Pippo is in no honeymoon at all."

"I'm surprised," said Vicenza. "You are always positive, and now, I'm worried." Vicenza walked around the balcony to approach Veronica, and Eileen took her place, putting the pasta into the boiling water.

"I don't want to be negative, but Pippo is opening a pandora's box."

"About his sexuality?' asked Vicenza.

"No. It's much more than that. He is now questioning what he did, how we live, and it reached a point that he doesn't even know what he wants."

"Wait. Slow down. I'm not following you," interrupted Vicenza.

"It probably started with his sexuality. Pippo discovered that he had a different pleasure with me, and it made him rethink his masculinity."

"Okay," Eileen interrupted. 's "If we want to really understand what is going on, let's go step by step. Why is sex with you so different? Vicenza and I had already talked about it, and we don't think we fully understand. Is it because he enjoys being penetrated?"

"It's not that. Pippo doesn't particularly like to be passive. Our sex is different than yours. I've seen you exchanging caresses on the couch. It was sweet and gentle. But that is not what we do or what Pippo likes. The words sweet and gentle don't exist when we make love. We are brutal, wild, almost violent. That's what he enjoys. I had never made love with such a powerful man. And I am not passive. I love to touch every inch of his body vigorously, and he does the same with me. Sometimes I feel as if we were fighting. I devour his penis as he devours mine, and he penetrates me with fury, what I like. It's probably difficult for you to understand. Pippo is not sweet, fragile, and vulnerable when we make love. And what he feels doesn't have anything to do with his stupid prejudices about machos and gays. But how can I make him understand that? He hated the behavior of your guests last week, and he cannot dissociate what we do from what they did, and it hurts him. But this was just how it started. Once he got depressed, it triggered a wide questioning process. His work, his life, and his future. Everything blew up at the same time."

Veronica continued. "He is powerful and rich. He has a magnificent house, a new Corvette, *Marinella,* and money to buy whatever he wants, but it doesn't mean anything to him anymore. There is nothing that he wishes for, and it hurts and depresses him. He can keep playing his games and developing strategies to expand his Sicilian friend's businesses, but there is nothing more for him there. I believe he would like to do something else, but he doesn't know what, and he knows that even if he chooses a new path, he will not be able to follow it. He is a prisoner of his own success. He loves boating and sailing, but he knows that he will never be fulfilled as a waterman or a sailor. I told him to leave everything and take *Marinella* to the Caribbean. But what would I do there? he asked me. And we know the answer. Nothing. I also suggested Sicily. He is always talking about this place, Ortigia. 'Go there with *Marinella*,' I suggested. But how can he do it? Pippo cannot be an unknown sailor anywhere in Italy and maybe nowhere in the world. And even if he could hide in a simpler life, he will miss the luxury of Las Vegas and New York, which he also enjoys."

While Veronica was talking, Pippo entered the apartment.

"From your expressions, I believe that you were talking about me," he said. "Do not worry; I'm feeling better."

"Great," replied Vicenza. "Why don't you take Veronica to sail for a few days. I can handle the phone calls."

"I wish," Pippo said, looking at Veronica. "But our Oaxacan princess doesn't like the waters."

"It's not that I don't like it," replied Veronica. "I love the land. I was born with my feet in the dirt. I can spend hours admiring *Marinella* with her open sails, but only if we are near the shore. When we get far away, I get in a panic. Sorry."

Vicenza served pasta for the four of them. Pippo fetched the wine from a cooler. "It's a memorable dinner. The first time that the four of us sit together, and we deserve a Montrachet to celebrate."

He opened the bottle, served the four glasses, and toasted. When they brought the glasses back to the table, Eileen grilled him with a question.

"Please, tell us, Pippo. From where do you derive your sadness?"

Pippo didn't answer immediately but noticed that Vicenza and Veronica were all ears listening to him.

"When you are older, you reflect on choices you made in your life. And you question if they were the best ones." He then stopped to look at Vicenza. "We did everything we dreamed, and I can tell you for sure that we accomplished all we wanted. We didn't choose the easy way, but even so, we made it, and I do not regret a single thing, but sometimes I wonder if we knew for sure what we were looking for. The ego is a bad advisor. Sometimes you aim high, not knowing precisely why you want to get there."

"But the whole fun could be in the journey and not in Ithaca itself," suggested Eileen.

Pippo didn't hesitate. "The journey was amazing, no doubt about it, but now a natural question arises, where do we go now? And I am not sure that I know the answer." And he looked toward Vicenza again. "Do you know what else you want? Is this luxury house the jail cell that we always avoided, with the difference that instead of iron, we have lavishly ornated golden bars?" And after a sip at the glass of wine, he added. "But now, let's eat. The pasta and the salad look tempting, the wine is perfect, and we could not be in better company. Time to enjoy it."

• • •

After dinner, Eileen felt tired, so they went back to Vicenza's bedroom. Vicenza was fully awake as Pippo's words were pounding in her head. "Go and rest. I can still write a few letters."

Eileen wanted to remain close to Vicenza and lay down on the couch near her. She looked at Vicenza for a few minutes and then said, "I admire, and in a certain way envy, the passion with which you write these letters. I neither have friends to write to nor something to tell them. Tell me, why do you write them?"

"Those letters are essential for us," explained Vicenza. "I believe that they are one of the main reasons for our success. All strength we have come from the Sicilian families. If we resisted for all those years, it's because they are pleased with our work. American families and those international groups such as the Albanians or Russians see us as occasional partners. We are helpful but not essential to them. They work with us because we can deliver, and we can do it because we have the families' support. Whatever Pippo is, it's because the Sicilian bosses want him to be. It took a long time for Pippo to understand that. For more than twenty years, we had to meet their expectations. Trust me, nothing is more fleeting than power. One day you could be at the top and the next in the gutter, and there were moments we struggled. We were far from our people, and Pippo was getting anxious. He knew that he could not trust all that was being said by Sicilian bosses. To lead, Pippo had to understand what was going on, and that's what my letters do. They are not from bosses but from my friends, their wives, and their daughters. Women who are not afraid of words. I started to write to them and quickly answer their letters. Today, I have with them the same kind of conversation we would have in Palermo on a Saturday morning in the Mercato di Ballaro or Vucciria.

"But isn't it dangerous? Those letters could reach the wrong hands."

"We learned how to write carefully," replied Vicenza. "We don't tell names or share secrets. We just gossip, and you know how revealing gossips could be."

"But I saw your expression while reading the last one, and you were worried," said Eileen.

"I am. My friends are asking about Pippo. Is he sick? Does he have the virus? Almost every single letter I receive includes a question about him. People in Sicily know that something is happening, but what can I say? That his *camurria* is because he loves a woman who is a man."

"What if you tell them that he got the virus?"

"I don't know. Many people could be willing to take his position, and if they believe he is sick, they might have wrong ideas."

"Tell that he got infected, survived it, and is now rehabilitating. It will make him look stronger. That's how I feel," said Eileen with her eyes already closed.

"It might be a good idea," answered Vicenza.

13.

What is going on? When Eileen awoke the next morning, Vicenza was in the kitchen hurriedly mixing a potato salad. Veronica was crossing the living room with a duffel bag, and Jimmy was at the door with his hands full of San Pellegrino water bottles.

"Pippo decided to go on a sailing trip and we are helping him," explained Vicenza.

"Sailing?" asked Eileen, not fully awake.

"Yes. Our conversation energized Pippo, and in the middle of the night, Veronica woke me up, telling me that Pippo wanted to sail. It's crazy with so many things oing on, and it's not the time for him to leave, but better have him sailing than inside the bedroom."

"And where is he?" asked Eileen.

"He is readying the *Marinella*. Jimmy and Veronica are helping him load the boat, and I'm preparing some food. He doesn't know when he will come back."

"Is he going alone?" Eileen asked.

"Yes. Veronica prefers not to go, and she will drive to meet him when he docks at night. It's absurd. We all know it. Sailing trips should be carefully planned, but the weather is supposed to be good."

From the window, Eileen could see the pool, and Pippo kneeling in front of the white stone. Jimmy was standing next to him as if waiting for Pippo to finish praying. She was puzzled but didn't bother Vicenza with questions. She helped put the potato salad in a plastic container and carried it to the boat.

"It's not much," Vicenza said, "but at least if he gets hungry he will have something to eat."

On the dock, Pippo was in an excellent mood. Once they loaded, he untied the boat and raised the sails. It was still early and the breeze was light. *Madness*, thought Eileen, but it was refreshing to see the big white sails of *Marinella* sailing away in the creek.

Walking back to the house, Eileen overheard Vicenza chatting with Jimmy.

"And what about Franz?" she asked. "What's he up to?"

"I'm worried," Jimmy answered. "He is going around talking with people and asking a lot of questions about the White Stone House and Pippo's activities. We know Franz told an FBI friend that he learned something new and bombastic about Pippo, but I have no idea what it could be."

Eileen kept following and listening to what they were saying.

"Franz can't have anything bombastic," said Vicenza, because there is nothing new. Plus, Franz has lost his credibility within the agency. Anyway, keep watching."

After Veronica and Jimmy left, Eileen asked Vicenza, "Could you tell me what exactly Jimmy does? No more half-truths, please."

"Jimmy does everything," said Vicenza. "He is Pippos' guardian angel."

Eileen looked at her with a puzzled expression, and Vicenza explained. "As you know from the company documents, he was baptized as Giacomo in honor of Pippo's father. His mother cooked for the family for many years, and she became close to Signora Paola. Her husband died, leaving her with eight kids, seven women, and only one man, Jimmy. Women didn't have many professional options at that time, and the only income they had was from Jimmy's mother's work. But she got cancer and died when Jimmy was still a child. The story is that Don Giacomo made a deal with Jimmy. He would support Jimmy's family if Jimmy would be Pippo's guardian for life. And that is how it happened. All Jimmy's sisters are married, and three of them went to college. Two are doctors, and one is a lawyer. They are all my friends. And Jimmy dedicated his life to protecting Pippo. When we came to the US, only Pippo's mother and Carlo, his older brother, knew where we were. Somehow Jimmy found us and said he would live near us. Since that day, he has been on our side. He could be an excellent chief, but unfortunately, he gets too excited and drinks more than he should when he cooks. That is why he kept working as an electrician, boring work, but that kept him sober. He is responsible for the property's security and became an expert on computers, videos, and all that security paraphernalia."

"Is he spying on Franz?"

"Franz could be dangerous, so Jimmy keeps an eye on him."

・・・

On her way home, Eileen passed by the post office to see if she could learn more about her friends. So many things were intriguing that she even forgot to ask Vicenza about Pippo's kneeling before the white stone.

The post office was particularly busy that morning, and Eileen waited to be alone with Miss Dillan.

"What else do you know about Franz?" Ellen asked. "I spoke with Vicenza, and she is worried."

"I don't know much more. Franz was a respected professional, and as I told you, he blames Mr. Giuseppe for all his problems. I cannot tell you why, but I know for sure that he hates Miss Vicenza and her husband. When Pietro, the gardener, started to say those surprising things—"

"What was he saying?" interrupted Eileen.

"He was drinking too much and accused Jimmy of being a murderer with connections to criminals. It seems absurd, but Franz believed that Miss Vicenza and her husband had connections with Mafia, and Jimmy worked for them. Nonsense, I know, but that is what he said. After the gardener went back to Italy, Franz decided to investigate why, and he only stopped after he retired. I cannot say for sure, but the rumor is that the false accusations about Miss Vicenza's husband cost him his job."

"And what is Franz doing now?" insisted Eileen.

"He doesn't do too much. He lives out of his pension. Like many others here, he drinks, and now he is asking around about the relationship Mr. Giuseppe could have with the Russians. It seems that he suspects that Miss Vicenza's husband is a Russian agent. A hallucination!"

Eileen knew Pippo was not a Russian spy. Nevertheless, after her visit to the post office, she recounted her conversation with Miss Dillan to Vicenza, and to her surprise, Vicenza immediately called Jimmy asking him to come to the house. While they were waiting for Jimmy, Eileen looked at the pool and asked Vicenza, "I believe I saw Pippo kneeling on the pool in front of the white stone. Am I nuts?"

"No, you are not. The white stone is something special for us. It permanently reminds us of Sicily. Pippo wanted to have it here, and having it delivered was a nightmare. Can you imagine? To bring that big stone from Sicily to Clairsville, but he did it. If you go to Sicily one day, you will see the *Scala Dei Turchi* and understand why we love it. It is a kind of a promontory near Agrigento on the same south coast where my village, Marinella di Selinunte is. It's limestone, and the Scala's shape is more or less the same as our stone, but the one near Agrigento is huge, and it descends from the mountain into the turquoise waters of the sea. Pippo used to say that if Sicilia were a woman, the Scala Dei Turchi would be her vagina. He wanted to have a piece of it, and he knew where to find it."

Eileen kept listening, fascinated.

"Pippo paid some divers to detach a similar stone from the bottom of the sea and take it to Reggio Calabria, where it was loaded in a merchant boat and brought to Baltimore. An adventure. Magical things that only Pippo could do. When he left, you saw him kneeling and praying to it. I saw it too. And please, don't be surprised if you see me, Jimmy, or any other Sicilian kneeling to the white stone. It represents our island, the one and only place we love. Looking at it, I don't fear anything. Pippo is sailing to heal himself, and no matter what problems we have, Franz, the Albanians, or the FBI, I'm not scared. We can fix it. We have on our side the white stone reminding us that we can."

Jimmy arrived while they were chatting, and Vicenza spoke freely in front of Eileen.

"What Franz alleges does not make sense," said Vicenza. "Nobody here works for Russians. Does he have a hideout here? Does he have family nearby?"

"I don't think so," replied Jimmy. "The only person he visits is his aunt, his mother's sister, in a retirement community."

"Keep a very close eye on him," said Vicenza.

"Why are you so worried about Franz?" Eileen asked after Jimmy left.

"Because he is good. Once he prepared a dossier about Pippo's contacts with Sicilian families that took us months and a lot of money to make it disappear. We developed a counter dossier, and we had to use all networks we had at the Department of Justice to discredit his accusations. Franz is dangerous."

"Are you a Russian spy, too?" quipped Eileen, smiling.

"No way. It's ridiculous this idea about Russians, but Franz must have something, and we need to know what it is. Remember Marlon Brando in the *Godfather*? 'Keep your enemies closer.' That is what Jimmy is doing. And now, let me go back to my letters. From what I read today, the problem with the Albanians is not as simple as we were thinking, and with Pippo off sailing, I must take care of it. I understood what you once said about Hemingway's leopard, and I would love to rest and enjoy what we achieved, but I don't think we can, at least not now. Our life is different, and if you want a metaphor, I prefer the Chinese juggler with the spinning plates. As soon as you finish turning one plate, another needs your attention. No matter where you are on the hill or what you have, you are always vulnerable. Pippo and I climbed high, but the higher you go, the more powerful your enemies are, and if you take a moment to relax or to enjoy sailing in your boat, your enemies will ambush you. I love your idea of stopping and enjoying the moment, but I'm not sure if I will ever be able to do it."

14.

Vicenza is in charge. Veronica received word that Pippo had docked at Hoopers Island in the Chesapeake Bay, so she eagerly drove down there to meet him. When she returned from Hoopers Island, Veronica immediately contacted Vicenza.

"He is much better," Veronica said. "Full of energy and tanned. He asked me to tell you that he is feeling great and that he is thankful that you are taking care of the house."

"Was he interested in knowing about something?" asked Vicenza.

"He asked about you and Eileen, but he didn't want to talk about any business. When I mentioned what Franz was doing, he instantly cut me off by saying that Vicenza will take care of it."

"Is he planning to come back?"

"No. He is planning to sail farther south into Virginia and maybe North Carolina"

"At least he is fine," said Vicenza, hanging up the telephone.

Vicenza had been on calls much of the night, trying to sort out conundrums Pippo would normally handle. Eileen came into the room sleepy and annoyed.

"Could you please tell me what else you are doing," said Eileen. "I woke up listening to your phone calls."

"What can I do? There is a six-hour difference between Sicily and us, and no matter how many times I had explained to them, I keep receiving phone calls at three and four in the morning." Vicenza added, "A lot of people are worried."

"Worried about Pippo?"

"No. I followed your suggestion and told everybody that Pippo was recovering from the virus. They had all wished him well. Our problem is the Albanians. Do you remember when I told you that some American families complained about the Albanians' aggressiveness?"

"Yes, and you told me that people you knew had business with them and that you could appease them," replied Eileen.

"Not so easy as I imagined. The Albanians are moving all around. They want a greater cut from the Americans and are pressuring Sicilian families too. Not only do they want a bigger share of European prostitution markets, but they seem to want to completely displace Sicilian families from Amsterdam, which is a cash cow. Initially, I thought it was absurd. The Sicilians are solidly established in European prostitution, and it would be impossible to challenge us. But now I'm worried. Two letters I received from my friends made me wonder. One is from one of Jimmy's sisters, who is married to a consigliere of a Trapani family, and other from a friend from *scuola primaria*, who lives in Ciavolo near Marsala. Both suggested that there might be something worrisome going on."

"And what would that be?" asked Eileen, curious.

"They heard about Albanians visiting their cities and having conversations with unusual people."

"What do you mean by *unusual*?"

"Sicilian families, don't play with foreigners. When they must do business with them, they assign one or two people to make contacts. Nobody else talks to them. What my friends are saying is that unauthorized people made those contacts, which might mean that someone in Sicily is betraying the families."

Their conversation was interrupted by Jimmy, who arrived with news from Franz. "He has photos," Jimmy said, upset. "But this time is not from Sicilians, but Russians. He has pictures of the Russian and Lithuanian ambassadors arriving to the White Stone House."

"How come he was able to take pictures," asked Vicenza, furious.

"The guy is smart. He took the photos at night from the driveway, and he probably crawled under the trees to escape our surveillance cameras."

"Do you have the pictures?" asked Vicenza.

"Yes," Jimmy answered. "I also seized everything he had in his aunt's apartment, including a computer and a camera. That's where he has been hiding out. He will flip out that we got there and realize that we are monitoring his movements, but I had to do it. And we need to know what else he has."

Vicenza looked at the pictures and exclaimed. "*Figlio di una putana*. The two ambassadors are inside the cars, and it's clearly our driveway. You did right. Let me think about what we should do." After a pause she added. "We should not rush. Let me think, and tomorrow I will tell you."

Eileen heard the conversation and once Jimmy left, she asked, "What do you have in mind?"

"All options are in the table," replied Vicenza. "If he shows the FBI pictures of Russians on our property, they will start to ask questions. Those Russian morons came here. What can we say? That they were discussing a gambling authorization for Italo-American families. We can't. Nobody in the Department of Justice knows what happens here, but if this son of a bitch raises the suspicion that we are Russian cohorts, they will be forced to investigate, and who knows what they will find."

Vicenza immediately called Pippo's private cellphone and told him about the photos.

"Franz is obstinate, and we know that nothing will make him stop." Pippo spoke calmly and firmly, seeming to be in complete control of his emotions.

Vicenza mentioned the Albanians, but again Pippo replied with a few words. "You are doing the right thing. Something fishy is happening in Marsala, and we must know what it is."

When Vicenza finished the phone call, Eileen piped, "How will you control Franz?"

"Pippo told us," answered Vicenza.

"No," replied Eileen, "He didn't tell you what to do. He just said that Franz is obstinate."

"And nothing will make him stop," added Vicenza.

"But if nothing is going to stop him, what can you do?"

"Halt him," Vicenza blurted, turning to leave the room and indicating with her hand that the conversation was over.

Eileen persisted." You can't halt him. If Franz vanishes, it will raise suspicions. Remember that he already accused you of the gardener's disappearance."

"I'm glad that now you're thinking like one of us," said Vicenza sarcastically. "I suspect though that your motivation is to protect Franz, and I remind you that we didn't get here by protecting enemies. Nevertheless, you deserve an answer. Pietro the gardener didn't disappear in the US. He went to Italy. His entry into that country was recorded by immigration. He stayed a few days at a hotel in Rome and traveled by train to Naples, where he registered into a hotel. The Italian police documented all these movements. He disappeared in Naples, and it's nothing that we could be accused of. Second, regarding Franz and your reluctance, we will be in big trouble if we don't stop him. All previous accusations he made were squashed by the FBI, where we have friends. Now, if the Russians are the issue, the CIA will conduct investigations, and there we don't know anyone. The essence of our business is secrecy, and if the CIA starts to go around checking our property and monitoring our meetings, we are screwed. And let me add a third point. I want you to trust our people. If they want to make someone disappear, they know creative ways to do it without leaving any trace. Let me remind you again. We didn't get here by making mistakes."

In the following week, Eileen and Vicenza had some time to themselves. Thanks to the virus, there were no more meetings, neither in Sicily nor in Clairsville. Vicenza had written to her friends asking about the Marsala families. Her sources were efficient and reliable.

On the Franz front, nothing happened. Franz was livid that his cache of information was stolen, and without his evidence his case against Pippo was derailed, at least for the moment. He would keep snooping and Jimmy would keep watching.

• • •

The summer days were hot and cloudless, and Eileen introduced Vicenza to kayaking. Most of the calls Vicenza received were in the morning, and late evenings were usually peaceful. They kayaked a few times, just the two of them sliding on the creek and watching the birds fishing and flying around.

Vicenza made her presentation to the same senior FBI agent who had been monitoring them.

The presentation was perfect, and she answered all questions patiently and charmingly. "It's good that Pippo is not here," said the agent. "He would not be able to do it better."

Pippo continued his sailing trip, island hopping in the Chesapeake Bay. "He is thinking about his life" said Veronica, when the three women had dinner one night at Veronica's place. The menu was one hundred percent Oaxacan, *temelas* to start, chicken and pork, with three Oaxacan sauces, *Mole Negro, Mole Verde* y *Mole Coloradito*, and a *Capirotada* for dessert.

"You would not believe," said Veronica, proud of her cooking, "I started two days ago, especially the *Mole Negro.* You have to soak red pepper in chocolate for more than twenty-four hours."

Veronica seemed anxious and said that she worried Pippo would not return to Clairsville or to her.

"Don't worry," said Vicenza laughing. "If he doesn't come back, I will chase him down and kill him. You might not be able to see him alive again, but I will bring you his body, and we will have the pleasure of burning him."

Veronica looked at her, shocked, and Vicenza explained. "If he disappears, our Sicilian friends would want to know where he is. They will send us some experts to find him. But before that, they will make our life hell believing that we know where he is."

"But he has always been so loyal to them," exclaimed Veronica.

"Don't be naive," scolded Vicenza "Whatever we did in the past doesn't matter. It's done. Those people want to know what we are going to do in the future, and if Pippo disappears, they will want to know why. And they will be worried that he might be planning to tell what he knows to the wrong people. The *pentiti* caused great damage to the families, and they don't want another Tommaso Buscetta. Pippo knows all this. He will never disappear. He loves us, and he knows that if he vanishes, we are the ones that will suffer the most."

While driving home, Eileen asked about the Albanians.

"What kind of news are you expecting from your friends."

"I want to know what they will tell me about a young boss in Marsala. He recently took control of his family. His grandfather died, and his father was killed. He is very ambitious. Older people rarely cause us problems. They are more predictable. They question and sometimes complain, but they follow agreements most of the time. Young people don't. They have their ideas and no boundaries. Pippo does not pay enough attention to them, and I think he is wrong. He forgot that he started to lead his family when he was in his thirties. I mentioned many times that we should think forward on the succession of the current capi, but he refused it. When everything is fine, people enjoy the present and ignore future challenges. This guy in Marsala is ambitious, and if there is anyone in Sicily trying to make a deal with the Albanians, I believe he could be the one."

Vicenza's phone rang. It was Jimmy with news about Franz, and Vicenza put him on the speakerphone.

"Franz had some kind of food poisoning and was taken to the hospital."

"And how is he?" asked Vicenza.

"I don't know," said Jimmy. "Claire might be able to tell you since the paramedics took him to the hospital where she works."

Eileen was staring at Vicenza with an edgy look, and Vicenza understood her suspicion. "Listen, Jimmy, Eileen is here with me, and I believe she suspects that you have something to do with this food poisoning."

"How could I?" he replied, laughing. "I only handle cameras and microphones, and they didn't invent remote equipment to poison someone. You can tell Miss Eileen that I'm not upset that he is sick, but he will probably be back very soon to his house. It's just food poisoning, and to be honest, I prefer him at home since I do not have cameras to monitor what he does at the hospital."

Vicenza reassured Eileen. "Jimmy didn't choose what Franz ate. He just monitors him to see with whom he speaks."

. . .

Claire called the next day with more news. "Franz is recovering. It was just mild indigestion, and he panicked thinking it was a heart attack. It seems that he ate some bad bar food. Tonight, he will go home. The hospital doesn't want to keep patients because they need beds for those with the virus."

Franz went home that same night, and on the following day, he was seen walking to the grocery, but, according to Jimmy, he still seemed somewhat weak.

After that, Franz didn't leave his house, and a cough started the following week. He had contracted COVID while at the hospital. The doctors did their best to help his recovery at home, but his oxygen levels became dangerously low.

Franz was hospitalized, transferred to the ICU, intubated, and died a week later.

15.

The nightmare begins. Franz was dead, Pippo was still sailing, and the news from the Albanians was not good. The Sicilian families were worried, and a letter Vicenza received confirmed that the Marsala family was secretly dealing with Albanians.

For a few days after Franz's death, their lives were calm. "Like on the eve of a storm," predicted Vicenza teasing, and she was right. The next day a friend from the Department of Justice called sharing good and bad news.

The good news is that her presentation at the FBI was so successful that they used it to lobby Congress, and thanks to it, received increased appropriations for the witness protection program. "You are now our showcase," the agent said. The bad news he shared was that that the CIA had requested information about previous FBI investigations. "It seems that they are now interested in your neighbor's house," said the agent.

"Fuck! Franz had sent them something before he died, and now we have the perfect storm—a Marsala family conspiring with Albanians, the CIA investigating our property, and Pippo behaving like a beach bum sailing *Marinella*. How we will deal with this?" she exclaimed, frightened. "If the CIA starts to ask questions, they will discover what we do!"

"Breathe," said Eileen. "There are certainly many ways to fix it, but panicking is not one of them."

"You don't understand," insisted Vicenza. "We are not talking about a crazy guy snooping our business. This is easy. Jimmy can fix it. We are now talking about the CIA. We cannot put a pill in their beer to send them to the hospital. We never dealt with the CIA, and we have no inside contacts there."

Eileen stood speechless. Vicenza had just divulged that Jimmy poisoned Franz.

Vicenza realized that she had said too much. "Okay. *Se vuoto il sacco*. Sorry. It is what it is. I never tell you what you don't need to know. The more you know, the more vulnerable you'll be, and I don't want that, but now we don't have time for this conversation. The CIA is a bigger problem. We must leave the property as soon as possible. You should take all your stuff and go to your home, and I will move our things to our fake house. They might come very soon, and I don't want them to catch us inside this mansion."

Vicenza called Jimmy, asking him to come and help her, and immediately began to pack everything they had inside the closets. Eileen put the few things she had into two duffel bags and helped Vicenza. After an hour of frantic work, Vicenza stopped to rest and approached Eileen. "Sorry for everything I said. I panicked. Jimmy indeed put the pill on Franz's beer. We just wanted him sick at home. We didn't plan the hospital, and it was unlucky that she got the virus."

"Okay, but now let's focus on the CIA. I will stay on your side, and we will find a way out."

"I thought you would leave me, and I was scared," said Vicenza hugging Eileen.

"Me too. I'm tired of your lies and half-truths, but now you need me. Let's think about what you will say to the CIA."

Vicenza agreed, and Eileen continued. "First, let's review what they know and what they might discover once they get here." For the first time, their roles were reversed as Vicenza was tense.

"They probably saw the Russian ambassador's pictures and learned from Franz that the photographs were taken at the property," said Eileen. "They certainly know from the FBI files who you are, and they will be aware of Franz's Mafia's accusations. I'm sure they will see your presentation's video to the FBI, but they likely don't have any hard evidence that ties you to Russians." After a pause to let Vicenza digest her words, Eileen continued. "For the CIA, you and Pippo are peanuts; you're just FBI informers. The reason they are coming is the Russian ambassador. Keep this in mind, it's not about you, it's about the Russians."

Eileen stopped to embrace her friend who was visibly shaken. "They know that the house belongs to a Panamanian company, and they will be curious about it," said Eileen. "We know who owns it, but we cannot say. We must invent a lie and trust me, I'm a writer, I know how to invent lies."

Vicenza nodded her submission.

"What they will immediately realize," continued Eileen," is that the house is hidden from external observers, with one blatant exception—your home. From your window, you can observe what happens here, and do not even try to say that you don't know. According to your own words in the presentation, you took care of the house for more than twenty years."

"And what do you want me to say?" asked Vicenza.

"We must deflect the attention from you and stick to the story we told the FBI. Tell them about the Russians, and other foreign authorities that you saw here, and tell them about American politicians and judges who, you know, have also been here. Make them believe that the target of the Russians was to lobby congressmen. And do not worry about privacy. The CIA is not charged with exposing espionage or spying. They use it as leverage."

"What about the judges and businessmen who were here? What do I say about them?"

"Were there many," Eileen asked.

"You won't believe how many," answered Vicenza waving her hand.

"And what about ambassadors?

"There were many of them, too."

"If you were only observing them from a distance, how would you know them unless you recognized them from news stories or photographs."

"True," said Vicenza.

"You do not need to expose everyone, only a few to deflect the CIA from you and Pippo. Remember, the CIA knows only what you have disclosed to the FBI, so stick to that plot." Make them show the photos to you before identifying anyone."

"That makes sense," Vicenza said, "but I'm sure that CIA guys will want to know who is running the property."

"You are right," replied Eileen," but there are alternatives. We can picture the Panamanians as powerful lobbyists who do not want to appear, which will make our task more manageable. But we need someone who could pretend to be a hostess for the house."

"What do you have in mind?" asked Vicenza, intrigued.

"Well, it needs to be someone close to us that knows the house. The CIA agents could be here very soon, and we do not have time to prepare anyone. It needs to be someone that knows the property. And the only people who know the house and work for us are Jimmy and the driver Pezzini, and we do not want them being questioned by the CIA."

"Yes, but there is another person who knows it," said Eileen.

"If you are thinking about yourself, forget it. Nobody will believe that you are working as a hostess for a secret Panamanian lobbyist."

"Not me. I only know one of the guesthouses and the apartment you have inside. We need more than that. We need someone who knows the house in detail and could convince them as a hostess. I'm thinking of Veronica. We trust her, and she knows each corner of the house and its history."

"It might work, but let me talk with Pippo first," Vicenza said.

"You can't talk with him by phone. Your phones are probably bugged."

The next step was to talk with Veronica. There were risks for her, too. It was not illegal to be a hostess, but she could be deported if her lie was uncovered.

Vicenza called her using Eileen's cell phone and only said she needed to see her urgently at her house. "The little one on the post office road," she explained to Eileen. "I don't think Veronica ever came to our fake house before."

Vicenza and Eileen also agreed that it was time for Pippo to return, but how to contact him? They decided to send him a text message from Eileen's cell phone, which was probably not bugged. She had never texted him before, and he would understand that something was amiss.

Pippo, I hope that Marinella is repaired and that you can safely sail home. I'm having problems with my phone and borrowed a friend's.

Veronica arrived almost immediately and didn't hesitate to help. Like Vicenza, she was amazed by Eileen's calmness.

"The main target for the CIA is not the White Stone House, itself, but some of the guests who have attended meetings there. We need to be able to implicate at least ten prominent Americans, preferably members of the House or Senate. You don't need to tell them their names, but both of you must recognize them by the pictures the CIA will show you. We must redirect their attention to them, otherwise they will keep the focus on Pippo and Vicenza. We also must agree on approximate dates, just say whether they came last month or last year. Particularly Veronica, since she supposedly hosted them." Eileen continued. "You also must tell them a coherent story about your contacts with the Panamanians. Maybe it's better if we invent someone; let's say a man called Rodrigo, a Panamanian, is the one who tells Vicenza how to maintain the house and notifies Veronica when the guests will arrive."

"Does this Rodrigo character contact us by phone?" asked Veronica.

"No, they could check your phones for verification. Better to say that all instructions are given in person. Let's say that the guy drives here . . . each time in a different car. Say as little as possible because everything you tell them could open new clues. You should show them the house, tell them about the parties with important guests. But that should come from Veronica, who should be as vague as possible or just say you simply don't know. It doesn't hurt to look stupid. And let's not forget to move some of Veronica's clothes into the apartment.

• • •

Jimmy and the driver, who was introduced to Eileen as Carlo Pezzini, helped with the moving. Vicenza and Pippo's clothes went to the little house, Veronica's stuff into the mansion apartment, and Eileen's bags to her car. Everything was done in less than two hours.

"I would like to stay with you, but it's better if they don't see me here," said Eileen. She turned and faced Vicenza. "You continue to lie to me, but despite all your shit, I love you."

16.

It's the CIA's turn. Vicenza and Veronica agreed on a list of politicians they would implicate, and Eileen had a long conversation with Pezzini. Vicenza had noticed that the Lithuanian ambassador was inside Pezzini's van in the picture that Franz had.

"It's not a problem," said Eileen," trying to appease him. "You will tell them that it was always Veronica who told you where to pick up the guests. It's better to have Veronica as the sole contact with our fictional Rodrigo. Where did you pick up the ambassador?

"At the local airport," the driver answered. "I picked up he and his assistants there, and three days later, I took them back to the airport, just as Don Giuseppe told me."

"And that is what you will tell the CIA. The only change is that instead of receiving instructions from Don Giuseppe, you will say that it was Veronica who always told you what to do."

Late in the evening, when everything seemed ready, Vicenza remembered. "Oh, *Dio*, we forgot Miss Tsuharu! She has been the gardener for many years, and they might ask her what she saw."

"Does she know Veronica?" Eileen asked.

"She probably saw her when she was cleaning the house, but you know Miss Tsuharu, for her, only the garden matters. It's better to take Veronica to her house and explain," said Vicenza.

"Let's not tell her more than she needs to know," insisted Eileen. "She only has to confirm that she saw Veronica in the house. And let's ask her not to say anything else."

"Don't worry. I will tell her that the CIA agents are looking for illegal immigrants, and, I'm sure, she will keep her mouth shut."

On the following morning, the CIA finally arrived. Two cars and six agents. Vicenza saw them from her window but waited. They walked around the garden, checked all closed doors, and came to Vicenza's house through the passage in her backyard.

Vicenza received them at the kitchen door with a mask, flip flops, and a naive expression.

They asked her if she was responsible for the house.

Vicenza gave them the Panamanian law firm's phone number and warned them. "It's a law firm, and whatever you ask them, it takes days for them to reply, but let's see if I can help you. What exactly do you want? I have the keys, and if it's just to see the house, I can take you there. No problem."

A senior agent accepted, and they walked together to the mansion keeping a prudent distance between them. One of the agents who was next to her pointed to Vicenza's second floor windows and asked what she could see from there.

"I can see part of the garden, the driveway, half of the pool, and the dock's entrance."

"So," replied the agent, "can you tell us what they do here?"

"I don't know what they do since I rarely come when they are here, but I see them at the pool or walking in the garden."

Vicenza acted perfectly as a friendly, easy-talking caretaker.

"They have many guests."

"A lot," answered Vicenza. "At least twice a month, particularly in the summer. Sometimes they have guests every day, but since the epidemic started, I haven't seen anyone."

"Who are the guests?" asked another agent, a young woman.

"Mostly old men. Sometimes, only men, and sometimes men and younger women."

"Women who look like wives?" insisted the young woman with a mischievous expression.

"Not at all," answered Vicenza laughing. "Rather the non-wives type, with beautiful bodies and tiny swimsuits."

"Do the men look like foreigners?" asked the senior agent in charge.

"Difficult to say. Some do not look like the typical American, but most guests were white males."

"Just men and women?" asked the young woman agent. "No men-with-men kind of gatherings."

"Since you are asking, let me tell you that on some of these parties at the pool, there were only men, and the young ones were adorable," said Vicenza smiling. "But wait, I'm not here to gossip. I can show you the house, but I cannot say who the guests were and what they did. I only saw them from my window, and not all the time. As you can imagine, it's not fun to watch people partying if you are not one of the guests."

"Would you be able to recognize them?" asked the agent in charge.

Vicenza pondered for a moment, then answered with an embarrassing look. "As you are CIA, I'm sure that you can talk with your friends in the FBI. They will tell you who we are, and you will understand why I would prefer not to be involved in your investigations."

"We know everything about you and your husband, and we will respect your status, but I'm sure you would not refuse to cooperate," the senior agent snarled.

"We *always* cooperate with the FBI, and we are thankful to them since they have been extremely nice to us, but I really don't know the guests. I think I have seen some of them on TV, but you can go to my window, and you will see that it's not easy to recognize faces from there."

"What if I show you some pictures?" the senior agent asked.

"Maybe," she answered. "One of them, I know for sure. He is a senator," and Vicenza mentioned the name. "He participated in some of the parties. Those for men only."

The senator she named was not someone that Pippo and her

particularly liked. Quite the opposite. Vicenza named him knowing he was rumored to enjoy young male partners, something the CIA could easily confirm.

The older agent took his cell phone and showed her the picture of the Russian ambassador.

"Yes," confirmed Vicenza with no hesitation. "I saw him once, and he looked important. I don't know who he is, but I can tell you that he walked surrounded by bodyguards. And this one enjoyed the young women."

"By the way, where is your husband," asked the senior agent.

"Giuseppe took our neighbor's yacht to fix at a boatyard in Virginia. Something in the mast rigging was broken. I am hoping he'll be back tomorrow. Do you want me to call him?"

"It's not needed. We still have a few things to check, and if he is coming back soon, we can wait for him," replied the senior agent.

Vicenza gave two more names of people who may have attended the parties. Of course, none of were friends with she and Pippo.

"Who lives in the house," asked a younger male agent.

"Nobody. The whole property is empty most of the time, and I'm the only one walking around. When they have guests, Madame La Vero comes to receive them, but when they go, she goes too."

"And who is Madame La Vero?" asked the agent.

"She is a Mexican artist who lives nearby. When she is here, Madame La Vero uses an apartment on the second floor that I can show you."

"Are there many Mexican guests?" asked the young woman agent, suspicious.

"Not that I know, but Madame La Vero would be able to tell you better than me."

Vicenza took them inside the house and waited while the agents walked all over.

Later the young woman agent approached Vicenza on the pool terrace. "Do you know that my grandfather was Sicilian?"

"From where?" asked Vicenza.

"Porto Empedocle."

"I know that place very well," said Vicenza. "It's the village where Andrea Camilleri was born."

"Yes, and I read all books of Comissario Montalbano," said the agent

"*Parla Italiano?*"

"No, unfortunately not. My grandfather died when I was young, and my grandmother was a New Yorker. Nobody in the family speaks Italian. The only thing that I know is one of my grandfather's expressions that my grandmother liked to repeat, Cummannari è megghiu ri futtiri."

"Vicenza laughed. "And do you know what it means?"

"I think so," the agent answered: "To lead is even better than to fuck."

Vicenza then asked. "Do you know other Sicilian families?"

"No, we were raised as New Yorkers."

"Have you been where your grandfather was born? asked Vicenza.

The agent answered never, which Vicenza thought was ironic since the FBI agent was talking to her next to the massive white stone, which was extracted from Porto Empedocle's shore.

The senior agent approached with a few more questions. "I presume you know Giacomo Palumbo. Do you know where we can find him?"

"Yes, but here nobody knows him as Giacomo. He is Jimmy, the electrician, and his house is near the post office. It's the blue one, and it's the fourth to your right if you are looking at the office. "

"And Madame La Vero. Where does she live?"

"At the end of Pine Woods Road, but I can give you her phone number if you want."

"I would appreciate it, and I want to thank you for all information. We will probably contact you again."

"You're welcome, but as you might understand, I'm curious about your visit. Is there something that you can tell me? As you know, I work for them. Are they doing something wrong?"

"We received an envelope with an anonymous tip, and that's all I can tell you now."

An anonymous tip? Vicenza wondered. *Wasn't it Franz?*

17.

They must be careful. Vicenza suspected that the CIA was monitoring her movements and phone calls. Eileen proposed a strategy. Veronica would go to the neighbor's house every day to meet Vicenza, while Eileen would be responsible for meeting Jimmy at the post office. None would use their phones, and Vicenza and Eileen would meet every evening at the grocery, hairdresser, or another public venue in Clairsville.

Pippo had finally returned and immediately confronted his wife. "I received the message Eileen sent me, and I returned as fast as possible. What is going on?"

Vicenza told him everything that had happened. "I'm proud of you," he said. "You girls are managing everything perfectly. I'm sure we can handle this, but we will have to prepare ourselves for a change."

"What do you mean by that?" Vicenza asked.

"We may not be able to use this house anymore, and if the house goes, we may have to go too. But I've been sailing non-stop for more than twenty-four hours, and I'm tired. Let me have a good night's sleep, and tomorrow we will talk about it. Meanwhile, please help Veronica. She is not used to situations like this. And tell Jimmy to tell the others to be careful."

The following day, Vicenza waited for Veronica at the terrace next to the pool, and she arrived wearing one of her stunning Mexican dresses.

"If I'm going to play the hostess, I will play it with class."

"You look perfect," said Vicenza, amazed by Veronica's relaxed expression.

"They came to my house last evening," continued Veronica. "Probably, right after they left you. We talked for a while, and they proposed to meet me today to explain what I do and what happened at the parties."

"Did they show you any picture?" asked Vicenza.

"The picture of the Russian ambassador, and as we agreed, I told them I saw him twice at the mansion's parties."

"Did they show you other pictures?"

"No. I believe today they would show me more."

"The important thing is to focus on a few names," said Vicenza. "The senator, those four congressmen that I mentioned to you, and the two deputy secretaries. None of them are our friends, and all of them had come at least twice for parties with young male and female models. Those names should be enough to get the CIA to back off. Tell them that you are unsure about any other picture they show you. As a hostess, your role is limited to receiving guests and making certain they're comfortable and entertained. You don't need to know their names or what they do at night. Just try to suggest, discreetly, that things were wild inside the guest houses. Tell them that you smelled pot and saw some quest snorting what you thought was coke. And now tell me, what do they ask you about the Panamanians?"

"They asked me who gives me the instructions, and I said what we agreed, that it was Rodrigo, a Spanish-speaking man. I also told them that I didn't know how to reach him. I said it was always up to him to contact me when there was a party, but I'm unsure if they believed. For me, this is the weakest part of our story. How come I received instructions from this guy for many years, and I don't even know his full name, where he lives, and how to reach him?"

. . .

Later that morning, Eileen met Jimmy in front of the post office. "How did it go with you?" she asked.

"They wanted to know about the house, and I said I'm just the electrician. They knew about Franz's accusations, and when they showed me the Russian ambassador's picture, I pretended I didn't know who he was."

"Did they mention Franz?" Eileen asked.

"No. "They only mentioned his accusations probably because they read the FBI files, but they didn't mention his name."

Eileen went inside the post office and, while she was waiting, she recalled that, on previous visits, she had seen Miss Dillan writing in a notebook.

"I noticed," Eileen said, pretending to be casual, "that you always write things in that notebook. What is it?"

"It helps me pass my time," answered Miss Dillan. "As you can imagine, my work is not exciting. My whole day is receiving the mail truck, distributing the mail into P.O. boxes, and posting the few things people bring. People chitchat about the weather and a few other things of little interest to me. I like to talk, but only with a few customers: you—Miss Vicenza, Claire, Miss Egger, who is always worried about our community, and Miss Fiets, who works at the county newspaper and likes to tell me about the news. Some of my colleagues play crosswords, others Sudoku, and those younger spend their time sending messages on their cell phones. My hobby is taking notes. I want to know my clients better, particularly those that I like. It makes me feel closer to them. I know, for example, who is your gardener, your electrician, and your contractor, and from our conversations, I also know the hairdresser you like, the pharmacy you use, where your kids live, and I feel happy every time Miss Vicenza receives a letter from her Italian friends since I know how much those letters are important for her."

"Fascinating," said Eileen. "May I see those notes, or they are confidential?"

"They are not confidential. Silly probably, but not confidential." Miss Dillan passed Eileen her notebook.

Eileen looked, and it was almost a journal with simple information such as *Miss Fiest has a new coat, it's green . . . Miss Cynthia's daughter is coming to spend two weeks with her . . . Klaus' daughter-in-law is pregnant again, . . . Miss Vicenza received two letters, one from Agrigento and the other from Bagheria.*

"Do you write about letters we receive?" asked Eileen disguising her surprise.

"No. Only Miss Vicenza's letters. She receives them from many cities in Sicily, and I like to check the map. I've never been there, but, thanks to her, I know almost all Sicilian cities."

Eileen thought for a few minutes and spoke authoritatively.

"Look, there is something that you must know. Some bad people are trying to hurt Vicenza and Mr. Giuseppe. They have raised false accusations against them. Some government agents will probably start to ask questions about them."

"I know," replied Miss Dillan, "Claire already told me."

"Claire?" said Eileen surprised. "How does she know?"

"All Italians are friends, and they always know what is going on with each other."

"Is Claire Italian too?"

"I thought you knew. Her name is *Chiara*, but she changed to Claire when she moved to the US."

"Is there a long time she is here?" asked Eileen, astonished.

"She and her husband came after Miss Vicenza. Her husband was a close friend of Jimmy, and I even think they were cousins. But he died in a car accident in Italy, and Claire decided to stay here."

If Claire was Italian, Franz's infection at the hospital was not by chance, but it was not the time to think about that. The crucial thing was to make Miss Dillan's notebook disappear.

"If those asking questions discover your notebook, they will certainly confiscate it." "They might even come today, and if you agree, I could take this notebook with me and promise you that I will return it when this nightmare is over."

"You can take it," said Miss Dillan instantly, "but I have others at home. I open a new one every year."

"But they don't know that, and nobody must know it. Not even Vicenza. She is so protective of her friends, and I believe she might get upset."

"But I only keep the city names. I don't know who wrote them," Miss Dillan said.

"Do not worry. You do not have to explain anything. I will take this notebook with me, and you will keep the others safe in your house. Nobody needs to know, and if someone asks about her of Mr. Giuseppe, tell them as little as you can."

Eileen left with the notebook, thinking she would prefer not to mention it to Vicenza. But, again, she was upset. Vicenza hid from her that Claire was also Italian and probably Sicilian. *Vicenza, Jimmy, and Claire killed Franz.* She was certain of it.

• • •

Eileen drove to the pier. She wanted to calm herself and talk with Klaus. It was crucial to prepare the watermen; the CIA agents probably knew about Pippo's sailing and would investigate.

Klaus was not there, but his son was, and Eileen approached him.

"How is your father?"

"He is fine, but he is at home."

"Listen, there is something that I want you and him to know. The other day, I noticed that you and your father greatly appreciate Mr. Giuseppe."

"Oh yes, he is a great man, and last night, I was crabbing and saw his boat sailing into the creek."

"He is a great man but also had some evil enemies, and people are trying to hurt him. Can you help?"

"You just have to tell me, and I will do whatever I can. And it's not only me. I know that many other fishermen will do the same."

"Some people are asking questions about Mr. Giuseppe, and we all must avoid talking about him. People can always misinterpret our words."

"I agree with you. I will shut my mouth and tell my friends to do the same."

Eileen returned to her car and drove home, still fuming. Vicenza was not only a liar, she was involved in a murder.

While Eileen was at the pier, the young CIA female agent had met with Vicenza and asked her to look at a series of photographs of suspected White Stone House guests. Vicenza pretended not to recognize anyone but slyly suggested, "What if Veronica and I look at them together? Perhaps we can jog each other's memory."

The agent agreed and Vicenza and Veronica looked carefully at each one of the pictures. Vicenza knew almost all of them but only chose the ones she wanted to incriminate, none of her friends, only the others. And despite their quick preparation, she and Veronica worked as a well-rehearsed couple.

"What do you think about this one," asked Veronica.

"I am sure I saw this one," Vicenza said, adding, "I believe I saw him in one of those parties with many women."

"Yes," added Veronica. nailing the coffin. "Now, I remember him, always running behind a redhead young model."

After reviewing the files, the agents were happy with a list of thirteen names. "And what do you know about the Panamanians?" asked the senior agent.

"I can't tell you who they are," Veronica said confidently, surprising Vicenza. "But I always suspected that they had something to do with drug cartels."

Vicenza, who had not talked with Veronica about mentioning drugs, kept looking at her while Veronica continued. "I heard a few conversations between guests, some of them who are in those pictures, that were drug related. You know, I'm Mexican, and they were talking about things like extradition of drug dealers, DEA activities, and even about Mexicans who are jailed in the US."

The CIA agents scribbled notes.

After the agent left, Vicenza grilled Veronica.

"What was that about drugs and a cartel? That could have tripped me up," she scolded.

"I saw Pippo this morning, and he asked me to say that. He wanted the CIA to think that Mexican cartels are behind the Panamanians."

• • •

After the meeting, Vicenza went to the supermarket to meet Eileen.

"Everything seems to be working according to plan," said Vicenza.

"On my side too," said Eileen. She told about her conversation with Jimmy and Klaus' son, but she didn't mention Claire and Miss Dillan's notebook. It was not the appropriate moment, but she proposed a new idea. "While talking with Jimmy, I thought, *'What if we say that Jimmy banged Franz's wife, and that Franz was seeking revenge?'*"

"Are you crazy?" said Vicenza.

"No, I'm not," Eileen replied. "That discredits Franz even more."

"Franz is dead and so is his wife," Vicenza said.

"So, that just might make the CIA guys think that all Franz did was a *cornuto's* revenge," added Eileen.

Vicenza liked the idea, and when she returned home, she walked to the neighbor's property to talk with the agents who were still inspecting the cottages. She waited, and when they were ready to leave, Vicenza mentioned to the young woman.

"As with most of the disputes, we will probably realize that it's all about a woman's betrayal."

The young agent didn't understand, and Vicenza explained. "Franz was upset because Jimmy was having an affair with his wife. That is why Franz started all these accusations."

The young agent was confused. "I don't understand. Are you talking about Franz's accusations about Jimmy and you guys made to the FBI? If that's true, it's water under the bridge. We are not here because of that. We received an anonymous tip about the Russian two weeks ago, and when we read the FBI files, we also thought Franz was the informant, but the letter was posted when he was already unconscious at the ICU."

18.

The plot thickens. "How could this be possible?" said Vicenza to Eileen and Pippo when they got together for dinner at Eileen's house. Vicenza was paranoid and believed her house was bugged. "If Franz was already dying, who sent the photos to the CIA?"

"Someone who wants to screw us," replied Pippo, "But who else had that photo? We know that Jimmy took the photos of the Russians that Franz had hidden at his aunt's.

"He probably had another copy," said Vicenza.

"Yes, but Jimmy found only one copy, and Franz was in the hospital when someone contacted the CIA and gave them copies.

"Franz might have left instructions with someone to send it to the CIA if he was killed," suggested Eileen.

"No way," replied Vicenza. "Those things only happen in books and TV series. Franz was not trying to blackmail us, but he was obsessed. He somehow knew that Jimmy eliminated Pietro."

"Wait a minute," interrupted Eileen. "Jimmy killed Pietro? You told me that Pietro disappeared after going to Italy."

"There is no reason to hide from you anymore. I trust you," said Pippo, shocking Eileen and even Vicenza with his candidness. "Pietro backstabbed us, and he was going to tell the FBI about our business for the Sicilian families. We had no choice. Jimmy put an end to it. It was not planned. Jimmy caught him when he was driving to Washington and forced him to get out of the car. Jimmy did the right thing.

"After that," explained Vicenza, "we sent someone to Italy with

Pietro's passport to trick the investigators. The FBI asked the Italian police to help them, but they couldn't find him. Our problem now is that someone here in the US sent a copy of the Russian photo to the CIA. Someone close to us is trying to destroy us."

"Hold on," demanded Eileen. "There is a bigger problem. Jimmy killed the gardener. You told me that Jimmy was responsible for sending Franz to the hospital, and that was all. You never told me that Claire, the nurse, also worked for you. How can I believe that Claire didn't inject the virus in Franz?"

"Eileen," Pippo answered, "we are not in the killing business, and we hate when someone must die. But we chose to live our lives under different rules. Vicenza and I wanted to be free to live our way, and we did it. I am very proud of it. When we started, the families were fighting with bombs, and innocent people died. Now it's different, there is peace in Sicily, and innocent lives have been spared. Guys such Pietro or Franz are pawns in a bigger game of survival. We learned that Pietro wanted to snitch us because his wife was sleeping around with me, and others. And Franz was stupidly obsessed with our success. It was either them or us."

Pippo continued. "We are under attack, and if it was not Franz who tipped off the CIA, we have a bigger problem. It must be someone from one of the families. Someone wants to replace me and expand their business. My guess is that it's either Lo Picollo or Inzerillo."

"No, you are wrong," Vicenza said. "It's probably someone from the families, but not those two. They tried to challenge you for many years, but they are older and calmer now. They understood that their families are better off having you where you are. All the old capos are pleased with you, and I know it for sure. The only ones that are questioning us are Nino and those from Marsala. That's what the women are saying. I told you many times, but you ignored it. After the *Commendatore's* death, Nino, his grandson, took control of the family, and he now is trying to expand their businesses outside their region."

"Could be," said Pippo, "but I must be honest with you, Vicenza.

I'm tired, and I can't bear this life anymore." Pippo was talking, looking at his hands, seeming incapable of controlling himself. "Thank God you are here keeping the boat afloat. I would not be able to do it alone. I want, and I need to get out of all this."

"Pippo. I already told you. I will help you to do whatever you want, but now we must defend ourselves. We should resist. I remember that there were times that I felt weak, and you made me strong. Now it's my turn to push you, and I will not fail." And after a pause, she continued. "Regroup Pippo, please. The CIA is a minor problem. What could really hit us hard is a threat coming from inside the families."

Eileen followed their discussion speechless. Pippo took a breath, composing his emotions, and started to talk more calmly. "Let's ask Pezzini. He is from Marsala," and he was finishing the sentence when he stared into Vicenza's eyes.

Vicenza immediately understood. "Pezzini is the same age as Nino. Do you think they know each other? *Figlio di una puttana.* We bought him the van and helped him launch the transportation business. *Corno. Lo uccideremo!*"

"Let's be careful," said Pippo, "and let me talk to Jimmy. We must be sure." "Keep checking with the women about Nino and see if you can discover which other families might be working with him. I will talk with the capi and let's see what they think."

"Be careful," said Eileen. "Our telephones might be bugged."

"Not this one," replied Pippo showing a cellphone he carried in his pocket. "This is the one I use to talk with the families, and nobody other than us knows that it exist." Looking at Eileen, he added, "May I borrow your car? I want to visit Veronica, and I do not want to go in Vicenza's pickup truck. The CIA agents might be around."

"And, of course, he can't use the Corvette," teased Vicenza.

When he left, Vicenza and Eileen remained on the terrace. Eileen was numb. She wanted to talk about so many things that she didn't know where to start.

Vicenza broke the silence. "I love your view of the creek. It's amazing to watch the moon's reflections in the water," and after a pause, she continued. "But I know that is not about the moon and the creek you want to talk about. We don't have any more secrets to hide, and I know you are overwhelmed, but trust me. Pippo and I have faced situations like this before, and we always overcome them. There is always someone trying to take Pippo's place."

"What does it mean to 'take Pippo's place?' Do they want to come to the US? This doesn't make sense."

"I know. It's complicated to explain," answered Vicenza. "Pippo has a very influential position among the Sicilian families, something like a special consiglieri, and that has made some bosses, like Lo Picollo and Inzerillo, feel jealous and threatened. They attacked us, and we fought back, but that was years ago. Now all families understand that Pippo is not a threat and accept his counsel and direction. I receive letters from women from all families, confirming that everything is calm. The only exception is the Genna family from Marsala. It has always been challenging to deal with them. They see themselves differently, probably because of the wine they produce, which has made them famous. Pippo was able to manage the Marsala families by working jointly with the Palermo families, which was considered impossible in the past. Now we have the *Commendatore's* grandson as the *capo*, and he is young, inexperienced, and ambitious. A bad combination. We must neutralize him, but I would not be too worried. His family is not as powerful as they think."

"So, there is such a thing as the Commissione," said Eileen. "Yes, Pippo is part of it. All families need to know what is going on, which is why one of each region gather from time to time. But there is no such thing as Mafia, and the Commissione does not have a chairman. There is no *capo di tutti I capi*. It is an invention. Sometimes one of them gets more renowned, and not necessarily for good reasons. Pippo is different because he is respected for his ideas—not for violence."

"What's with this Nino character?" Eileen asked.

"Nino wants more power, and as he is young, hot-headed, and

rebellious, challenging older bosses. That is what we have to deal it now," Vicenza said, "That and the CIA agents."

"You know," said Eileen, "I think you never tell me the whole story, and when pressured, you just unveil piecemeals."

"Could be," answered Vicenza trying to lighten Eileen's mood. "I might be trying to keep up the suspense, or maybe I'm trying to protect you. It could even be that I'm afraid that if you knew the entire ruth, you might have abandoned me. If you leave me, how would I be able to sleep without your body by my side."

• • •

Pippo was fully energized and wanted to speak with his brother Carlo, before arriving at Veronica's house.

He called, knowing that his brother was always awake before sunrise. Carlo confirmed that strange things were happening.

"Interesting that you mentioned," he said. "Recently, I heard from Carluccio Pessina something about Nino. As you know, Carluccio runs the prostitution in partnership with the *Albanians* on the North, including Milano and the Adriatic Coast. He told me about his suspicion that Nino was contacting them. It seems strange since Nino has only a small prostitution ring in Calabria, which is peanuts for the Albanesi, but who knows, the kid might be pushing to expand."

"Or it could be that the Albanesi want to screw us all and are looking for partners who could help them break the families," said Pippo. "Better watch out. They might be looking for a larger share in Italy. You and I were expecting that would happen one day. Maybe it's now. The Albanians want to challenge us, and we need to respond to it quickly. Otherwise, they will get stronger and even more aggressive. Those guys might be playing with Nino's inexperience and ambitions, and we should not underestimate their threat."

After that phone call, Pippo passed by Jimmy's house, who opened the door in his pajamas.

"Are you comfortable with Pezzini?" Pippo blurted.

"Yes, he is good. He is dedicating a lot of effort to building the van business, and he helps me when needed. He did a great job with Franz. He is the one who put the powder in Franz's beer."

"Are you sure he is loyal?" insisted Pippo.

"Until now, yes, but I will watch him more carefully."

"Did he have access to the Russian ambassador's picture taken at the White Stone House?"

"Oh yes, he is the one that grabbed the suitcase from Franz's aunt's bedroom."

"And you think he saw what was inside."

"For sure, we opened it together. I wanted to know what Franz had."

"Are you sure he saw the Russian's picture?" Pippo insisted.

"Yes, we talked about how explosive that picture could be on the wrong hands. And there was also the other picture, the one with the Lithuanian ambassador where Pezzini appears."

"Is he loyal to his Marsala family or us?"

"Difficult to answer. He came here because he killed an Italian prosecutor who was causing problems for the *Commendatore*, and he is probably still loyal to them. But since he got here, he did everything we asked and did it well. Why do you ask? Is there a problem with the Genna family?"

"You know how arrogant they are, and now the *Commendatore* is dead, and Nino is in charge. We don't know him well. Try asking Pezzini about his family, but be careful. I don't want to arouse his suspicion."

"It won't be a problem. Pezzini loves to talk about his family. I'm the one who always cuts him off. I don't like to talk about Sicilians when we are drinking in a bar."

After leaving Jimmy's house, Pippo went to Veronica's place, and he only returned home the following morning.

19.

A different approach. The CIA agents had pressed Veronica for more information about the mysterious Panamanians, and she shared her concern over dinner with Pippo and Vicenza at Eileen's house. She cooked lamb, Pippo's favorite dish.

"I knew that they would press for more information," Eileen said.

"Yes, Veronica said. "The agents want to know who they are and why they keep the house."

"No problem," said Pippo, surprising them with his renewed energy and clarity. "We can hire a Panamanian lawyer serve as a front. but Veronica must tell them that the lawyer prefers to have the meeting in Panama City, where nobody would consider detaining him."

"Let's see if they accept," Veronica said.

"Of course, they will," said Pippo confidently. "Any CIA agent would love to travel to Panama, particularly if you assure them that the law firm will pay all expenditures, including hotels and generous extras for the night.

"And what will the lawyer tell them?" asked Eileen.

"I don't know, you tell me. What do you want them to say? You are the writer, and we trust your creativity," challenged Pippo, grinning.

Vicenza intervened. "It's not easy. We don't want the lawyer to say that they work for Sicilian families or us."

"We can blame the Mexican cartels," said Pippo, tasting the Chianti that he had just opened. "Everybody hates the cartels. Let's blame them."

"Are you going to say that the Panamanians, and I, who is their hostess, work for Mexican cartels?" questioned Veronica.

"No, that is not acceptable," said Vicenza. "She is Mexican, and they will suspect that Veronica is part of the cartel."

"Panamanian law firms are known for hosting illegal business," offered Eileen. They could say that they expanded their services to help their international clients curry favor with American politicians and businessmen. The lawyer can say that his clients identified lobbying as a priority and that they bought the White Stone House estate as a safe and remote place to bring people together. The lawyer can say that the clients include Mexicans, Europeans, Russians, and even Chinese. All of them lobbying the American Congress for different reasons."

"Do you see why I trust her?" said Pippo looking at Vicenza. "Writers are good at designing strategies. Thank God that they don't have the guts to implement them. If they did, we would be thrown out of the market."

· · ·

Veronica extended the invitation to the CIA agents, and after consulting their bosses, they agreed to travel to Panama.

Meanwhile, Eileen scouted around town, asking locals if they had contact with the agents.

"The agents tried unsuccessfully to talk with many locals, and nobody said anything. The only thing they repeat is that Miss Vicenza is a great woman."

"And what about the fishermen?" asked Pippo.

"For them, you are more important and trustworthy than the president," replied Eileen looking at Pippo's proud face.

Despite the good news, Eileen was gloomy, worrying about her relationship with Vicenza. Was she considering a divorce? It didn't seem so. Pippo was comfortable with their relationship, meaning that he didn't feel threatened, and if he wasn't, what was her future?

Vicenza was a different woman. Different values, different morals. Was for that reason Eileen was so passionately in love?

• • •

The following day Pippo came with bad news. "Carluccio was killed, as well as the older son of Don Domenico from Trapani. It's a coup of the Albanesi to control the prostitution business in Italy," he told Eileen. "Don Carluccio controlled prostitution on the north and the Adriatic Coast, while Don Domenico in the West, Marseille, and the French Mediterranean. They were the big players, and other families, like the Gemma from Marsala, had only small operations. But now, it's a war."

"Is Nino challenging the other families?" asked Eileen.

"He doesn't know what he is doing, and he is not the problem," answered Pippo. "He probably believes that he had the Albanesi support to challenge other families. *Stronzo*! He didn't see that they used him. We knew that the Albanesi would challenge us one day, but I didn't expect it so soon."

"Why now, then" Eileen asked.

"The Sicilian families have always been concerned with the Albanians, which I warned about many times to the other bosses. The Albanesi are different than us and more violent. Sicilians are equally brave," Pippo added, "but we've become more sophisticated. Our people now are smart hackers who deal with bitcoins. We have access to FBI computers' networks, and recently some kids from Messina developed a scheme to fraud banks, driving Swiss and Germans crazy. It was still a small scam but a good beginning, and we have routes to smuggle weapons faster than the American army transport them. The Albanesi are rude. They know how to beat, shoot, and kill, and they do it almost for fun. A war with them will be bloody, but we cannot lose control over prostitution. That's crucial for all other businesses we have," he explained.

"Many families were forced to make deals with the Albanesi since they didn't have access to Eastern European countries. In the past, Colombians, Dominican, and Brazilian women were all European men wanted, but it changed. They now prefer blond Romanians, Ukrainians, and Russians. And the Albanesi bring them. But that was it. We just wanted them to get us the women. We never wanted them to share in our other businesses. Prostitution is crucial for drug distribution. If the families lose one, they may soon lose the other."

"I might have an idea," said Eileen. "But first, I need to know what kind of deals you had with the Russian ambassador. Was it gambling?"

More than that, we discussed weapons," replied Pippo. "The Russians wanted to send light weapons to Venezuela, but they didn't want to do it directly. They knew that the Americans had good intelligence inside the Venezuelan government, and they did not wish to appear in the deal. They asked us, and we did it through our European dealers. All weapons arrived in Venezuela with no Russian traces."

"And what did you get in exchange?" Eileen asked. "I doubt that you did that only for money."

"I'm impressed," replied Pippo. "You are correctly grabbing the essence of our philosophy. If you have the opportunity to please the Russian government, there are things much more valuable than money to get in return, like, for instance, licenses for gambling in the four Russian gambling zones. At that time, we were also having problems in Europe with some aggressive Russian mobs who, thanks to the ambassador's influence, let us operate our business with more freedom and less competition." After a pause, he challenged her. "Now that I told you, go ahead and explain to us what you have in mind?"

"Well, it's a long shot, and we will have to think about it carefully. Still, it is worth trying. We can take advantage of the CIA investigation. They want to know who is using the estate, and we can suggest to them that in addition to Mexicans, the Albanians are frequent users We can even suggest to the CIA that we suspect that the Albanians are negotiating weapons smuggling with the Russians. The CIA will be delighted. They get to target the Albanians, Russians, and Venezuelans. It's everything they want. We turn their attention away from us and at the same time screw the Albanians."

"Bravo," said Vicenza. "It makes sense, and we can ask our Panamanian lawyer to suggest to the CIA that the Albanians were their clients."

"You are right," said Eileen. "We can also ask Veronica to say that the Albanians were here when the Russian ambassador visited the property. We have the pictures, and we can adjust the dates and perhaps coincide their visit with the time the Venezuelan deal was discussed. After that, we will let the CIA agents draw their own conclusions."

Pippo and Vicenza look at each other, pleased.

"And what do we do with Pezzini?" asked Vicenza. "He might be working for Nino, and we cannot have a *traditore* among us?"

"I know what we will do," answered Pippo. "Let me ask Jimmy to whisper to Pezzini that Carlo, my brother is sick, and our family is vulnerable. It is a lie. Carlo is stronger than ever, and our family is prepared to fight any enemy, Sicilian or not, but let's see what happens. If Nino moves to attack Carlo, we will know that Pezzini is betraying us. This will give us an excellent excuse to end him and seize his family operations in Calabria. It's a small but profitable business that might bring us additional income."

• • •

After three days of work and three spectacular nights of whores and fun, a CIA agent returned from Panama with a much clear vision. The young woman who had become Vicenza's friend confided it to her, "I knew there was something," she said, "a Russian ambassador will never visit the Eastern Shore of Maryland to watch exotic birds or fish in the creeks, and now we know he was here dealing with Albanians. Let's see if that Ladyman Veronica could help us fill in some blanks."

"I'm sure she will," replied Vicenza curtly. "Veronica is a serious woman that deserves all our respect, and she is a *muxe*, not a ladyman. Muxes are a respected and long established third gender in the Mexican and Aztec world."

Veronica was exceedingly helpful to the CIA agent. She lied that she remembered hearing conversations about weapons, and offered the names of three women who entertained the guests on the weekend the Russian ambassador was there.

"One of them was talking about weapons for Venezuela. Another said that the Albanians have intimate knowledge of Maduro. And another of the women said the Albanians mentioned that Colombian leftist groups were interested in buying Kalashnikovs."

The CIA took the bait and redirected the investigation to the Albanians. Vicenza and Veronica identified some Albanian faces from pictures shown by the CIA. Many of them had never come to the Clairsville house but were people that Pippo wanted on the CIA radar. Eileen didn't know at that time, but Pippo and Vicenza were conspiring with Sicilian families to destroy, once and for all, the threat Albanians posed to the families.

When talking with CIA agents, Veronica also kindly added that she recalled other Albanian meetings attended by Venezuelans, Colombians, and Mexicans, which, according to the CIA, indicated that Albanians were undoubtedly supplying weapons to Latin American leftists. Everything she did was directed by Pippo.

"But we are not yet there," Pippo warned. "The Albanesi's business is prostitution, and that's what they do. They are experts in smuggling women, but they never dealt with weapons. We must think of something else to help convince the CIA, and we must find something sooner than later. There is a war going on. We already had incidents in Naples and Rome, which are no longer limited to Don Domenico and Don Carluccio's families. The Albanians are making it clear that they want to control our prostitution operations, and we should strike back."

Eileen had an idea, but she preferred to talk to Vicenza first. Later, when the two were alone in the room, Eileen pitched her idea.

"I'm planning another party."

"Good, and who are your guests?" asked Vicenza.

"The Albanians."

"Okay, *Avanti*, I'm sure you have something else in mind. Spill out."

"We can invite the Italo-American families and the Albanians, as you did last time. We could tell the Albanians that the Americans plan to propose a bigger deal, like a partnership in Europe or America."

"And why would the Americans do that?"

"Because you will ask them. From what you told me, American families are Sicilian families' partners."

"Okay, if the Americans invite the Albanians for a meeting, I'm sure they will come, but what will we do if the CIA is monitoring our movements?"

"That's exactly the reason why we will throw the party. In addition to the whores you brought last time, the CIA would love it if we also invited some Venezuelans and Colombian political groups."

"And what will make them come?"

"We can tell them through the Panamanian lawyer that some Albanians want to talk about a weapons-for-women deal. Allow us to import your women and we can help you get guns."

The idea seemed crazy but exciting. Vicenza proposed it to Pippo, and he agreed but reminded, "We must continue to act very carefully. The CIA cannot know that we are in contact with the Panamanians. For them, we are only the caretakers of the property."

20.

Party time. The idea of entrapping the Albanians energized Pippo, and the Sicilian families got actively involved. Pippo contacted the Panamanian lawyer and approached the South Americans through the lawyer's firm. "We don't want bosses, just representatives. It's only a first meeting to listen to a proposal."

Vicenza reached the Italo-American families, telling them that the Albanians were willing to improve their offer. Pippo suggested that she should remain vague about the details.

"We can explain it to them later," Pippo said. "Our target is the Albanesi, and we must be careful not to hurt our credibility with our American friends. We're getting a lot of attention, so we will probably have closed our operation here in Clairsville, but we will remain in the country."

The official reason for the meeting was that Italo-American families were ready to make new concessions and were even willing to support Albanians expanding their prostitution rings in Europe. Pippo also mentioned that a stellar selection of the most beautiful Venezuelans, Colombians, Dominicans, and Brazilian women would attend the meeting to make the invitation more appealing.

Vicenza was preparing Veronica for her hostess role and did not have time to waste. The meeting would occur as soon as possible to deter the further escalation between Albanian and Sicilian families.

Pippo received a phone call from his brother Carlo confirming that Nino requested a person-to-person meeting with him, and Vicenza explained it to Eileen. "A person-to-person meeting between capos does not happen very often. Traditional bosses rarely leave their family compounds. Nino requested the meeting because he obviously heard rom Pezzini that Carlo was sick and decided to check. That shows us that Nino is careful and smart, and that Pezzini is betraying us."

"And what will you do?" asked Eileen.

"Nothing. Let my brother and Nino talk, and I'm sure they will smooth out everything. No deaths this time. I promise you."

On the next day, Pippo came with more news. "The Panamanian lawyer had contacted the CIA. They will help the CIA catch the Albanesi and, in exchange, the CIA would get off their back.

"Let's play dumb and be ready." Pippo said. "If the CIA agrees, the party might happen soon." He asked Vicenza, "Do you think Veronica will be ready to host them? "

"La Vero is a natural," Vicenza confirmed. "She doesn't like to be around people, but she knows superbly how to act. I am sure that she will be a better host than anyone you have seen. Beauty, class, and intelligence. What else does a hostess need?"

• • •

The senior CIA agent contacted Pippo a few days later. He wanted to come to Pippo's house and arrived the same evening bringing with him the young woman agent.

"We need your help," said the senior agent as soon as they sat around the kitchen table. "We identified a dangerous group who had used the neighbor's house to cut weapon smuggling deals, and we want to catch them. We agreed with the Panamanian lawyer to entrap them."

"And do you think those Panamanians are reliable," asked Pippo pretending to show suspicion.

"I would not say that they are trustworthy," answered the senior agent. But I can tell you that they have a lot to lose if they misbehave. I told them that we would immediately cancel their US visas. And I also threatened them with a full investigation of their clients in the US. I'm sure they will cooperate."

"And how can we help?" asked Pippo, acting worried.

"We will use the neighbor's house, and the Panamanians will ask Miss Veronica to host it. We want you to keep taking care of the house as you always did, assuring that everything will be in perfect order, and when the meeting takes place, we will have to use your house to monitor their actions and prepare a raid."

"Won't it be dangerous?" Pippo asked.

"I don't think so, but if you feel more comfortable, you can leave and be far away when the meeting takes place."

"Yes, I would prefer that," replied Vicenza jumping into the conversation. "We don't want to be involved with those groups. We take care of the house, but, as you know, we are part of the FBI program, and we like to keep our peaceful life and stay out of the limelight. We can help Veronica prepare the gatherings as we always did, and after that, we will travel to Ocean City and stay there until the meeting is over."

The young female agent gently grabbed Vicenza's arm. "I believe you should go away. We never know how things could evolve on a raid."

• • •

Pippo's brother called from Sicily to talk about his meeting with Nino. "A very good one," Pippo told Eileen and Vicenza. "Nino was surprised when he saw Carlo in good health, and Carlo teased him, mentioning that some people were spreading rumors about his health. I think they hit it off. Nino was a soccer player, and Carlo managed the Palermo soccer team for a while. Nino might not like older bosses, but Carlo is an exception."

Pippo continued. "Carlo told him that the families would retaliate for what the Albanesi did to Carluccio and Domenico's family, and any Sicilian who might be working with them will suffer. Carlo told

Nino to be patient and that time will reward him since he is one of the smartest among the young generation. They ended the conversation on good terms, and Carlo told him that it would be safest for Pezzini to return to Sicily."

"Great conversation," congratulated Vicenza. "The younger ones are not our enemies, and we just have to trust them and help them avoid the mistakes we made."

"Okay, but now we have a small business problem," Pippo reminded. "Without Pezzini, Jimmy will have to manage the vans we will need for our guests."

"Don't worry, this kind of problem is easy to solve," replied Vicenza.

They helped Veronica with the preparation, and only on the eve of the meeting did Pippo call the American families, warning them not to come. "There is some tension with the Albanesi. It's better to postpone any negotiation with them. Stay where you are, and we will keep you posted."

With everything prepared, Pippo and Vicenza traveled to Ocean City. "It's time for us to go," Vicenza said to Eileen. "Stay at your house, and if there is any problem, Veronica will call us, and I will immediately tell you."

• • •

The Albanians arrived on two private jets at the local airport and were transported to the mansion, where Veronica was waiting for them. She was elegant and colorful as ever, leading a team of twelve Latin models. Gorgeous, and all of them well known by Pippo. Some Albanians stayed in one of the guest houses, and others, the VIPs, were accommodated in the guest apartment on the mansion's second floor.

The second guest house was left empty, supposedly to accommodate the Italo Americans, whose, according to Veronica, flights were delayed for technical problems.

At night, while the Albanians were partying with the models, a

Venezuelan lawyer and a colleague representing the South American leftist organizations arrived. Jimmy picked them up at the airport and they immediately joined the Albanians at The White Stone House. "Tonight, it's just *puteria*," Jimmy said in Spanish, causing laughs among the lawyers.

The CIA agents waited until Albanians and Latin Americans were stoned or wasted, and at two o'clock in the morning, twenty well-armed agents stormed the property. None of the guests dared to resist.

The CIA agents took all guests to Washington. There, the Albanians were questioned.

"Are you planning to provide arms to Maduro and Colombian revolutionaries?"

"Of course not!"

"And what was the purpose of the meeting?"

"Whoring with some American friends," was the most common answer the Albanians gave to the agents.

"How come if there were no Americans at the property?" And for that question, the Albanians didn't have a clear answer.

The Latin lawyers were cleared, as the CIA was not interested in them, they were sent back to the airport in a few hours.

For the Albanians, the interrogation continued. The CIA wanted to know why they were discussing weapons smuggling, and the Albanians insisted that their only interest was prostitution. The CIA agents were not convinced and kept them for two days. The two Panamanian lawyers continued providing additional information about Albanians' contacts in Europe likely involved with the weapons deal.

"Time is all we need," said Pippo to Eileen when they returned from Ocean City and went to Eileen's house."

"Time for what?" Eileen asked.

"We wanted to divert CIA's attention, and we did it, but this was just part of our plan," said Vicenza. "The Albanesi have been neutralized, at least for now, and the CIA no longer suspects us."

Eileen was surprised by Vicenza's tone and enthusiasm. "They are ruthless, and their power is growing, but they still lack organization and a solid international network. In five or ten years, we won't be able to challenge them anymore. Our chance was now, and the Sicilian families are going for the throat. They are attacking them in all their positions, using our contacts in high places to strangle their operations completely. When the CIA releases those who are here, they will not know where to go, and we will finish them."

"Gosh, Vicenza, you seem to have pleasure in massacring," Eileen said.

"Sorry, it's not a pleasure. It's euphory, perhaps. They attacked and threatened our people, and we are fighting back. *Cu pecura si fa, u lupu s'a mancia.* Act like a sheep, and the wolves will get you. We are not sheep, and we will never be. We are lions. That is how the Sicilian people resisted centuries of invasion."

Eileen was stunned by Vicenza's words. She wanted to help Pippo and Vicenza get rid of the CIA investigation, but she didn't want to be part of a mobster massacre.

"I want you both to go home. You are tired from your trip, and I am too," said Eileen, walking to the door and indicating that she wanted them to leave.

"Eileen__"

"Tomorrow, Vicenza, we will talk. Not today."

Eileen filled a glass with scotch and ice and sat on the terrace. She watched the creek until she heard her doorbell ring. *Vicenza,* she taught, but she was wrong. It was Veronica, and she was tense.

"We need to talk. I'm worried," Veronica said walking into the terrace. "If you are drinking, may I have one? And please, make it a double."

21.

Worse to come. "Vicenza called me and told me what happened. She is miserable. I'm sure she loves you a lot, but I agree. We all need to better understand what is going on. In the last days, Pippo spent all his time on the telephone talking with his Sicilian friends. I cannot follow everything he says, but I understand what they are talking about and can see that Pippo is not a simple consigliere. He talks and behaves like a boss. And it's not only recently. I've often seen him talking with his friends, and I can tell you for sure that he gives orders. Last week was crazy. He planned the attacks against the Albanians. He hates them, and I heard him repeating the expression, 'take no prisoners.' I even asked if he was worried about the CIA, and he said no. 'I don't fear judges, only killers,' he said. I insisted that he could go to jail. He calmly answered me that 'only a big ego takes you to jail and good lawyers will always set you free.' That is what he believes," Veronica stopped to take a sip trying to calm down.

"For Pippo and Vicenza, it is all about the Sicilian families," she continued, "and they have their support and money to protect them, but what about us? You at least had money to buy this house, but I live from my work, and I would never be able to hire a good lawyer. I am worried. I know that Pippo is trying to find a way out of this. He told me. But he doesn't know how. Meanwhile, he acts as if everything is fine."

"Did you talk with him about your fears?" asked Eileen.

"No. I don't believe it's the right time to do it, and I'm afraid he may not understand. He may think I'm weak or begging for some kind of protection."

Veronica took a deep breath, took another sip of scotch, and continued. "You were not here when Pietro died. Pippo was with me when Jimmy called to tell him that he had stopped Pietro. I heard Jimmy said that Pietro was a poor guy who didn't know what he was doing. Do you understand what I'm saying? Jimmy pleaded for him, and Pippo coldly replied, "Can you be sure that he won't snitch us to the FBI?' And when Jimmy recognized that he couldn't, Pippo said. 'He knows too much. You must silence him once and for all. Don't let him suffer, but go ahead. Eileen, let's not fool ourselves. We both know what Pippo is."

"I don't believe that they will do anything to harm us, but you have a point, Veronica, we know too much. Not only that, the CIA will not go away as easily as Pippo thinks. There is too much intrigue around him and the White Stone House. Pippo and Vicenza will have to redefine their operations and take on an even lower profile."

"You didn't get it," Veronica interrupted. "Pippo cannot get out. There is no hiding. He is a Mafia boss. I know they always insist that Mafia doesn't exist, but he is the boss of whatever exists, and I can tell you, it's not something small. I thought that you had already pictured it. They didn't come to the US to run away, but to continue to lead their organization. He is and has always been his family *capo*. All of this has been a farce."

· · ·

They met the next day. Eileen was gloomy, but Vicenza seemed fully revigorated. "I'm feeling fresh because of a long conversation I had with Pippo. He knows what he wants, and I know it too. I want to spend the rest of my life with you, and I will do whatever I can to help him move on with his life and convince you to live by my side. Trust me."

Eileen was astonished and murmured, "And can you tell me what you are going to do?"

"Yes. We will sell the property, but first, Pippo and I want to propose something. We want you to keep the white stone at your house. I know the white stone is huge, but we're willing to pay for you to redo your pool. We can sell the estate, but we cannot sell the white stone."

Eileen could not avoid laughing. "I'm here worried about our future, and you are thinking about how to preserve a stone!"

"Don't' worry about your future."

"How could I not be worried? You and Pippo choose what you will do, but what about me? Veronica and I are also in danger."

"You didn't get it," replied Vicenza. "You still don't understand how we Sicilians are. We screw our enemies if needed, it's true, but we will give our lives to protect those we love. You and Veronica are part of our future. Trust me, and stop asking questions."

"I can't, Vicenza. There are still many things that I don't understand."

"Okay. You keep asking your questions, and I will try to answer them, but now, we need to have the white stone moved and sell the property. We want to put the house on the market immediately. It will be complicated because our names are not on the deed. The Panamanian lawyer can help with that. We're hoping for a private, confidential sale."

"Can I ask you something?" said Eileen shily. "Where are you planning to live?"

"Here, near Clairsville, of course, but not in the little house by the estate. Pippo and I will buy a house on one of the creeks, something secluded As you know, Pippo can survive without you, me, or even Veronica, but he absolutely needs the *Marinella*. We know some waterfront properties that we like, but first, let's get rid of the big mansion and all the past that the property represents."

"And what about the work you do with the Sicilian families? Are you going to stop with it?"

"No, but it will be different. Pippo and I will continue to live here, but we will not have meetings close to our house. You can fool the FBI once, but not twice. We will be looking for a place closer to Washington."

• • •

Eileen went to Veronica's house to share what she had learned. Veronica seemed unsurprised.

"They know what they will do, and if Pippo assured us that we will be fine, then we will," Veronica said. "We have no reason to doubt his intentions."

Eileen traveled to California to see her kids and spend Christmas with them, while Vicenza frantically helped Vicenza and Pippo prepare the estate for sale.

The transfer of the stone to Eileen's house was a big ordeal. It could not be moved by land since the rural roads were not large enough for the stone's wide truck, so Pippo had to rent a barge to take it by water, which is how it had arrived years earlier He also hired a contractor to prepare Eileen's yard and deck for the monstrous stone. The result was fantastic. The stone could be seen from the creek and started to attract the attention of a few watermen who slowed down their vessels to admire it.

The mansion was quickly sold to a bitcoin billionaire who had frequented the property, someone Pippo had reached out to. The transaction was handled through the Panamanian lawyer as planned.

Pippo eased Veronica's concern over her future by fully paying off the mortgage on her house. Vicenza enjoyed staying at Eileen's home, and when the weather got better, Pippo started to sail *Marinella*. All seemed to be going as planned.

• • •

Suddenly, on a dreadful Tuesday, Vicenza received a call from Pippo's cell phone. The woman on the other side didn't seem to know what she wanted and asked, "Who is this?" Vicenza refused to say her name and replied, "What do you want?" The woman hung up. Vicenza called back three times, but nobody answered. Pippo had left the day before with *Marinella* to sail south, and his telephone was supposed to be with him.

Vicenza called Jimmy, and he confirmed that Pippo was planning to sail straight to Deal Island, and he added, "I am supposed to drive Miss Veronica there tomorrow and meet him."

Vicenza attempted again to call Pippo, but he didn't answer. Eileen tried to calm her down, saying he was probably sailing with no signal.

"And how is it possible that this woman called me from his phone?" replied Vicenza. "Is it possible that *questo strunzu* is betraying Veronica with another woman?"

Veronica called after an hour, asking if Vicenza knew where Pippo was.

"I'm worried," said Veronica. "Jimmy called me asking if I knew, and Pippo never goes anywhere without telling Jimmy, you, or me."

Vicenza didn't want to mention the women's call, and Veronica continued. "He called me last night telling me that the winds were pushing him faster than he was expecting, asking me if I could go and meet him today. I told him I couldn't. I had a client coming to pick up a big commission of five benches, and I promise Pippo to meet him tomorrow."

Vicenza hung up and spoke aloud to herself. "Pippo cannot be with another woman if he wanted Veronica to meet him." She immediately called Jimmy. "Something is wrong. Call the marinas where he usually docks and check if someone has seen *Marinella*."

It didn't take more than twenty minutes for Jimmy to call Vicenza back. "There was a fire on a dock in front of the seafood restaurant in Hoopersville, and it seems that *Marinella* was one of the boats involved. I'm going there right now."

"Okay, but first, come to Eileen's and pick me up. I'm going with you."

Vicenza and Jimmy drove to Hooper Island, a one-and-a-half-hour ride. Eileen stayed at home and Veronica joined her there. Veronica called a woman she had met on one of her trips to meet Pippo. The woman, who managed a seafood deli, confirmed that a fire burned the dock and two boats, one of them, *Marinella*.

Eileen and Veronica immediately got into Eileen's car, and they had just crossed the Cambridge Bridge when Vicenza called crying. "There was a fire. *Marinella* was completely destroyed, and Pippo was inside it."

22.

The boat had sunk. When Eileen and Veronica finally got there, the police had blocked the road to the docks. There were fire trucks, police cars, and a crowd milling around. They approached a policeman standing guard. "Are you from the victim's family?" Eileen, dazed, answered, yes.

Only the bow and the mast of *Marinella* were visible; the rest of the boat was underwater. Next to it, another boat and part of the dock were burned. The fire department's vessel was anchored close to the remains, and two divers worked on *Marinella's* wreck.

Veronica was hysterical. She tried to get closer to the boat, crying desperately, "Where is Pippo?" Jimmy consoled her and took her to the seafood restaurant. Eileen followed, solemn and shocked.

Inside the restaurant, Vicenza was surrounded by a policeman and the restaurant staff. When she saw Eileen and Veronica, she started to cry and hugged Veronica.

Eileen was the only one who paid attention to the policeman's precise explanation.

"Mr. Giuseppe Vittorini arrived in Hooper Island yesterday evening a little before five, and he came to the restaurant. He was alone and sat at the bar where he ate fried calamari, a slice of apple pie, and drank four beers. While having dinner, he spoke with some locals, and Miss Reece, the waitress took a few pictures that we have copies of. He said he was having electrical problems on the boat, and part of the instruments were not working. He agreed with Mr. Goody, a local fisherman and expert in boat wiring, who had agreed to look at the boat the next day. According to Miss Reece, Mr. Vittorini went back to the boat at eight forty-five, and he left with her his cell phone because the outlet inside the boat that he normally uses to charge his phone was down. Mr. Vittorini then walked to the dock, and at nine-thirty the restaurant closed. During the night, probably around two-thirty, a fire started inside the *Marinella* and quickly spread. An explosion was heard. When the first resident arrived, both boats, the *Marinella* and *Sis Hellen*, a fisherman boat that belongs to Mr. Kiffer, were on fire. A group of residents extinguished the fire on the dock and on *Sis Hellen*, but by then the *Marianella* was partially sunk. The keel reached the bottom. Otherwise, the whole boat would be now underwater. When the fireboat from the Wingate Fire Station arrived, a firefighter dove and found Mr. Vittorini's body."

"Oh God!" Eileen blurted.

"The body was almost entirely burned, but the pieces of clothes found inside the cabin and bathroom match what he was wearing the night before. We still need to do further forensics and check dental records, but there appears to be little doubt at this time that the body was that of Mr. Vittorini.

"It might not be him," said Eileen. "They still need to confirm with dental matches."

"It's him," Vicenza whimpered, "and it's pointless to deny it. Jimmy showed me the photos they made from the body, and we could see around his neck the medal of San Gerlando, the patron of Agrigento, that Signora Paola gave to him when he was a kid. He never took off that medal. Never!"

Eileen saw Jimmy chatting with another man, and she got closer to listen. It was the county sheriff, and Jimmy was talking about the boat. "I told him that it was time to change all wiring harnesses. They were old. Every winter, Mr. Giuseppe varnishes the whole boat but has always postponed the harness maintenance. He had agreed that next winter, we were going to do it. It would be a big job, but I promised him that I would do it in less than three months. Now it's too late," said Jimmy, teary eyed.

"There is nothing else that Vicenza can do here," said Eileen to Jimmy. "I will take Veronica and her to my house, and you please stay."

"Yes. I think it's better to take Miss Vicenza home. And please help her. She will have to call Mr. Giuseppe's family in Sicily to tell them what happened, and it will be horrible. As soon as the police and the fire department finish their jobs, I will join you."

• • •

Most of the drive back to Clairsville, the three women remained speechless until Veronica dared to say what she was thinking. "He is not dead. It was not him inside the boat. Pippo often talked about a new life. You know it, Vicenza. He knew that the families would never let him go. He said to me, and I'm sure he also said to you that only dead he could be out. He is faking his death."

"I know," replied Vicenza. "We talked about it, but we always knew it would be impossible. I'm sure the families will send their people here. They will be discreet and respect us, but they will be more thorough, and ruthless, than the FBI or the CIA."

"If Pippo was killed, do you think the families were behind it," Eileen asked.

"Maybe, but I don't believe it," Vicenza said. "Pippo and I agreed to work less for the families and dedicate more time for us and both of you. He had recently informed the Sicilian families that they would have to choose another person to be the liaison with the American families, and, to my surprise, the Sicilians agreed. Pippo would continue to be their consiglieri, but with fewer responsibilities. That is what we were going to do. What happened yesterday is a disgrace. *Ci siamo fregati dal destino*. This was supposed to be the beginning of a new life."

When they got back to her house, Eileen helped Vicenza make a list of everyone she had to call, including his family, the FBI and

CIA agents, the DOJ friends, judges and politicians, and all Sicilian families. But the first call, and the most difficult one, was to Pippo's brother. Eileen and Veronica helped her. Carlo burst into tears and then swore revenge if his brother's death was murder.

That night, Veronica slept on Eileen's couch and Vicenza in the bedroom. Eileen stirred all night, her mind spinning with scenarios of Pippo's death and worries about what would happen next.

The Dorchester Police proceeded with the body identification with informal help from FBI agents. The dental records matched perfectly, and a DNA comparison, done using bone fragments, also confirmed that Pippo was dead.

Vicenza sent Jimmy to see if it was possible to save *Marinella*, and he returned frustrated. "Impossible. The only part that was not destroyed was the bow. The boat sunk, stern first, and touched the bottom, only the bow remained above water, but from the mast back, everything was destroyed. We saved the sails stored in the bow compartment and the anchor. I took the mainmast from the boat. Someone could use it, but the high temperature damned the boom and the mizzenmast. If you agree, I will keep a piece of the transom where you can still read the final four letters of the *Marinella* name. All the rest is lost."

Old pictures of the boat were published in the Baltimore newspaper which described the *Marinella* as one of the most beautiful boats to navigate the Chesapeake Bay.

"They wrote more about the boat than about Pippo," complained Veronica in tears.

● ● ●

As expected, two Sicilians arrived from Palermo to double-check details of Pippo's death, and Vicenza only met with them once. "Sorry, but I have to take care of Pippo's funeral, and Jimmy will help you with whatever you want to know or see."

The only pleasant surprise came from the watermen. A group of them visited Vicenza, confirming that they would continue to pay what they owed to Pippo despite the lack of any documentation. "He was nice to us, and we will repay every cent he lent us." They also offered to participate in the funeral. "Mr. Giuseppe told us once that he wanted to have his ashes thrown into the creek. If you agree, a few of us would like to join you in doing that."

Their proposal gave Vicenza an idea. She wanted to organize a memorable funeral for Pippo, but she didn't want it in a church. They never attended church, at least not in the US, and thought it would be hypocritical to do so for his funeral. "If it were a church in Sicily, I would accept, but a church here never meant anything to Pippo. It's better to do it on the creek," Vicenza said.

The date was set for the funeral, and Vicenza told Miss Dillan to help her invite all locals. "On Sunday," she said, "we will celebrate his life at the pier. After that, I will spread my husband's ashes in Clairsville Creek, and some watermen will join me. We will not have a church service, but rather a boat procession."

Vicenza immediately realized that she had a problem. All Sicilian families wanted to express their respect to Pippo, which would raise suspicion among the FBI. Pippo was not supposed to have connections with Sicily, and a large presence of Sicilians at his funeral would be unexplainable.

The first to complain was his mother, Signora Paola. She wanted to come, which would reveal Pippo's identity. Carlo convinced her to instead honor Pippo's memory with a mass at the San Domenico Church in Castelvetrano, inviting family and friends. Vicenza also let it be known that no one should send flowers or gifts.

Eileen and Veronica helped with the arrangements. Eileen suggested renting a tent for the pier, but Veronica was not pleased. "A white tent is boring. Pippo deserves better." So, she bought a tent that she painted with warm and shining colors. "Pippo loved my reds and yellows." Once she finished, Veronica went around borrowing from current owners the benches she had painted and sold to them.

• • •

The day of the funeral, the Clairsville Pier looked like an Oaxacan Plaza, entirely filled with colorful spring flowers. On land, there were more people than expected sitting on the colorful benches or standing around. In the water, at least thirty boats tied one to the other, ornate with flowers, waiting for Vicenza to spread Pippo's ashes.

Two large pictures, one of Pippo's face and another of him at *Marinella*'s helm, were at the tent's entrance, and after Vicenza talked about her life with Pippo, Klaus's son described how much Pippo loved the creek. Even the FBI senior agent attended out of respect for Pippo, introducing himself only as a family friend.

Vicenza, Eileen, and Veronica step inside Klaus's son's boat and sailed to the open creek. Behind them, other fishermen's boats carried guests who wanted to join the procession. It was a perfect early spring evening, and they only returned to the pier when the sun was already setting and the sky was bright red, making Veronica's tent glow even more.

That same night, Vicenza and Eileen sat at Eileen's terrace to share a bottle of wine. "Now it's you and me," said Vicenza. "And let me tell you, life will not be easy," she joked. "Until now, my life was a Bonnie and Clyde adventure. From now on, it will be Bonnie and Bonnie."

"Maybe," replied Eileen. "But between Bonnie and Clyde, there were no secrets, and I am sure that you still haven't shared all of yours with me."

"Okay," answered Vicenza. "I propose a pact. I will keep only one secret. And this one is to protect you. One day, before I die, I will tell you. Other than that, I promise to tell you everything. I swear on my mother's name. Go ahead. From now on, you can ask me whatever you want, and I promise to tell you."

23.

No more secrets. "Are you sure? Can I ask you whatever I want?" questioned Eileen, who was tired from the day's events but thrilled with the proposal.

"Whatever you want," replied Vicenza.

"Okay. Here is the first one," said Eileen, adjusting a pillow on her back. "Tell me, once and for all, and honestly. What have you and Pippo been doing for the Sicilian families? I know pieces of it, but I feel I didn't get the entire picture."

"Okay, let me fill in the gaps," Vicenza said, pouring both of them more wine. The creek was calm and quiet. No boats and no wind. Not even the moon, just restful stars watching their conversation. "Pippo became head of our family during a time of crisis. The *mattanza* times, or the Great Mafia War, as some newspapers preferred. Some powerful leaders, the Corleonesi, advocated a full confrontation with state authorities, and most families obliged. We knew it was a lose-lose situation, but any reluctance from our family would be seen as a betrayal.

"Pippo got involved with some stupid violence. It was something that he later regretted, but it's true. He participated in a decision to attack and execute prosecutors. It was atrocious, and we soon realized it was a mistake, but the whole process of reversing that strategy took years. Pippo always believed in preserving the Sicilian families' unity, and he didn't want to push for a division, particularly when we were under attack. It took months and long conversations, suggesting that we could be better by adopting a less confrontational posture. Slowly Pippo convinced them, and later, with the imprisonment of Toto Rina, he became one of the most trusted voices among all Sicilian families."

"The *capo* of *tutti capi*?" asked Eileen, thrilled.

"Not exactly, at that time, Benedito Provenzano was unquestionably the most powerful *capo*, but Pippo was close to him, even though there were some disagreements between them."

"What kind of disagreements," Eileen pressed.

"Pippo advocated a less aggressive posture, and Provenzano preferred violence to show strength. Initially, Pippo wanted to avoid the internal war and supported Provenzano's decisions. That is why Pippo was accused and prosecuted as part of the bombings and assassinations. But later, more and more bosses started to listen and respect Pippo's ideas."

"If Pippo was so respected, why did you come to the US and go into hiding?"

"That was the irony; the more important he became, the more we had to hide. First, we hid from prosecutors, and it was relatively easy. In Sicily, most small villages are on the top of mountains with only one or two access roads. We were immediately warned whenever a police car or a suspicious vehicle appeared."

"And nobody snitched on you?"

"No. The *Omerta* rules!" replied Vicenza. "Anyone who snitches dies, no exception. That rule might look barbaric, but I can assure you, it's extremely effective. And it was not only that. Most locals were friendly. They were Sicilians and had no interest or pleasure in denouncing us, and for those who, for hate or financial benefit, considered it, the *omerta's* weight was implacable. But as I said, those were the easy times. Later, it got worse. Most families supported Pippo's idea of a new relationship with state authorities, but the Corleonesi resisted, insisting on confrontation. It was the worst period. You could not recognize who our enemies were since they were also Sicilians. Even the *Omerta* law was flouted since some were loyal to us and others to the Corleonesi. It was a war soaked with Sicilian blood. And in a war like that, you could even win a battle, but you would never enjoy it since those you beat were Sicilians like you. We knew that we were right, and we didn't hesitate a single second, but we never had a moment of peace."

"That is when you decided to come to the US?"

"No, we only decided to come here later. Pippo and I were paranoid, but we never thought about giving up. We fought using all the weapons and rage you need to win. You can't fight and win without dirtying your hands, and again, we did stuff that we were not proud of. We had to. After the families finally reached a peaceful agreement, the capi decided to add another member to the Commissione, a consigliere generale, who would not represent a single group of families or regions but care for all of them. And they invited Pippo to the position. And I want to be sure that you understand the difference. Pippo was never the *capo di tutti I capi*, as you say. This position does not exist. He was the *consigliere di tutti gli familie*, which is even more honorable since it is based on trust and not fear. Pippo transferred control of his family to Carlo, his brother. And thanks to Pippo's leadership, the families today are out of the newspapers, living in peace and prosperity."

"Wait," interrupted Eileen sarcastically. "Peace and prosperity to traffic drugs, smuggle young prostitutes, and sell weapons?"

"Yes," replied Vicenza angrily. "Sicilian families helped you have the pot and the coke you had in college. And although I'm sure you never enjoyed prostitution, let me tell you that Sicilian families were instrumental to the US government in selling weapons to Iran to finance the Contra revolution in Nicaragua. And not only this. We were by far the main provider of weapons acquired with generous US resources to Colombia. On a softer note, Pippo and I laughed once because we were simultaneously coordinating actions of a Sicilian family working with the Colombian cartels and the guerrillas, and another supporting the Colombian paramilitary groups fighting against them."

"And you think it's funny?"

"Of course, it's funny. I've never been to Colombia, nor do I plan to go there, and we, respectable American citizens protected by the FBI, were coordinating actions on both sides."

"Vicenza. You don't have any morality," Eileen scolded.

"I have my own. I might not be comfortable with napalm being used to bomb plantations in Vietnam or drones killing children and civilians in the Middle East. The difference is that we are not hypocritical. Sicilian families smuggled marijuana to the US when pot was illegal, and now some of us are large investors in legal pot-growing businesses. We were bootleggers during the prohibition and alcohol distributors after it. We profit from illegal gambling and now legally partner with Native American casinos. We proudly provide young and beautiful Russian ladies for the pleasure of European politicians and Middle East princes, and so what? With all due respect Eileen, don't talk about morality. I know American judges and politicians much better than you. We are partners in many deals, and I can tell you that moral imperative is a relative concept. I met prostitutes, brave women raising their families who are worth a thousand times more than some politicians we dealt with. Who has power and money dictate values, and whenever they need to change them, they do it with no shame." And she continued confidently. "Pippo and I always had a moral compass. We robbed, smuggled, and, when necessary, killed, and none of these actions ever gave us any regret. We robbed from those who had, we smuggled stuff that people wanted, and we killed those sons of bitches who tried to hurt us."

"Okay," said Eileen. "You made your point. Calm down, and tell me more about what happened after Pippo became the consiglieri."

""The title is *consiglieri generale*. Do you remember that I told you that as a family *capo*, he made a deal with the communists to tear down Palermo mansions and build apartments? As a consiglieri, he reached an agreement with the right-wing politicians from the North of Italy. They helped stop the bad press and prosecutors' attacks on us, and we assured their party the majority of Sicilian votes. Because Pippo could not personally participate in the negotiations, he sent me to meet with the Italian prime minister."

"Did you do it?" asked Eileen, laughing.

"I did. You can't imagine what a ridiculous man he was. I met him at ten o'clock in the morning, and he was wearing more makeup than you at a night wedding. His hair was dyed black as charcoal and fixed with a tone of hairspray. Disgusting. And he invited me to a private dinner at his weekend mansion. Do you understand why I hate politicians? They are ugly and fake. But despite hating them, Pippo made a deal that brought peace to the island and smooth sailing for all families.", and she smiled. "At the meeting we had, I agreed with the prime minister to finance his party campaign on the island in exchange for full control over contracts for new roads. Can you believe it?" They both laughed. "Remember when I told you that the Roman politicians controlled most of the public works done in Sicily. That ended with the new agreement. Since that meeting, we, the Sicilian families, controlled infrastructure bidding on our island."

"And how important was this?"

"You can't imagine how much money you can make out of roads construction. Sicily is full of mountains, and you need either a tunnel or a bridge to cross them. Roads on our island cost a fortune. So much money that people have no idea if it is too much. By controlling the bidding process, all contracts are awarded to our companies, and we pocket at least ten percent of the contract value. To give you a rough figure, just one road, the Palermo-Messina's highway, cost hundreds of millions, and ten percent of that were split between our families and used to pay bribes to local government officials. Do you understand why Pippo was a genius? Instead of putting bombs and killing judges, the families today build roads modernize the island, make money, and delivering to the prime minister's party. Please, let's make a toast for Pippo. He deserves it."

"And after that, your life improved."

"Unfortunately not. For a while, we felt good. Most of the bosses were happy with the agreement. But you must remember that Pippo was still on the most wanted list of the Sicilian police, and we continued to live on the run. Every three or four days, we had to move to a different place, but with the new position, we lowered our guard. The Corleonesi were calmer, and the police who were still searching for us became less enthusiastic. We relaxed, and that is when we almost got killed. Pippo and I only survived thanks to Jimmy.

"We were distracted, but Jimmy never was. He has a special instinct, and he noticed some strange coincidences and some *polentones* from other parts of Italy, popping up here and there around us. Pippo and I were traveling light at that time, and our security only included four guys in two separate cars. But Jimmy, without telling us, had increased it. We were in Salemi, one of those cities where we could hide at the top of the mountain, but a larger one, where it was more difficult to keep us secure. For precaution, Jimmy put a few additional guys guarding the house where we were staying, and thanks to it, we survived," and she paused remembering what happened. "Pippo and I were sleeping, when we heard raffles of automatic weapons near us. Some guys from Calabria, hired by a Catania family who wanted to destabilize us, launched a massive attack believing that we had light security. Jimmy and his men stopped them, but it was dreadful. Four of our men died before they retreated, leaving five of their men behind. In the next hours, thanks to a general warning issued for all the island, we caught the remaining assailants in Messina. Two days after the attempt, the Catania boss who ordered the attack received in his house a truck with all nine bodies, properly executed and packed. We survived, but we were tired, and that is when we decided to come to the US. And no more talks. Now I want to lay on your bed naked and have all my body touching yours. And don't even try. It was a big and emotional day, and we will not have sex. Just love."

24.

Moving on. Vicenza couldn't wait. The following morning, right after they had breakfast, she proposed, "Let's go for a walk. There are many challenges ahead of us. Tough ones, and as we do not have more secrets, let's talk about them and decide together what we want to do."

They walked towards the pier, and when they crossed the pool deck, Vicenza kneeled in front of the white stone. "We will need her help."

On the road, Vicenza continued, "Things seem calm, but let's not fool ourselves. We still must untie some crucial knots."

"Regarding your work?" asked Eileen.

"More than that. In my life."

"You are scaring me," responded Eileen.

"It's not my intention, but I need to share everything with you. Pippo died, but it doesn't mean that I'm free to do whatever I want. I know a lot of stuff, and the Sicilian bosses are probably legitimately wondering what I will do next."

"Like what? Do they want you to keep working for them?"

"It's not as simple as that. We have already suggested some names to do the work inside the US, and they will not have problems finding someone. The other big issue is the Commissione. Maybe they will choose a new general consiglieri, perhaps they won't. I cannot think of someone as good as Pippo, and it might take a long time to rebalance power between families and regions, but they will sort it out. There is, however, something much more significant. They probably don't realize it yet, but in the short term, they depend on me.

"How come?" asked Eileen.

"They took Pippo's work for granted, and they totally relied on him. All international contacts, especially in the financial world and international organizations, are Pippo's contacts. Those people only know Pippo and I. The families might know who they are, but they don't know what they are doing or how to reach them. It took us years to build our network, it's a network of trust, and it's ours. It will take time and patience to transfer all that to other people. And when they realize it, the crucial question will be, What Vicenza is planning to do?"

"I believe they know that they can trust you," said Eileen.

"Maybe, but one of the main laws of our business is never to trust anyone. Those who are with you today could betray you tomorrow. And they will be wondering, 'Can we really count on her?' Don't forget, Eileen, that I've spent all my life with them. I know how they think."

Vicenza paused for a few seconds and continued looking at her own feet as if she was talking and listening to her words at the same time. "I believe they are not afraid that I might talk. They have known me for many years, but who knows? People who were above suspicion started to talk, surprising us. Would I be a new Tommaso Buscetta? I know I will not, but do they know.

"But from what I read, Buscetta started to talk to get out of jail. You are free. Why would you talk?"

"For the same reason that Buscetta did, to feed the ego. I learned how an inflated ego could be the worst of our enemies. Some people betray to shine under the stage lights, and many did it."

"But you won't."

"I know, but how can they be sure? Please understand, Eileen, I'm trying to anticipate what they could do. I've been there before, and I know how they think. I'm sure that one day someone will say. What about her friend? She's a writer, isn't she? Are they planning to write about us?"

"I'm listening to you, but I think you are exaggerating," scoffed Eileen.

"I'm not. They are not like you and me, and their expectations differ from ours. I'm not the first widow. Trust me, there were many before me. And you know what all of them had in common? They all dressed in black and lived secluded within the walls of their houses. Signora Paola is an example. Since Don Giacomo died, she only leaves her house to go to weddings, mass, and funerals. Twenty years later, she still wears black, and she is not the only one. Ninetta Bagarella, the wife of Toto Riina, has always been admired for her sobriety and silence. That's the parameter they will use for me, and you know that I don't fit. We will work together to transfer all information Pippo and I had. Still, I'm sure they expect me to go back to Sicily and live the rest of my days among olives and oranges. And I don't think either you or I will be happy cooking pasta on a Sicilian farm. We are different, and it's up to us to convince them that we are not a threat. To bury our heads in the sand will not solve our problem. They will be suspicious."

"But you have all friends that you write to. They will vouch for you."

"They are Sicilian women, and they see me as the widow of Giuseppe, il *consiglieri di tutti familie*. Sicilian women are not supposed to discuss their husband's business. Do you know that women never attended a Commissione meeting? Never! My women friends will be the first to be surprised if I don't behave as a cloistered widow. They have an image of me, but they don't know me, and they will probably be surprised once they see who I really am."

"Okay, and what is your point? What should we do?"

"I believe I must go to Sicily and face them all, eye to eye."

They kept walking in silence until Eileen asked Vicenza. "Do you want to go alone?"

"No," answered Vicenza. "There is nothing in my life that I want to do without you. I want you to go with me, but I don't know what will happen there. I know for sure that staying here and acting as if it were business as usual will not work. I'm proud of what I did,

I'm proud of what I am, and I want to be by your side. Yes, I know it would be risky for you and me, but if we want to be together for the rest of our lives, we must cross that bridge and cross it together."

"Do you think you might go to jail?" asked Eileen.

"I don't think so. First of all, they cannot prove that I am who I am?"

"What?" said Eileen surprised.

"I already told you that my Sicilian documents were made with false fingerprints. When I did my documents, we were already stealing, and Pippo paid a woman to put her fingers on the paper for me. The only documents I have with my fingerprints are the ones I made in the US. That is my sole legal identification; I'm an American citizen. How can they throw me in jail? They have photos of me twenty-something years ago, and I might look similar, but they cannot prove who I am based on that. But quite probably they will try. I'm sure prosecutors will think they can make me talk in exchange for less jail time, but I honestly believe it will not be possible. And do not worry about you, since there is nothing you know that could interest them. They want the Sicilian names, and other than Carlo and Jimmy, you don't know any."

"When would you like to go?"

"The sooner, the better. They are not yet talking about me. I know them, they are very respectful. Pippo's funeral was moving, and I wore black as an honorable Sicilian widow. They will wait at least a month before asking questions, and I want to be ready by them."

"That means that we have a month before we travel?"

"No, I want to travel now. Twenty-three years ago, I left Sicily, and although I always dreamed of my return, the simple idea of buying an airplane ticket scares me. I'm terrified, and I need to overcome my anxiety before meeting them. That is why I want to go to Sicily right now. Not to see them immediately, but to get acquainted again with my country. We will not tell anyone that we are going and before we go to Castelvetrano, let's travel around a little bit. I can take you to

Taormina, Ortigia, Agrigento, and I can surprise two or three of my friends to practice."

"To practice what?" asked Eileen.

"Everything. My Sicilian, my manners, and even my thoughts. I feel like an actress who needs to research her role. I must be confident when I see Signora Paola, and I must be extra confident to visit the other *capos*."

"Are you sure that you want me with you?"

"Every minute, and even if you don't understand what my friends are saying, you are the only one who understands me, and I would not be confident if you were not there by my side."

Eileen didn't need time to think and instantly answered. "I doubt we can leave tomorrow, but why not the day after? Let's see if we can find tickets."

"According to Pippo, the best and safest way is to fly from here to Amsterdam and buy a ticket from there to Palermo."

"Did Pippo travel to Sicily?" asked Eileen.

"At least twice a year for the *Commisione's* meetings."

"You two were amazing," said Eileen. "And as we are talking about Pippo, we also have to talk about Veronica. She is worried."

"She is sad because she loved Pippo. Veronica will have to deal with her loss and redefine her life as much as we. Of course, it would be better if we could spend more time with her, comforting, listening, and sharing our sorrow, but I can't. I'm also sad that Pippo is gone. He was my partner and best friend, but I know that if we don't deal with the families, they will deal with us, which I want to avoid. And do not worry about the financial part. The house, and her parents' house in Oaxaca, are fully paid for and in her name. I know how much he loved her, and I will care for her. By the way, something that you must know. Money is not a problem for us. As you always suspected, the big house belonged to us, but this is just part of what we have. Neither Pippo nor I cared about money, but we have more than we could spend. Pippo and I have a few accounts in Grand Cayman, and I can easily access them. We have more money than you, Veronica, and I will need for the rest of our days," Vicenza continued. "You know what I am thinking for Veronica?" Eileen stopped walking, and Vicenza continued opening her arms. "Alluring and exotic like she is, I'm sure that she can find a European prince," and excited as a kid. Let's give Veronica a few weeks to mourn, and then we can rent her a nice apartment in Florence where she could study European art. From there, she could travel to Roma, Milano, and Venezia. I am sure she will find a rich prince, and I even know some names that I can suggest to her."

"And what about Jimmy? Will he be okay?"

"Easily. Very soon, he will return to Sicily. He has always been a loyal man, and Carlo already told him that he wants Jimmy there, by his side. It's just a matter of days for him to sell what he has, and travel. Chiara, or Claire as everybody knows her, might want to stay. It seems she has a new love, but I will help her with a generous savings account. She could also take care of our houses while we were gone. Do you see how smooth it is to start a new life when you have a family protecting you?"

"*Vaffanculo*, as you like to say," joked Eileen. "And on another matter, I also have a secret that I must tell you." Eileen told her about Miss Dillan's notebook.

"What did you think? That we were going to kill her because she knew too much?"

"I was not sure," replied Eileen, embarrassed.

"You were right. Those notebooks could be a problem if the CIA had access to them, but you know what we can do. Let's make a deal with Miss Dillan. We will buy them for a good price and burn them. I like Miss Dillan, and we already helped her a long time ago when she needed money for her mother's surgery. Let's reward her for her silence, and we will continue to need her help with the mail. I will ask her to send us every week, through UPS or DHL, the letters we receive in the post office. I still want to know what my friends are writing me."

25.

Flying to Palermo. Eileen and Vicenza immediately went to Veronica's house to pitch the idea of travel, and she received it well. "I was planning on going to Oaxaca to stay with my mother for a while. It will be easier for me to process my sadness if I'm at home."

Vicenza mentioned Florence, and Veronica liked the idea. "I think we all need a break, but I still have a few commissioned works to finish, and as soon as I return, I will get rid of them. Give me some time to think, but I believe I will go."

Next, Eileen and Vicenza scurried over to the post office to speak with Ms. Dillan about her notebooks.

"You want to pay me for them and then burn them? Is my writing that bad?" she quipped.

"It's best if they don't get into the wrong hands," Vicenza said.

At the end of the evening, Miss Dillan brought all her notebooks to Eileen's house, and they burned them together.

While accompanying Miss Dillan to the door, Vicenza said, "We will tell you where you should send the mail, but please don't tell anyone where we are, not even Claire. We don't want to be bothered."

Miss Dillan nodded, agreeing.

Vicenza next spoke with Claire. "We will travel for a few weeks. It's time to regroup. Our first stop will be Amsterdam. After that, we don't know."

Vicenza didn't want anyone to know that they were going to Sicily.

They packed, closed their houses, drove to the airport, and

boarded a flight to Amsterdam the following day. Inside the plane, Vicenza confessed that she was anxious.

"Other than Sicily, Clairsville, and four quick trips to Naples, Rome, Chicago, and New York, it is the first time I have traveled anywhere."

"I can't believe it," replied Eileen. "Have you ever been to any other European city?"

"Never," answered Vicenza, half embarrassed, half excited. "Pippo was the only one doing the traveling."

"And you never joined him?"

"No. For Pippo, traveling meant work and whores, but now it's different. Not only do we have serious stuff to do in Sicily, but I'm also eager to visit new places with you."

. . .

Amsterdam was a surprise for Vicenza. "Not the chaos of Palermo or the coldness of Washington," she said in the taxi. Grabbing Eileen's arm, she also whispered, "Did you realize that here there are no homeless? America is supposed to be rich, and Washington streets are full of junkies, beggars, and tents. What a shame!"

They spent the day wandering through the city and decided to stay an additional day to enjoy the canals and the tulips that were starting to blossom. On the third day, they flew to Palermo. Vicenza was apprehensive.

"For more than twenty years, I dreamt about this moment, but now I'm terrified. I imagined myself driving to my old house a thousand times and my sister Simona waiting for me with a black scarf on her head. Of all people I know in Sicily, she is the one I missed the most. Would she be pleased to see me?"

During the flight, Vicenza calmed down. She told Eileen about her fears and expectations, and Eileen's support reassured her that going back to Castelvetrano was the right thing to do.

When Vicenza finally looked through the window and saw Mount Pellegrino on the outskirts of Palermo, her expression changed. There were tears and a resplendent smile as she climbed down the airplane's stairs.

The first drive inside Palermo was a shock. "We should not have gone to Amsterdam before," complained Vicenza, "because by comparison Palermo looks so ugly."

"I know," replied Eileen ironically. "I heard that they destroyed all their historic houses and replaced them for those colorless and hideous apartment buildings."

The taxi driver seconded her. "It was the Mafia."

Vicenza smiled and winked at Eileen.

They booked a room in a discreet downtown hotel and only left their apartment to dine on Osteria Lo Bianco. "I came here a few times with Pippo a hundred years ago," teased Vicenza. "It was our favorite restaurant in Palermo." After dinner, Eileen wanted to walk. The streets were empty but Vicenza felt uncomfortable. "I'm not yet ready to meet anyone," she said, and they returned to the hotel.

The following day, they rented a car and drove to their first destination, Cefalù. "It's a beach town, and I have an older cousin who lives there. She isn't close to the family anymore, and I won't feel pressured. It's just a first rehearsal."

Vicenza also told Eileen about her cousin. "Carmela and her husband were wild, and Pippo and I cherished their adventures. Later, her husband died in a confrontation, and she always carried a gun in her purse, which was not common for women. She moved to Cefalù and opened a restaurant for tourists. But from her letters over the years, I can tell she is still bitter over her husband's death." Don't be surprised if she calls me Cenzina, my childhood name. The last time we saw each other face to face, I was fourteen years old."

While they were driving, Vicenza mentioned, "You see how good this highway is? Well paved and cutting distance with nice tunnels and modern bridges. It was built by our family's construction company."

Vicenza had the address of a cozy hotel built in between rocks with a panoramic view of the sea. It was Carmela's suggestion. They walked a little with their feet in the sand, Afterwards, Vicenza went to Carmela's restaurant. Eileen chose not to go.

"I want you to be relaxed and at ease," Eileen said. "You both will feel more comfortable speaking Sicilian, and I don't want to be a drag."

Vicenza and Carmela chatted for hours, and Eileen only joined them later for dinner. Carmela was tall with an imposing presence and a kind smile. She could barely speak English, but her *Gamberi Rosso* didn't need translation. "Best red prawns I ate in my life," laughed Eileen. Later back at the hotel while drinking a Sicilian wine at their room's terrace, Vicenza told Eileen about their conversation.

"She finally told me what happened. Her husband was from the village of Partanna, and when they got married, she went to live with him there. According to her, I was a *damigelle d'onore*, a little bridesmaid at her wedding, but I don't remember. I was four years old. Her husband was a tough man and worked as a driver and bodyguard for Pippo's father. After they married and moved to Partanna, he started his own business. He was a mechanic, who liked to race cars, and he gave protection to local businesses in exchange for a payment."

"The famous *pizzo*?" asked Eileen.

"Yes, the *pizzo*," confirmed Vicenza with reluctance. "He had a few men working for him, and if needed, he could always count on Don Giacomo men's help."

"I understand," said Eileen. "He was an honorable man, establishing his honorable family, selling protection to neighbors."

"Yes," agreed Vicenza, opening her hands as if saying, "It is, what it is."

"When he died," Vicenza continued, "Carmela wanted to keep with the protection business. She was the one who managed it and collected payments while her husband handled the car repair. Carmela was tough and, as I told you, liked to have a weapon handy. She sold the auto repair and continued with the protection, collecting the *pizzo*, but Don Giacomo asked her to stop. He told her that it was not something that a woman should do. But Carmela was stubborn and continued. First, Don Giacomo pressured her men to leave her, and as she insisted, he sent his second son Gino to Partanna, spreading the message that he would take care of their protection personally," and lowered her head as if trying to excuse Don Giacomo for what he did.

"Carmela asked for a meeting with Don Giacomo and Signora Paola. According to Carmela, Signora Paola offered to finance any new activity that Carmela would choose. But the couple quite straightforwardly told her that she could not continue with her protection activities. Don Giacomo even told her something that I never heard before."

Eileen moved on her chair to better listen, and Vicenza repeated Don Giacomo's words with a somber expression. "He told her that many wives are the right hand of their men, and that he never makes an important decision without consulting Signora Paola, but he insisted that women never get involved in family business for their own protection, and he explained her why: If everybody believes that men solely handle all business activities, enemies will never come for women."

"Do you understand his point? Vicenza asked Eileen. "He told her that if Carmela insisted on selling protection, she would be suggesting to prosecutors that Sicilian women were not innocent bystanders," and after pausing for a moment she continued. "Don Giacomo had a valid point, since no woman in a Mafia family had ever been charged by Italian prosecutors."

"Never?" insisted Eileen.

"Never," repeated Vicenza. "Many men were convicted, but no women. The only name that I can remember is Maria Licciardi from the Neapolitan Camorra, but in Sicily, never. Toto Riina and Bernardo Provenzano were hunted, prosecuted, locked in jail, and Ninetta Bagarella, and Saveria Palazzolo, still live restfully in Corleone, one not so far from the other. A few women caught with drugs were accused of drug traffic but never of managing operations. There was a traditional saying, *Noi Siamo le donne. Non sappiamo niente.* We are the women. We don't know anything."

Vicenza was not pleased with her own conclusions.

"I hate the idea that women only take care of the house and kids seem to have proved its effectiveness. Why do Sicilian women need special protection? Are they different and more vulnerable than men? I know that we are not in the US. We are in Sicily, and men here have a different view of things. But they are wrong. They don't want people to believe that a woman could be a local *capo*, and if that is how they think, imagine how they will view me. They will probably want me to step aside, entirely, and prance around for the rest of my life wearing a black scarf like my sister. No way. *Una minchia for them*."

"Let me understand," said Eileen. "You are upset because Don Giacomo asked Carmela to renounce their criminal activities, but do not forget that he financed her cozy restaurant on the beach, which she keeps until today?"

"You are missing the point," huffed Vicenza. "I'm upset because Don Giacomo asked her to renounce her chosen life, just because she is a woman."

"And what exactly does this conversation mean to you, and us. Are you another Carmela wishing to assume Pippo's position?"

"No. I don't want that. But I also don't want to spend the rest of my days hiding inside a house dealing with a dreary routine. And it's your fault?"

"How it could be my fault?" replied Eileen.

"You made me want to live again. Now I would only settle for the best. With you, I know that tomorrow could be better than today, and I don't want any stupid *capo* telling us how we are going to live our life. If we want to travel, we will travel. If we want to rob or walk naked on the beach, we should decide where and when. Do you understand now why it's your fault.? You made me love life again."

26.

Time for surprise. "We are going to Taormina," said Vicenza. "And let's not spoil our trip talking about negative things. Let's enjoy that place the same way I did with Pippo."

"But we don't have to do the same things you did, okay?"

"I agree," replied Vicenza with a mischievous look. "Let's spend our time doing more pleasant things, but I have important business in Sicily, as you know." "Yes, I know that you want to pass your contacts to the other capi."

"Yes, but I have to be clear about who to pass them to."

"Explain it to me," Eileen said.

"The contacts are very precious, and I want to be sure that we are passing them to the right people. I trust some capos, but not others. Some are greedy and will not necessarily share the contacts with others. That could start a war.

"Do you trust Carlo?"

"One hundred percent. Pippo's brother is a great man who cares about Sicily and the families, but he doesn't have the stamina or desire to lead. He can run the family and all its businesses, constructing companies, banks, and farms, but he cannot lead the Commissione. He is a good shepherd, but not a lion, and what's ahead are tumultuous times. I will work very close with Carlo, he is our anchor, but we need others. "

"And who would they be?"

"I don't know, and that's the problem. I can tell you which ones I like, but that is not what matters. We must wait for the dust to settle and see if a new balance of power emerges. The beauty is that the capi need us alive."

"Got you. You want to have some say on the future of the organization," said Eileen.

"It's not that I want," said Vicenza. "We need to do that. Otherwise, all we did could be lost."

. . .

They spent dreamy days in Taormina. The hotel was on the cliffs, and Vicenza chose the room.

"According to Pippo, this specific room has the best view in town," she explained. "I've never been there, but it was the room of a rich German woman who Pippo seduced and later pinched," Vicenza laughed. "Can you believe it? As teenagers, we were in Taormina chasing rich tourists, and now we are here as two wealthy ladies."

Pippo was right; the room was stunning, and the best part was the terrace, with two lounge chairs, an open view of the ocean on the left, and Mount Etna jutting over their shoulders to the right.

They rented a scooter and visited Castelmola. Vicenza wanted to show Eileen the tiny apartment she had rented with Pippo. It took some time for them to get used to the scooter, but they soon were cruising the island with confidence, visiting every beach from Catania to Messina.

Vicenza insisted on renting a powerboat. "Pippo liked sailing, but I rather go fast," she said, "and I want you to navigate the *Stretto de Messina*."

On the boat, when they were getting closer to Punta del Faro, Vicenza explained, "This is the same strait that Ulysses crossed returning from the Trojan War. *Scylla*, with her long necks and six ghastly heads, was on the left, ready to eat his sailors' heads, and on the right, *Charybdis* waiting with her gigantic mouth, anxious to swallow the whole boat. He followed the advice of Circe. "You must steer close to Scylla's rock and sail through it as fast as you can. It is far better to lose six men than have your whole crew and the ship devoured by Charybdis."

Vicenza continued talking, inspired by the colors of a looming sunset. "That is what Taormina is to me, a place where past and present blend to feed my soul."

After Taormina, they drove to Syracusa. "I want to talk to someone I've known here since my crazy teenage years. He lives in Ortigia, part of Syracusa, and is someone I trust and know."

They stayed two days in Ortigia, as it took Vicenza some time to locate her mysterious friend. Once she talked with him, she joined Eileen for lunch at Piazza del Duomo.

"Now I know what we will do," she said, surprising Eileen with her confidence. "He is someone that I trust, and I mentioned to him our plans and told him about our conversation with Carmela. He suggested we use what we learned from Carmela. If we tell the capi that we want to quit, we will be in a weak position, strengthening their hand, but if we tell them that I am ready to replace Pippo, we will corner them."

"Okay, slow down for me to follow you," asked Eileen.

"They will never let me replace Pippo, and they will have to make me an offer, just as Don Giacomo and Signora Paola did for Carmela. To buy us out, they will have to pay much more than a restaurant in Cefalù. And the amount doesn't matter. You and I already have more than we need."

Eileen made a toast, and Vicenza continued. "My friend also reminded me that in the US, Pippo and I were on our own, but here in Sicily, I belong to my Castelvetrano family and owe loyalty to Carlo. He should be the first to hear my plan, and my friend made a wise suggestion—only to pass the information I have to the Commissione."

"What does that mean?" asked Eileen.

"He suggested me not to give information to any of the capi, but only to the Commissione as a whole, which means that they should call for a meeting where I will be the special guest."

"And why are you so excited about this?"

"Because it will be the first time that a woman will join the capi on a Commissione meeting," Vicenza laughed. "They would rather die than meet with me, but they will have no alternative since I have the financiers' network, and the secret codes for their accounts."

"Great," replied Eileen. "So, what do we do next? Do you want to go to Castelvetrano?"

"No. First, we go to Agrigento. Our honeymoon is not over, and I have a surprise for you there."

・・・

First, they visited *Noto*, where Vicenza showed the little house she had also rented with Pippo. They spent two days visiting vineyards and went to Ragusa. Eileen was so fascinated by the baroque architecture that she wanted to spend an additional night there. "It's like being part of a Commissario Montalbano movie," said Eileen, who had read all books about the Sicilian police inspector.

In Agrigento, the city of Signora Paola's family, they didn't need to stay in a hotel. Gaetana, or Tana as Vicenza called Pippo's sister, insisted, "Our daughters are away, and you can stay in their room."

Tana was one year older than Pippo, and was his favorite sister, an admiration that Vicenza also shared. She was the only sibling to attend university, and went on to become a pediatric physician. Tommaso, her husband, was also a doctor.

"She couldn't live in Castelvetrano with the family and her mother trying to rule every single detail of her life," explained Vicenza.

Tana's husband was very welcoming, especially to Eileen. He had studied at Johns Hopkins University in Maryland and was fluent in English. They talked about Agrigento and the Chesapeake Bay, where Tommaso had great memories. "It's a pity that Tana never told me that you were living there. I would have visited you," he said to Vicenza. Tana immediately added, "That is exactly the reason I never told you. Other than Carlo, my mother, and me, nobody in the family knew where Pippo and Vicenza lived."

They discussed the family and Vicenza's plans for her conversation with Carlo. They opened a few bottles of a Nero D'Avola wine Vicenza had brought from Noto.

Tommaso retired earlier since he had surgery very early the following day, and the three women continued to drink, becoming less inhibited into the night.

"So, I assume by your obvious affections, that you two are together as a couple?"

Vicenza and Eileen didn't reply, and Tana proposed a toast. "To both of you. I admire your courage, and looking to Eileen she continued. "I always suspected that there was something more than a friendship from how Vicenza described you. In her last letter, Vicenza spent many paragraphs talking about 'her friend Eileen'. But it was just a hunch, and now, after observing how you both behave, I can bet my right hand that you are lovers."

Eileen and Vicenza remained in silence.

"Don't be embarrassed. I'm the one who should be embarrassed since I never had the courage that you had." Looking back to Vicenza, she said, "You don't know, and nobody in the world knows, but my great love was a woman." Tana filled her glass again before continuing. "Her name is Susan, she is British, and we lived together while we were in college. But I chose to come back home and didn't let her come with me. Stupid, I know, but that was what I did. I came back to Sicily, met Tommaso, and accepted when he asked me to marry him. He is a lovely man, always attentive, a great professional, and a perfect father. No regrets. But there is not a single day that I do not think of Susan."

"And you never saw her again?" asked Vicenza.

"I saw her a few times. After my second daughter was born, I felt depressed, and I pretended to have a medical conference in London to meet her. We spent three weeks together, and I returned to my husband, my daughters, and my Sicily. A few years later, we met again. It was in Switzerland, at a medical congress. Again, a week of love in Geneve and two more weeks of heaven in a little cottage in the French Vosges, and I came back. I'm sure that if I called her now, she would be here by tomorrow, but I won't. I'm the honorable pediatric *Dottoressa Gaetana*, happy wife of a brilliant surgeon and mother of two beautiful and smart daughters, one studying to be a journalist and the other a psychotherapist. But you can be sure that I miss the touch of her hands on my skin every single night."

Vicenza and Eileen kept looking at her in silence, and Tana asked, "Did Pippo know?"

Vicenza nodded, confirming. "You know Pippo, what he wanted was his freedom."

"I knew very well my brother, and now I wonder what is happening in heavens. If God let him free, virginity would be fully abolished in weeks. His *minchia* would not spare a single attractive saint. But be careful. I love your idea of forcing the capi to invite you to their meeting, and I hope you can convince Carlo, but don't dare let him or any other man know about the two of you. Sicilians are not prepared to understand the love between two women."

27.

The white stone. The following day, they visited the Valley of the Temples with its Greek ruins, and after a long walk under a shining spring sun, they sat in the shade of an olive tree for a rest.

"Are you worried?" asked Eileen.

"A little. I won't say that it was a surprise. It was never my intention to announce our relationship loudly. Whatever we do, it's our business, or *Cosa Nostra*, as we say, but it was hard to listen to it from Tana and sad to hear her story."

"I agree. Let's deal with the families first, and after, we will live the way we want. Here we will be friends. During the day, we will be discreet, and at night we will be on our own since nobody objects to two women sharing a room or even a double bed. It's amazing, no? They consider us sexually harmless."

They spent the rest of the day searching around Porto Empedocle to rent a boat. "It could be small but must be powerful and comfortable," said Vicenza. Finally, they found one and left Porto Empedocle's harbor at the end of the evening, navigating towards the west.

"Are you sure we will be able to come back at night," asked Eileen.

"Easily," replied Vicenza. "Tonight, we will have a full moon, and I want you to see the sunset on a unique spot."

After a quick ride, Eileen saw a cliff made of the same white stone, which was now at her house. "It's La Scala dei Turchi," explained Vicenza. "You might remember what Camilleri wrote. Commissario Montalbano felt so dazzled when he saw the Scala that he had to close his eyes and cover his ears with his hands for a moment. Pippo and I used to say it was our spot."

And she continued excited. "I know, many people here think the same, but we felt re-energized every time we came here. We often sailed by to watch the sunset, especially with a full moon like tonight. You will see. While the sun disappears in the west, coloring the sky with red, the moon appears, magnificent in the east. From where we are anchored, we will see everything: the moon's reflections in the water and the shining white of the Scala Dei Turchi."

And as Vicenza predicted, they both sat in silence on the boat's bow, hand in hand, watching. There were no words, just emotions, and the only thing they managed to do was to gently cry.

• • •

From Agrigento, they hit the road to Castelvetrano. It was time to meet Carlo and Pippo's family, but Vicenza wanted to pass by Marinella de Selinunte and see her sister. "Marinella is at the mouth of a river that brings prosperity to all western Sicily. But sadly, the river is polluted, and I heard the village is now crowded with tourists. I'm sure you will be disappointed to see it, but that is the place where I was born."

Vicenza's sister Simona lived on a farm. She was a few years older than Vicenza, but they looked like twins with remarkably opposite tastes in clothes. Vicenza was wearing safari pants, a green and yellow T-shirt, and a turquoise scarf, while Simona was entirely dressed in black. Black shoes and socks, a black dress, and a black silk blouse. Vicenza had a green trek hat, while Simona covered her head with a black scarf.

"Didn't I tell you?" Vicenza said to Eileen, laughing and hugging her sister. "She is still mourning our mother's death. And who can blame her? Not even ten years had passed since mom died."

"*Zita*," Simona blurted, asking Vicenza to shut up. "First you hug me, and then you can start criticizing everything I do." And after tears and a prolonged hug, Simona explained, "We look the same, but we are completely different. Everything I do, she hates, and everything she does I deeply despise."

Eileen stepped away to allow the sisters time alone. "I will take your daughter with me to show me the village?" she suggested. They all agreed, and Eileen left with Mimma, a twenty-year-old girl with big bright childlike blue eyes.

Mimma proposed taking Eileen to visit the Greek ruins, but after Agrigento, Eileen had enough monuments, so they went to the Marinella Pier.

While talking with Mimma, Eileen noticed that she said Vincenza instead of Vicenza. She asked, and Mimma clarified. Her name was Vincenza, but when the FBI registered her new identity, instead of Vincenza, they wrote Vicenza on the passport. For you in the US, she is Vicenza, but here, for us, she will always be Vincenza or *Cenzina*."

Mimma told Eileen that Pippo and Eileen loved to go to the pier when they were teenagers. "Pippo liked to sail, and his father gave them a boat, the *Chiaro di Luna*."

Eileen showed Mimma pictures of Pippo's *Marinella* on her cell phone, and the girl immediately reacted. "*Chiaro di Luna* looked the same but smaller. She also had the small second mast on the back."

"What happened to the *Chiaro di Luna*?" asked Eileen.

"When the police chased them, they apprehended the boat and left it anchored here. The prosecutor thought Pippo or Vicenza would come back to see it, and they would catch them. But it didn't fool them. My mother begged the police to allow her to take care of the boat, but they did not let her. Wooden boats require maintenance. The *Chiaro di Luna* started to leak and over time sunk. It's a pity. People who knew it say it was a splendid boat."

"Both Pippo's boats sunk," commented Eileen. "*Chiaro di Luna* here and *Marinella*, there" and she added. "It was sad to see *Marinella* burned. Almost nothing was spared from the fire."

Later, Vicenza and Simona went to the pier to meet them and

watch the sunset together. There, Simona told Eileen with pride, "People say that our village is unappealing, but they keep coming, if not for other reasons, at least for the sunset."

"Now you know us," said Simona passing her arm over Vicenza's shoulder. "My sister was like our father with big dreams, always wishing to do something different, and I'm more like our mother, comfortable with a simple life. Tonight, you will meet my husband. It's olive harvest time, and he is delivering our olives to the mill. And you will also meet my son and my daughter-in-law, Carla, who married last year. Mimma's boyfriend, Alessandro, will also be there. We all take care of sheep, olives, and mandarins, except Alessandro, who works as a car dealer, but is quickly learning how to make a *pecorino* cheese. You will not hear from us the great stories that Vicenza certainly can tell you. Here we live out of the land, honoring our traditions, and always far from *Don* Giacomo and Pippo's family businesses," and looking at Eileen, she added, "I believe you know what I mean by that." After kissing Vicenza's cheek, she continued. "Despite being an old-fashioned *campesina*, there was not a single week in the last twenty years that I didn't receive a letter from my sister."

"And what do you think of her plans?" asked Eileen.

"I never questioned her plans. She knows that I always hated her *Cosa Nostra* acquaintances, but I love her, and even Pippo, despite the stupid and crazy things that he made my sister do."

"Or that I made him do?" teased Vicenza. "You will never know."

"Anyhow, I recognize that since Pippo took care of his family business and the Cosa Nostra affairs, things improved a lot. There are no more bombs or executions, and today nobody talks about Mafia anymore. But there is still a lot to be done. Pippo, Carlo, and others fought for the Sicilian families, and they always helped us in Selinunte. People here are very thankful, but others in Sciacca, Marsala, and Trapani are still involved in drug trafficking. I can easily recognize when suspicious boats dock on our harbor, and those people do not care about Sicily or us. They only look for power and money."

"Okay, no more talk," said Vicenza. "You promised to cook a *Pasta Norma* for us, and trust me, my sister's sauce is much better than mine. She uses secret ingredients that she hides from us."

"I told you many times. I do not have any secret ingredients. Just patience. A good sauce needs hours on the burner, and I know that you are too impatient for that."

• • •

Eileen and Vicenza ate the pasta and slept deeply after a few bottles of wine produced in the Marsala region. They drove to Carlo's house late the following morning, and inside the car, they talked about money.

"You mentioned that you have the codes of Swiss accounts owned by the family," said Eileen. "I don't understand those things. What exactly do you have?"

"This is our greatest leverage with the capi, and don't be embarrassed if you don't understand. I believe that they didn't understand either," and Vicenza explained. "A big issue for those who deal in the illegal markets has always been how to safely launder money. Large sums of cash or currencies from different countries cannot simply be deposited into a bank account. Pippo became a master at moving cash around and converting it into legitimate deposits. We put together a network of experts to help us, but any mechanism was expensive since financial institutions always charged a large percentage for their services."

"What about the cryptocurrency part. That stuff is still a mystery to me.?"

"Pippo didn't understand it either, at first. He eventually acquired some cryptocurrency and made payments with them to see how it works. It became a godsend. When you use crypto, nothing is registered. The digital money is transferred electronically, and no fees are paid to financial intermediaries. After the first initial transactions,

Pippo made more significant ones. Today, most payments for illegal businesses are made with those currencies. But there is something else. Pippo saw the future potential for crypto and started buying it early, before it caught on. The value of the currencies went sky high, and Pippo made a lot of money for the families, and himself, secretly trading and selling crypto.

"Are you saying that they have more money than they think?"

"Exactly. All this extra income from crypto gives us tremendous flexibility. The bosses might not want to deal with women or accept our relationship. But if they want to keep riding the crypto train, they have to deal through me, for now. Let's go to Castelvetrano, talk with Carlo, visit Signora Paola, and enjoy being back to Pippo's family."

28.

Back to where it starts. Vicenza was surprisingly calm when they drove into Pippo's family compound and saw the villa on a small hill perched above a vast field of olives, the city of Castelvetrano, and, far away, the sea.

An older man approached the car at the gates.

"*Bentornata Signorina Vincenza. Tutta la famiglia vi aspetta con immensa gioia.*" Vicenza had called before, and the entire family was there.

The first person Vicenza greeted was Signora Paola. After that, she hugged Carlo, his wife, and Adriana his older sister. Eileen noticed that Vicenza was carefully following a seniority protocol. Adriana was the one who had introduced Eileen to each family member starting by Signora Paola who thanked Eileen "We are glad that you are comforting Vincenza in this difficult moment"

The main house, built more than two hundred years ago, was large, but nothing that could be compared with Vicenza's Clairsville White Stone House mansion. Adriana explained that the first floor was used by employees and Gino, who managed the olive fields and the oranges. They climbed a double staircase leading to a terrace that Carlo, and in the past, Don Giacomo, had used to receive visitors. On one side, a view from the city, and on the other, a pergola covered by pink bougainvilleas. Adriana explained to Eileen, "Beyond the terrace is the house where Carlo lives with his wife and his kids. My mom, Camilla, Gino's family, and my family live in those three houses that you can see from here. And there is a fifth house you cannot see, built by Pippo and Vincenza, on the top of a nearby hill."

They walked into Carlo's house, and Eileen was surprised. There was nothing there that would attract the interest of an auctioneer, only old furniture and a few paintings, nothing comparable to the refined taste and luxury of the Clairsville mansion.

"I told you," said Vicenza when the two of them were alone. "The word luxury doesn't exist in the villa of any Sicilian capo. They are rich and powerful, but above all, they are proud to be simple Sicilian people."

Adriana suggested that both should stay at her house, but Carlo wanted Vicenza to remain with him for at least one night. "We have plenty of things to talk about," he said. "Tomorrow, she will stay with you."

Eileen followed Adriana to her house and met Vicenza again at dinner in Carlo's house. There were nineteen people, Eileen counted. All comfortably accommodated around the table in the dining room. In the center, on one side, Don Carlo with Vicenza on his right, and Signora Paola on his left, and in front of them Carlos's wife Constanza.

During dinner, they talked about Pippo. They were all proud of him, and Eileen could notice that some were sadder than others. Curiously Signora Paola didn't seem sorrowful; she mentioned that Pippo, her husband Don Giacomo, and her mother would always be by her side—whether dead or alive.

After dinner, they moved to the piano room, and Eileen was amazed by the number of musicians in the family. A nephew played piano and a niece the accordion. Soon, the entire family, except for glum Signora Paola, was singing and laughing.

Between songs, Vicenza quickly said to Eileen, "I spoke with Carlo, and he fully supports us."

· · ·

The following morning Eileen and Vicenza met early.

"What does it mean that Carlo supports us?" asked Eileen when they started to walk among the olive trees.

"He agreed that I should only talk with the Commissione, not the capos individually."

"Does he know about the financial accounts and the cryptocurrencies?"

"He always knew everything. He doesn't know the actual amount, but he knows that the money exists and that the only one who had the codes was Pippo, and now, me."

"I think this whole idea is crazy. If something happens to you, nobody will ever have access to the money."

"Don't worry," said Vicenza smiling. "If something happens to me, you will be the one to have access to it."

Eileen stopped walking. "What are you saying?"

"Pippo and I were always afraid of forgetting one of the keys since, for each account, there is a different code, and there are many. That is why we wrote down all of the codes and put them into a metal box that we hid under the white stone, which is now in your backyard. And so, if something happens to me, you can withdraw all money and become a multimillionaire." Vicenza continued teasing. "The only problem is that you will have a few Sicilian bosses trying to kill you."

"*Vaffanculu*," said Eileen. "And what are you going to do next?"

"If Pippo were alive, it would be up to him to call for the meeting, and as he is not, Carlo suggested that he should call for it. The transfer of Pippo's information will be the single item on the agenda, and Carlo insisted that until a new general consiglieri is appointed, I should keep doing everything Pippo was doing."

"You must plan what you will tell them."

"Not so fast. Carlo will propose the meeting on my behalf, but I am not sure they will accept it."

They walked in silence for a few minutes. "I'm worried," Eileen said.

"Don't' be. Things are going fine," said Vicenza.

"I know, but—"

"They will not hurt me," Vicenza interrupted. "Carlo is telling them about the extra crypto money. "

It's not them that worries me," said Eileen. "It's you. I'm afraid you might be on some kind of selfish ego trip. I noticed that you were upset while everybody was praising Pippo at the dinner but not mentioning you."

Vicenza tried to interrupt her, but Eileen continued. "Don't forget that I know you better than them, and I can tell you for sure that you were upset, and I understand. We know that you and Pippo always did everything together, and credits go only to him. Now it's your turn. And understandably, you want to take the opportunity to show them who you are, but let's think about what you really want. Are you willing to be like Pippo and continue guiding the families' businesses? If it's what you want, let me tell you, I will not be in this with you. I love you, and I can deal with whatever you did in the past, but I would not be by your side if you keep doing the same. Franz and that Albanian massacre are still on my mind, and I swear to you that I will never be part of anything like that again."

Vicenza walked in silence, and Eileen continued. "Please try and see things from my perspective. Everything I had, career, house, family, seems now so far away. I'm happy with you, and I don't regret anything. I'm delighted with my new life by your side, but I want to know where we are headed."

"I understand, and I appreciate your concern, but there are things that I must do. Maybe I'm a little euphoric, perhaps you are right. But keep in mind that I must preserve Pippo's memories and accomplishments. I feel I owe him that, and there is more, I need to make sure they will let us live the life we choose. And, I need assurances that they will do that. That's my goal."

They could not resist and embraced each other.

"I will do more," said Vicenza cheering Eileen. "I will tell my women friends that I'm here and invite them to come and see me. I will ask for their opinion and advice. And as we do not want to bother Carlo, let's receive them at Adriana's house. She has a lovely pergola, where we can receive them."

"Why don't we move to your house?" asked Eileen. "Adriana told me that you have one inside the compound."

"The house has been closed for twenty years."

"And so what? Let's open it, clean it, and move in. We will be much better in our own place than as guests in Adriana's home."

"Okay, why not," replied Vicenza. "But I can't go now, Carlo wants to talk to me in the evening, and I don't want you to go there without me. Let's go tomorrow, I promise. First thing in the morning."

"And by the way," said Eileen, "the package of letters that Miss Dillan sent us is at Adriana's home."

They walked there and Vicenza looked at all letters, opening just one of them, and returning the others to Eileen. "The others I will read tomorrow."

Vicenza went back to Carlo's house with the letter she picked, one with the sender's name and address: *Concezione Vittorini,* the same family name Vicenza adopted in the US. *Via Belle Signore, 49 – Vizzini, Sicilia,* and it sounded familiar to her. Later, Eileen recalled why. *Concezione* was the name of the main character of *Conversazione in Sicilia,* written by Elio Vittorini. Eileen found the book at Adriana's house, browsed it, and noticed that the narrator met a soldier at Via Belle Signore in the last chapter. She looked at the post office postmark: *Ortigia,* the same city where Vicenza met with her special and secret friend.

29.

A new hideout. "Take me to your house?" said Eileen when they met the following morning.

"It's a little farther from here," explained Vicenza. "We decided to live away from the others, and we wanted to see the sea. That's why we built a cottage on a hill. It was lovely, but I'm afraid you will be disappointed in its condition."

They walked on a gravel road surrounded by olive trees, and only when they started to climb the hill did they see the bougainvilleas.

"Oh my God," said Vicenza. "I didn't know that the bougainvilleas were still there. I planted them around the house, and I thought they had all died."

The road led to the back of the house, and as they got closer, Eileen could see red bougainvilleas covering the roof.

"That is how I dreamed the house would look," said Vicenza, almost in tears. "And thanks to whoever took care of the plants, it looks even more beautiful than I had imagined."

The house was small but had little pergolas covered by bougainvilleas on both sides. "Pippo always complained that the pergola at his father's house was unbearable under the afternoon sun. That is why we did pergolas on both sides. One in the west, protected from the morning sun, and another in the east for the afternoon. Here, the summer sun is too strong."

Vicenza excitedly looked around. "As we didn't want to have kids, we built it just for us. Living room, dining room, and kitchen on the first floor and one single bedroom for us on the second."

Nothing seemed abandoned; the walls were painted, the wooden door and windows were varnished, and when Vicenza opened the door, she was surprised to see that the house was relatively clean, and that the furniture was covered with cloth.

"The only person that I can think of is Camilla. I remember once she asked me to use the house, and I agreed. But this was more than fifteen years ago. Let me call her," said Vicenza.

Camilla immediately acknowledged on the phone of using the house every time her boyfriend Duilio came to *Castelvetrano*. "But wait for me, I didn't know that you planned to stay there, and I didn't prepare it. Give me five minutes, and I will join you."

Camilla arrived worried. "Sorry, there is no bedclothes. When we stayed here, I borrowed them from my mom's house, and there is nothing in the kitchen since we never cooked."

"Don't worry," replied Eileen. "Tomorrow, Vicenza is going to Palermo, and I will buy what we need."

"We can borrow," tried to say Camilla but was immediately interrupted by Vicenza. "No need to borrow anything. You did wonderfully by keeping the house and the bougainvilleas, and I'm very grateful. If you want, you could help Eileen with the shopping."

"But you will have to sleep in the same bed," said Camilla concerned.

"No problem, we already did this before, and none of us snore," replied Eileen, smiling.

Eileen couldn't stop looking, she was impressed with the furniture. Everything there looked at least one hundred years old. "It's my grandmother's furniture," said Vicenza. "When she died, I got the bed, the table, and a few more things. I know. Nothing here is cozy and comfortable, but it is how a Sicilian house is. We rarely stay inside. Only in the winter."

• • •

Vicenza left for Palermo the following morning, but before, she tried unsuccessfully to convince Carlo that she could go alone.

"I know you can go by yourself," Carlo said. "But here you are not Vicenza from America. You are *Vincenza,* my brother's widow, and I'm the one who makes the rules. You will go to Palermo with a driver. Jimmy volunteered to go with you, and I do not care if you need him or not. You will meet Don Rini, and you cannot arrive at his villa driving your own car."

Carlo also warned about Don Rini. "He will receive you in his library. It is a dark room with a lamp next to the chair you will sit in. He will see you, but you will barely see him, and he will probably have a blanket covering his legs, but do not fool yourself. He is old but sharper than you and me. Be ready to talk a lot. Don Rini listens more than he talks. He wants to know everything. You requested the meeting, and it's up to you to do the talking. He might ask you a few questions on some specific issues, and whatever he asks, think carefully before answering. If he asks you something, he has a reason that may not be apparent. Maybe it is something that he wants to know, or perhaps, he is testing to see if you are trustworthy. And keep in mind that he is thankful for the strike on the Albanesi. Don Rini's central business is to bring Colombian drugs to Europe, and without the threat of the Albanesi, he has an open road ahead."

Vicenza had never met Don Rini, but she exchanged letters with one of his daughters, Andrea, and she called her. "After meeting your father, I would like to see you." Andrea agreed.

• • •

The meeting at Don Rini's villa started exactly how Carlo anticipated. His wife received Vicenza at the door and took her to the library, where Don Rini made her sit in one of the two chairs separated by a slightly inclined lamp allowing for more light at the chair reserved for Vicenza. She could barely see his face, and the entire conversation was in Sicilian.

He started by telling her how much he appreciated Pippo, and he even surprised her by saying, "I trusted him more than any member of my own family."

Vicenza thanked him for his words, knowing that Don Rini had sent men to investigate Pippo's death. Vicenza told him in detail what happened on the day *Marinella* caught fire. Don Rini interrupted, asking, "Why did he like to sail by himself?"

Vicenza realized that she should be careful not to shed suspicion on Pippo. "He always loved to sail, but my Giuseppe was also a Sicilian stallion. It seems that there was a young mare supposedly awaiting his arrival."

Don Rini nodded his consent, seeming satisfied with the answer, and Vicenza told him about the financial accounts. Don Rini listened in silence and thanked her, mentioning that he was happy that Pippo had left clear instructions for her.

"I am sorry, Don Rini, but my husband never left instructions for me. The truth is, we always managed our work together. The decision to come here and tell all members of the Commissione about the cryptocurrency accounts was my decision. I wanted to do right by the families. My husband is not with us anymore, and now it's up to the Commissione to decide who should manage the information we have."

"Who do you think this person should be?"

Vicenza knew well what to say, but she preferred to wait a moment and give the impression that she was surprised by the question. "You might need more than one person since it would probably be impossible to find someone with all the skills and trust required. I believe that my husband had already mentioned that you will need another person to keep in contact with politicians in the US and the other American families. We have already suggested some names. The person in that position should be efficient but doesn't need to be from one of the Sicilian families. Perhaps someone born in the US, whom we trust, could do the work. There are a few options, and you certainly can select a good one. A bigger problem, however, would be to replace my husband in dealing with financial issues." He nodded and she continued. "Over many years, we developed a network of financial experts to help us with money laundering and financial investments. And whoever you choose for this job could be tempted to embezzle our money. Nothing is fully registered, particularly in cryptocurrency transactions, and even the amounts in those digital accounts is unclear. The finance network Pippo and I managed is very complex and unwieldy, involving international finance, cash businesses, banks, and currency fluctuations. It is why the whole network we built might be unsustainable unless properly managed."

"Please, explain," Don Rini insisted.

"Money is fungible, and in our case, there are no documents. The cryptocurrency value floats every day. Your accountants know how much you have to pay to a Colombian or a Mexican cartel, but they have no control over the transaction, nor do they know the real financial costs involved. Currency exchange rates come into play, as fees must be paid to have money secretly transferred without a trace. It takes many hands to move hundreds of millions of dollars around the world, undetected. You have trusted us to do it for you all these years. The amounts are so large now that we could have embezzled millions without raising suspicion."

"And how did you and your husband avoided being cheated?" asked Don Rini.

"By doing all transactions ourselves," answered Vicenza. "My husband and I have experts, who help us plan the operations. They advise us on the currencies we should use. But experts only advise. Who pushes the button to do the deal has always been my husband or me, no one else. And as we always had your trust, you never asked us to provide a balance sheet. I can provide that, and you will realize you have more money than you were expecting. Like I said, a lot of our holdings are in cryptocurrencies, and those values change daily. We have done very well holding your money."

"Don Carlo warned me about that, but I have some difficulty understanding."

"It is very complex, which is why you will need trusted experts to guide your decisions. And, it's why you need more than one person or group to handle transactions."

"What specifically do you suggest?"

"My advice is to split the accounts and operations by two or three. The son of Don Brancato, Guido, who is in charge of the bank you and Carlo have, is trustworthy. The niece of Don Galiano from Agrigento lives in Switzerland, and she is one of the experts we use for our operations. She is good and trustworthy too. We also have the son of Don Curcio from Caltanissetta, who works for an international bank in Milano, and has helped us many times. And let me be clear, I'm not suggesting splitting the families' operations. It's good for all of us to operate together. More money means more power and fewer costs. What I'm saying is to split the operations, keeping one single command, that if you ask me, my choice would be the son of Don Brancato."

Don Rini was visibly impressed and had adjusted the lamp cover to bring more light to Vicenza's face.

She continued, full of confidence. "And there is more. My husband had an essential and delicate position as the general consiglieri, and it would be very valuable for the families to have someone with the same moderating skills he had. He believed in making money, not in bloodshed. We all know how difficult it will be to agree on a name for this position." Vicenza teased, "It is easier to choose a new pope than have all *cap*os agree on a single name to be the general consiglieri. Meanwhile, if you all consider it appropriate, I can continue to help you. My husband and I have been on this together, and there was not a single piece of advice he gave you in the last ten years that was not discussed with me." and she concluded, looking into Don Rini's eyes, "I know, better than anyone how to keep things smooth until we have white smoke going out of the chimney, and I will gladly do it to be sure that nobody would destroy what my husband did for the families."

30.

The Belle Signore. As soon as she left Don Rini's villa, Vicenza called Carlo to update him about the meeting, and from there, she went to a restaurant to meet Jimmy. She wanted to discuss a few things that were still pending. It was a lengthy lunch. They sat at a table far from the other customers and spoke for more than two hours. Pippo always trusted Jimmy more than himself, and Vicenza learned to feel the same. After lunch, they went to Don Rini's daughter's house, and Andrea received Vicenza with great news. "My father was very impressed. He said that you are honest and capable, and he even expressed that you were *like Giuseppe*, which means a lot since your husband was like a son to him." Andrea continued. "When we heard that your husband was sick with the virus, there were a lot of talks among the families. Some people whispered that it was time to replace him, but my father and others opposed it. Later, when you told us that he died, the same bastards started to insinuate that his death could be fake, suggesting that he was planning to run away with families' money. My father always trusted your husband, but the pressure was intense, and he was forced to send some people to investigate what happened. Thanks to their report the bastards retracted, but there were still rumors. Now that you confirmed that the money is still there and that there is even more than families were expecting, we will shut them up, and as my grandmother used to say *ta stari mutu i va' a fatti fùttiri, scecca!*" A Sicilian expression that could be poetically translated as shut up and fuck you, asshole!

Vicenza laughed but asked, "And who were those bastards?"

"Some from Corleone, many from Catania, and I believe some from Marsala. Don Nino and those from Marsala are now behaving like sheep, regretting the whole mess they made contacting the Albanians, but I still don't trust them."

"What you just said is an example of what we have talked about in our letters. Women could do much more for the families. You mentioned your grandmother, who was wise and polite like mine, but who could use the right words at the right moment. You also showed me how precise you are in assessing the Marsala family. Despite all that, we continue to accept the image that Sicilian women are good only for cooking and taking care of the kids. Fuck it! You know that the capi, including your father, refuse to let me join a Commissione's meeting just because I have a vagina instead of their voracious *minchias* between my legs. We should not accept it. The families want their money, and I will give it to them because it belongs to them, but like it or not, they will have to meet with me and my vagina."

Vicenza didn't have to say another word. Andrea was a strong supporter. She worked at the bank that Don Carlo and Don Rini's families had established as a direct assistant to the bank CEO, Guido Brancato. Vicenza pointed out, "I told your father that Guido is an honorable man and could take charge of the financial operations. But you know how busy he is, that is why I also told your father that there is a woman, Michaela Galiano from Agrigento, who is very good and trustworthy.

"I met her," interrupted Andrea. "Once, she came here for a meeting with us, and we were all very impressed with her."

"Do you understand what I am saying?" pressed Vicenza. "We can have a Sicilian woman from one of the families managing the money. *Cosa Nostra* doesn't mean men's only."

They talked about other Sicilian women in high professional positions. Then Andrea surprised Vicenza by asking, "As we are talking about women, I'm wondering if you are planning to go to Corleone?"

"That is an excellent question. As you know, Pippo and the Corleonesi had some disagreements. Still, Toto Riina and Provenzano are gone, and their representative in the Commissione is Don Petruzzello, whom I never met. I planned to talk with all members before the meeting, but what do you think? Is he one of the bastards?"

"Not sure, but I have a suggestion for you," replied Andrea with a naughty look. "Why don't you talk with those who really matter?"

"And who are they?" asked Vicenza, curious.

"Ninetta Bagarella and Saveria Palazzolo."

"Are you nuts? Toto Riina and Bernardo Provenzano were for a while the main enemies of my husband, and now you want me to talk with their widows."

"Exactly. From widow to widow, and from woman to woman. Let me explain to you what I think."

Vicenza opened her arms as if saying, "Go ahead, I'm all ears."

"The disagreements between families led us to war with prosecutors, and worse, a war between Sicilian families. But from what I've seen, most past disagreements were caused by testosterone, which our men have undoubtedly in excess. The Corleonesi chose to fight the prosecutors, and everybody else, but today, thanks to your husband, we do more business than before without that ridiculousness of putting bombs and killing prosecutors."

"And do you think those two women would accept to talk to me?"

"I met them already, we talked, and I'm sure they will. Times are different now. My father keeps the drug trafficking business, but he is also a banker. Our family is financing tech upstarts, and my cousins are the main sponsors of the Palermo anti-Mafia museum. We are smarter, and part of the secret is that we don't think with dicks anymore." Andrea paused to let Vicenza absorb her words and concluded, "I believe you will be surprised once you meet them. They are almost in their eighties, and they are wise women. Most importantly, you don't have anything to lose. If they don't like you, nothing will change, but if you have a good conversation, I can bet that Don Petruzzello will immediately approach you."

"Do you have their telephone number?" asked Vicenza, determined. "I want to call them right now, and I want to be in Corleone tomorrow. Let's surprise them. I don't want to give those women time to discuss our meeting with those bastards you mentioned."

Andrea agreed and called Ninetta, who didn't hesitate and welcomed the meeting.

• • •

"Change of plans," said Vicenza to Jimmy when they left Andrea's house. "Tomorrow morning, we are going to meet Toto Riina and Bernardo Provenzano's widows."

"But—" Jimmy tried to interrupt.

"No buts, Jimmy, I know that we have to inform Don Carlo, and we will do it together now, but I am going to Corleone, and if you don't go with me, I will rent a car and go by myself."

"Okay," said Jimmy resigned, "but let me tell you that Don Rini must also be informed. See that van there," Jimmy said, pointing to a black van parked on the other side of the street. "It was sent by Don Rini with four bodyguards to protect you."

Vicenza looked at him, surprised, and Jimmy continued. "I told them that it was unnecessary, but they confronted me by saying they respond to Don Rini and not me. They will follow you and protect you wherever you go. I already called Don Carlo, and he told me to accept the protection. His exact words were, 'Now that Don Rini knows how much Miss Vinceza is worth, he doesn't want anything happening to her.'"

As soon as Vicenza got into the hotel room, she called Eileen to relate the news. She mentioned her conversation with Don Rini, Andrea, and her plans for the following day. "Remember Marlon Brando," Vicenza said, "keep your friends close and your enemies closer."

"What do you want to achieve?" Eileen asked.

"I don't know, but if Andrea suggests it, I want to go. She is smart and one of her father's main advisers. If she proposed the meeting, she knows that her father would approve."

After talking with Eileen, Vicenza made another phone call, but this one was from a cell phone that she had hidden in her bag, and not even Eileen knew about it.

• • •

Early on the following morning, Vicenza left Palermo with her bodyguards to go to Corleone. She wanted to take advantage of the calm hours of the morning to have a soothing conversation with her former enemies.

Before seven, she got to Ninetta's house, the widow of Toto Riina, the most ruthless boss the Sicilian families ever had, and Ninetta received her cordially, but reserved.

Her house was humble, and only Ninetta and Saveria were there. Granita, *brioche*, *crocche*, the typical Sicilian breakfast, and coffee were over the table. The three of them spoke for more than two hours, and when they finished, Ninetta accompanied Vicenza to visit the neighborhood where Riina and Provenzano grew up and became friends. As soon as they finished, Vicenza returned to Castelvetrano where Carlo and Eileen were anxiously waiting for her.

It was past two when she arrived, and they went straight to the table. Constanza, Carlos's wife, had prepared a table for two at the pergola, thinking that Carlo and Vicenza were going to lunch alone, but Vicenza insisted that Eileen join them.

"Tell us," said Carlo. "How did those Belle Signore receive you?"

"Initially, they were aloof but straightforward. Later, as the conversation evolved, we became more informal, and I can tell you that the meeting turned out very pleasant."

Carlo smiled, and Eileen relaxed.

Vicenza continued. "First, we talked about the main differences between Pippo and their husbands. Saveria suggested that their different visions and behaviors could be explained by their childhood. While Toto and Bernardo struggled to survive, Pippo was born into a comfortable family. And by the way, both women showed great respect and affection to your mother. Saveria even said that when Provenzano was being chased, Signora Paola had personally let her hide for months in a house your mom had near Raffadali."

Vicenza asked Carlo, "Did you know that?"

"I know that mom has a house in Raffadali, and I know that she let a few runaways use it, but I must confess that I never heard that my mother had sheltered Provenzano's wife."

"Anyway," Vicenza continued, "Saveria said that Provenzano and Riina were bitter and could never understand that they could peacefully settle disagreements. For them, only the most powerful could survive. That is why they choose to scare their enemies, and even their friends, with violence. She also suggested I visit the place where they were born, what I did with Ninetta after our meeting since Saveria's health is not so good." Vicenza added with an angry look, "That part of Corleone is still indecently poor. More than thirty years passed, and nothing there changed."

After a pause to bite the *arancini* prepared by Constanza, Vicenza continued. "While Saveria tried to justify their violence, Ninetta was more critical. She told me that they built their power with brutality and mistakenly believed that strength would take them wherever they wanted. They never understood that there was a world beyond Sicily and their businesses. Ninetta also recognized that Riina believed the whole country would fear him when they killed the prosecutors. In essence, she approved what Pippo did. Still, she has a lot of resentment towards other families that took advantage of Riina and Provenzano's fall. They swiped their properties and operations. *Pirates!* she called them. People who ignored that Riina and Provenzano were from our land and only fought for Sicily and our people. This humble house where we live now, Ninetta said, showing me her place, is the best Riina ever got for us, and she got emotional saying that they shared their money with members of the families who worked with them, but when they needed it, very few showed up to support."

"And what about your meeting with the Commissione?" asked Carlo.

"They fully supported it," Vicenza declared. "And I mentioned the names of Guido Brancato and Michaela Galiano to check if they would object, but they didn't. Until now, it seems that we have a clear road ahead."

31.

Unexpected troubles. After lunch, Vicenza and Eileen walked to their cottage, and Vicenza asked, "Was there any argument between Constanza and you while I was away?"

"No. I didn't even see her. Yesterday, I went shopping and I spent the whole morning cleaning and organizing the house. I just saw Constanza when you arrived. Why do you ask?"

"I have the impression that she was upset with you when we sat for lunch."

"I saw, but perhaps, she was upset with Carlos," Eileen suggested. "Don't you think it was weird that he didn't ask her to join us at the table?"

Vicenza thought for a moment and then agreed. "Maybe. For Carlo, our lunch was business, and he didn't feel the need to invite her."

"Well, it might be the Sicilian way, but business or not, she is his wife, and we are their guests. She should have been with us."

"I agree with you, but it's not our problem. We have more crucial things to deal with than Constanza's mood and let me tell you that the meeting with the ladies was delightful. There was no dispute, but Ninetta has a grudge against Carlo. It seems that when the war between families was over, some Trapani families took over part of the smuggling business of the Corleonesi, and Carlo sided with them. And worse, Toto Riina had a warehouse near the Palermo port that apparently Carlo took from him.

They kept walking in silence, but Eileen couldn't control herself.

"Everything is going perfect, but we still have a secret between us."

Vicenza stopped, smiled, and gently replied, looking into Eileen's eyes. "Yes, I have a secret, but it's only one. And yes, I will tell you one day, but now I can't. Trust me."

"Okay," said Eileen. "I will wait, but there is something else that we should fix immediately—the beds. Adriana will probably talk to you about it."

"Oh no! But let's wait. Now I will keep traveling, and you could come with me. I have to go to Trapani, Marsala, Caltanisseta, and Catania. We will sleep in hotels, and we may even have time for sightseeing. Unfortunately, we must travel with Jimmy, and I don't know who else Carlo or Don Rini will assign for our security. I will meet the capi by myself. None of them speak English, but I'm sure you will find something to do. And tonight, we can make a big sacrifice and sleep uncomfortably in the same bed. But we still have to pass by Signora Paola's house. She must be anxious to talk to me."

"She didn't look like it," commented Eileen.

"She has always been cold to me," said Vicenza. "I believe she was jealous I stole her baby boy, but now that she knows about my meeting with Ninetta and Saveria, she might be curious. And I also want to talk to her about the warehouse. But first, let's go to our place. I want to see what you bought and kiss you at least ten times. Later, we will go there, and I promised it would be a quick visit."

• • •

Constanza's was more upset with Vicenza than she had imagined. The previous night, Signora Paola went to dinner at Constanza's house, and during the whole meal, she and Carlo only talked about Vicenza. Carlo mentioned the phone call he had received from Don Rini praising Vicenza, and Signora Paola told of how impressed she was with Vicenza's self-confidence and determination. Constanza barely spoke a word during the meal.

That evening, when Vicenza and Eileen walked to Signora Paola's house, Constanza was already there. Signora Paola was in the kitchen with Camilla preparing *granitas*, and Constanza was beside them. When Vicenza entered, Signora Paola stopped what she was doing and kissed Vicenza. Constanza and Camilla looked at each other surprised. Signora Paola had never done that, and while preparing the granitas, Signora Paola began to talk about Pippo. She even mentioned that Pippo went through an emotional crisis before his death, and Vicenza was firm on his side.

When they were bringing the *granitas* to the terrace, Eileen and Vicenza were alone for an instant, and Vicenza mentioned, "I'm surprised by her attitude. It seems she decided to be nice to me."

"Be careful," said Eileen. "Constanza will be jealous."

"It's her problem, not mine," replied Vicenza.

They sat at the terrace, and the sun was almost touching the horizon, but it was still hot. Vicenza told about the meeting with the Corleonesi women, and *Signora* Paola agreed to talk with Carlo about the Palermo warehouse.

"Our men are selfish," she said, "and they believe they are immortal, often leaving widows in trouble."

They continued to talk, until dark, revealing an astonishing number of stars. Signora Paola told old stories about Sicilia family wives, and she was so comfortable speaking with Vicenza that even Constanza chose to enjoy the evening and forget her sorrows.

. . .

The following day, before leaving for Marsala, Vicenza mentioned the warehouse to Carlo. "According to Ninetta, it's closed and falling apart."

Carlo made a phone call to Palermo and confirmed to Vicenza. "Ninetta is right. It's abandoned. We needed to put some money into it, but it was not a priority. It's a small warehouse, and we don't have any use for it other than renting it out."

"If it's small, why don't you transfer it back to Ninetta. We can ask Guido Brancato to give her a long-term loan to renew it. She could rent it and repay the loan. My feeling is that she does not need the income now, but she would like to have something to leave for her four kids when she dies."

Carlo agreed, and Vicenza left for Marsala in a van accompanied by Eileen. A driver and a bodyguard sat in the front seats, and Eileen and Vicenza in the back. Jimmy rode in the car behind with Don Rini's bodyguards, who still had orders to protect Vicenza wherever she went.

The meeting in Marsala was with Nino, the young *capo* who created the Albanian problem. After the conversation with Carlo, he had shown appropriate behavior, but as Andrea had warned Vicenza in Palermo, "It's too early to trust him."

Eileen spent her time visiting the city. When they got together later, Vicenza proposed a walk. "Pippo and I came here a few times, sailing to the Aegadian's Islands, but our favorite route was to Agrigento and the east coast. Our family was never friends with those from Marsala."

They bought two granitas, and Vicenza told him about the meeting she had. "Nino is young but will have a great future. As his father was murdered, he became the *capo* when his grandfather died. Their family has a large wine business, and they control a prostitution network in parts of Sicily and Calabria. Nino's younger brothers work at the family winery, but Nino's passion has always been the prostitution business. When he assumed control of the family, he tried to expand their activities. Still, he was blocked by those Sicilian families who controlled the markets in the northern states of Italy. He was impatient, and instead of bringing the disagreement to the Commissione, he chose to ally with the Albanians. A great mistake! The Sicilian families often make alliances with foreigners but never side with them against other Sicilians. That is what he did, but he paid the price, and I believe he learned. He even told me that thanks to the families' strong action against the Albanians—"

"The massacre that you and Pippo launched," Eileen interrupted.

"Yes, thanks to the massacre, if you prefer to use that word, Don Nino is now expanding his prostitution operations in the south of France. He also told me about a conversation he had with Pippo about new options for the future. Nino knows that our family focuses on selling goods and services to the government. That is why we established the construction company and other businesses where the government is our sole client, and thanks to professional management—"

"And a lot of bribes," interrupted Eileen.

"Okay, and thanks to professional management and many bribes, we are making good money from it. And let me tell you something, my lovely nun. We didn't invent government. We only take advantage of its weakness and inefficiency."

Eileen smiled, and Vicenza continued talking about Nino. "He also knows that we opened a bank with Don Rini, and where, by the way, we legally collect subsidies from the government, which are given to honest bankers under the honorable justification of fighting the COVID crisis and boosting the economy. Don Nino liked the bank idea so much that he bought the license of an insolvent bank with another Marsala family, and he is willing to associate it with our family. Still, he recognizes that Carlo and Don Rini will take some time to forgive him."

Vicenza talked excitedly. "I liked his enthusiasm, and I even offered him a piece of advice. He is the newcomer, and the other capos are all well-established. He should not appear too anxious to grab new areas for his family. First, he must show respect," and looking at Eileen, proud of her words. "Don Rini's drug trafficking goes hand-in-hand with prostitution. Nino could start by offering something instead of grabbing stuff. I even suggested that he approach Andrea Rini, who, in my opinion, is a brilliant woman."

"Here she goes again, the Godmother Vicenza, thrilled to be a *capi Mafiosi* again," teased Eileen.

"Shut up," replied Vicenza with a smile. "As Carlo proposed, I should act as general consiglieri until a new one is appointed. Don Nico is bright, and like Andrea, younger than the other bosses. That is what we need now, people with youth and vision. He talked about something Pippo mentioned many times—hacking businesses. Casinos are losing their market to betting companies, and everybody will soon have access to legal betting from their homes. Drugs are also becoming legal. Don Rini, for instance, is partnering with some Sicilian-American families in legal pot production in the US. But hacking is a whole new market to explore. Nino has alliances with Russians, Eastern European groups, and North Koreans, using them to access aggressive hacker groups, and I strongly encouraged him to proceed. What I want you to understand is that hacking will occur, and I prefer it to be a Sicilian family. We are Sicilians and Sicilia is Cosa Nostra.

"Finally, we talked about Pezzini, and he acknowledged his mistake," continued Vicenza, but this time with a troubled face. "Nino said that he never ordered him to betray us, and it was Pezzini's decision to send the photos to the CIA.

"Do you believe him?" asked Eileen.

"No, but I prefer to turn that page. Don Nico showed me the photo of Pezzini terminated with a shot in his forehead, and he apologized and swore to me that his family would work under Carlo's leadership. I will talk to Carlo again. What he did in Clairsville didn't hurt us, and to have Marsala, at least temporarily on his side, will give Carlo a stronger grip over the Commissione."

. . .

Back at Castelvetrano, Vicenza reported her meeting to Carlos, who was more positive about Nino. "I think he made a few rookie mistakes, and I agreed with you, he can be a great capo, but *Prima deve fare la gavetta*, pays his dues, as any beginner, and be patient." Carlo then switched to another subject.

"I already called Ninetta, and she was delighted. The warehouse is small, but as you said, it is something that she could leave for her kids. And the interesting part is that less than an hour later, I received a phone call from Don Petruzzello."

Vicenza explained to Eileen that Don Petruzzello was the representative of the Corleone families at the Commissione. "We talked about your plans of visiting him, and he proposed that instead of you going to Corleone, he would like to come here to talk to you, me, and also to visit our olive fields and the oil processing facilities. I have already asked Gino and Constanza to help us organize the visit, and he will lunch with us. We have not had peace with Marsala and a Corleonesi family visiting Castelvetrano for a long time"

32.

A storm within a storm. The following days, Vicenza and Eileen stayed in Castelvetrano. Most women with whom Vicenza had exchanged letters already knew that she was back and wanted to see her. The pergola on Eileen and Vicenza's house was as crowded as Don Carlo's terrace, and cars drove up and down the compound. Camilla teased Vicenza, "I could not ride peacefully my bike this morning with all those cars coming into the property and asking me where is Signora Vicenza's house. If I were Carlo, I would be jealous."

Don Carlo was not jealous; on the contrary, he was happy. He knew that he was doing what his brother would have wanted, and everything was going according to plans. The same could not be said about Constanza. She used to be Signora Paola's favorite, and now it was impossible to talk to her mother-in-law about any subject other than Vicenza. Signora Paola even prepared her *panna cotta* for Vicenza's guests. There were visitors in the morning in the west pergola and others in the evening who Vicenza received on the east side, all women. Eileen, Camilla, Adriana, and Signora Paola, did their best to help, and Vicenza was delighted. Everyone wanted to see Vincenzina, born in *Marinella di Selinunte che era diventata una Lady negli Stati Uniti*. At the end of the evening, even the men, Carlo, his brother Gino, and Onofrio, Adriana's husband, went to Vicenza and Eileen's house to drink prosecco and hear stories of the day. Only Constanza and Adelaide, Gino's wife, didn't come. They were preparing for the Corleonesi visit.

The sun was exceptionally bright on the day of the Corleonesi visit. No clouds in the sky, and from Don Carlo's terrace, they could glimpse the turquoise colors of the Mediterranean. Don Petruzzello arrived with pomp, bringing a large entourage that included Signora Ninetta.

Don Carlo had his family received them in front of the main house as a show of respect. After the patio greetings, Don Petruzzello's wife, daughters, and Signora Ninetta walked into the house with Signora Paola. Don Petruzzello's sons joined Gino and Onofrio visiting the olive fields and the oil mill, and Don Petruzzello, Don Carlo, and Vicenza sat at the pergola to enjoy lemon granitas.

Eileen was lost, and while walking next to Camilla, she vented. "I don't know what to do and where to go?"

Camilla' smiling, replied, "Do you understand now why I prefer to play my piano?"

The lunch and everything else were exquisite. Constanza did a stunning job. Vicenza shined and captivated everyone's attention, particularly during lunch, when she described the Sicilian things she missed the most. However, the real journey's star was Camilla with, playing Sicilian songs and a few modern tunes at the end of the lunch. Everybody, guests and family, sang them loudly and cheerfully.

It was a perfect day, and Eileen insisted on telling Constanza how impressed she was with everything, but it was not enough as Constanza appeared somber and aloof.

• • •

Early on the following morning, Vicenza and Eileen went to Trapani. The plan was to speak to Don Maltese, the Trapani member at the Commissione, and have lunch with a few women friends. They had booked a room near the port so they could visit the islands of Favignana and Levanzo the next day.

Eileen and Vicenza were comfortable in the back seat of the van, talking about the events of the day before.

"Did you see how much Signora Paola and Ninetta chatted the whole day?" Vicenza asked. "Who could imagine our families were at war a few years ago?" Suddenly, a white van approached them with three masked men brandishing weapons and signaling them to stop.

Jimmy was in the van behind with Don Rini's guys and immediately ordered the driver to speed up, crashing into the back of the white van. Everything happened fast, and the three masked men were surprised and fled.

Eileen and Vicenza heard Jimmy instructing her car's driver by radio. "Jimmy is telling our driver to stop the car and not follow them," said Vicenza.

Their car stopped, and Jimmy and Don Rini's bodyguards surrounded Eileen and Vicenza's doors holding automatic weapons.

"Better to let them run away," said Jimmy. "It could be a decoy. They may want us to chase the van while attacking them with another car."

They waited for a few minutes, and nothing happened.

"Let's go back to Castelvetrano," said Jimmy. And he got inside the car with Eileen and Vicenza, machine gun in his lap, instructing the driver, "Go at one hundred miles an hour, and do not stop for nothing."

Jimmy called Don Carlo, who sent two cars to join them. It took them more than one hour to reach the point where they were attacked and less than thirty minutes to drive back.

"Who could they be?" Vicenza asked.

"Here, you never know," Jimmy said. "My instincts tell me they are police agents," answered Jimmy. "Otherwise, they would not have run away so easily."

"But they were wearing balaclavas," replied Vicenza.

"It's not uncommon here. The police do not want their identities known. We were lucky. They probably didn't know about the second car, and they aborted the attack when they saw us, but we will check all this out. Don Carlo has good contacts, and if they were cops, we would know it very soon."

They were already near Castelvetrano when they were joined by the two cars Don Carlo sent, and when they arrived at the compound, he was at the stairs with news about the attack.

"They were agents of the DIA, *la Direzione Investigativa Anti-Mafia*, who is part of the Department of Justice, and they were looking for Vincenza Leone."

"Never heard of her," Vicenza said. "I'm a Vittorini."

"I know," said Don Carlo, "But let's not take this lightly. Anti-Mafia legislation allows police to hold you for more than one day without contacting anyone, and it's better to prevent it. Let's have a phone conversation with our lawyers. Meanwhile, please stay inside the compound."

Don Carlo and Vicenza had a conference call with the lawyers in the afternoon. Eileen joined them. The situation was clear. The Department of Justice suspected that Vicenza was Vincenza Leone, wife of a wanted criminal Giuseppe Leone, but did not have proof. In a picture when she was seventeen, Vicenza looked similar to the Leone woman now. Should police officials pursue her, Vicenza Vittorini had a passport proving that she was an American citizen.

The lawyers recommended Vicenza request an appointment with the operational center of the DIA in Palermo, preferably for the next day, to give them proof of her identity."

Vicenza agreed and asked the name of the American ambassador in Italy. "I will give him a phone call," she explained to Carlo. "He participated in one or two of our special weekends in Clairsville, and he and Pippo were friends."

"It's important not to overshoot," said the lawyer. "They might think you are scared, but let's keep the ambassador informed since those anti-Mafia guys are powerful and could always surprise us."

Vicenza reached the ambassador in Rome late in the evening. She explained that she was a victim of mistaken identity. "It seems the police are after a Mafia woman who looks like me," she explained. The ambassador instantly called the head of the US Consular Agency in Palermo, who called Vicenza suggesting she stop by his office before the meeting with DIA."

"Don't worry," Vicenza said to Eileen when they were alone at their place. "We knew that this was going to happen. We talked about it, and the sooner, the better. I have documents, and they are one hundred percent legit. There is nothing that the Italian prosecutors could question."

Eileen barely rested that night, but Vicenza woke up calm and perfectly composed the next day. She left for Palermo with Jimmy and the bodyguards, and Eileen stayed in Castelvetrano.

"There is no reason to expose you," said Vicenza.

In Palermo, Vicenza first went to the US Consular Agency, where the consul general checked all her documents to ensure that everything was in order. "*Tutto a posto*," he said. "I would be pleased to join you at your meeting if you deem it convenient."

Vicenza thanked him, mentioning that the letter was enough, and from there, she went to the DIA office where the lawyer was expecting her.

Following his advice, Vicenza didn't say a word during the interview; only the lawyer talked. He politely expressed that Vicenza was there to present her identification documents and noted that Vicenza was volunteering to have her fingertips taken to avoid any misunderstanding.

Once they finished, the director addressed Vicenza. "It seems that you have many Sicilian friends. We know that you are a guest at Don Carlo's compound, and I believe you also met Don Rini and Don Nico."

The lawyer answered, explaining that "Miss Vicenza does not see any reason to answer questions about her personal life, and if everything is concluded, we would like to leave. We have provided all the proof you need to verify Miss Vicenza's identity, including fingerprints."

Indeed, Vicenza's prints were clearly different than those of the wanted woman.

The director was not convinced by the information provided but had to release Vicenza. "Be prudent, we are in Sicily, and those DIA prosecutors believe they could do whatever they want," The lawyer warned.

Vicenza left DIA's office and called Carlo. "The son of a bitch is following our movements. He knew I was with Rini, and Nino."

"Why not?" replied Vicenza, "I'm not ashamed of my past. I was young and wild, and I'm proud of what I did and the new opportunity you guys gave me."

Vicenza returned to Castelvetrano in a great mood. But when she was almost getting there, she received a phone call from Gaetana.

"They know it," Tana said.

"What do they know?" replied Vicenza.

"They know about you and Eileen."

Vicenza was speechless, and Tana continued. "Adriana called me. Constanza and Adelaide went to her house saying they suspected that you and Eileen are lovers. Adelaide can see your house from her bedroom window, and seemingly, she saw you hugging and kissing Eileen."

"Her house is far away, and I can barely see her roof from my terrace. How could she see us kissing?"

"With a binocular, and don't tell me that is pathetic, of course, it is. Why should she use a binocular to spy on you? The fact is that she did, and when you add the story of the bed and that Adriana and Camilla had both seen you and Eileen walking among the olive trees holding hands and hugging each other, it's more than enough for them."

"And what are they planning to do?" asked Vicenza.

"Adriana doesn't plan to do anything, but she is appalled. For my sister, lesbians only exist in TV movies. She even told me by telephone that she believes there are no lesbians in Sicily. Please understand that Adriana is not a bad person, and she loves you, but she only left Castelvetrano once, and it was for her honeymoon in Puglia. I think you should talk to her. Camilla is okay, but she thinks that my brothers will be mad, and I agree. Still, the bigger problems are Constanza and Adelaide. They believe that Signora Paola should know, and if they tell my mom, I have no idea how she would react."

Vicenza was furious, and when she arrived in Castelvetrano, she went straight to her house, where she found Eileen and Camilla talking under the pergola.

"We have a problem," said Eileen when Vicenza approached her.

"I know, Tana called me."

Vicenza looked at Camilla and asked, "What do you think will happen?"

"From what I know, Constanza and Adelaide plan to tell my mother today. According to Constanza, my mother is the one that should decide what to do."

"And Adriana?"

"My sister is crying. You have always been her reference point, and she cannot understand. Pippo just died, and a few weeks later, you are with a new lover, and worse, a woman. It's too much for her."

Vicenza thought for a minute and then said confidently, "Okay. The storm has started, and we have no choice. We must sail through it. Please tell your mom that Eileen and I need to talk with her this evening. But first, Eileen and I will see Adriana."

33.

Sailing rough waters. "It will be tough," said Vicenza while walking to Adriana's house. "At least Ulysses could choose the less damage between Scylla and Charybdis, but we have no option. We will have to cut through the storm. Do not be worried about Carlo. He already knows it. Pippo and I never kept secrets from him. Carlo was aware of Pippo's depression and everything else happening in Clairsville. I'm not sure if Pippo told him that Veronica is not a woman, but other than that, Carlo knows everything. He told me he was worried about us on the first day we got here, but I made it clear that we would never deny it. I understand that we must deal with other matters first, and that you and I would be as discreet as possible, but we would never hide our love. You are my woman, and there is nothing more important to me.

"Our conversation with Adriana will not be easy. I always knew that she would never understand. And be ready for Gino and Onofrio. For them, lesbians are whores who they see in porno movies, but I don't care. The toughest will be Signora Paola. But what can we do? It is, what it is, and I hope Carlo can help us, but be ready for the worst."

The conversation with Adriana was long. Vicenza didn't justify her love for Eileen but felt compelled to explain that there was no disrespect to Pippo's memory. "It started before his death. Pippo knew it and supported us from the beginning. He liked and respected Eileen," she explained. "Your brother and I were still best friends, but there were already many years that we were not husband and wife."

Adriana felt better, she would never accept a betrayal to her brother, and even if she could not understand a lesbian love, she liked Vicenza and Eileen enough to respect whatever feelings they had.

From Adriana's place, Vicenza and Eileen walked to Signora Paola's house. Adriana went with them, and when they got there, they faced Constanza and Adelaide standing next to Signora Paola with a triumphant expression.

"It seems that everybody wanted to talk to me today," said Signora Paola. "I prepared a tea and some pastries." Camilla was also with her mother, and a few minutes later, Carlo arrived.

"While Camilla helps me serve the tea, I think we could start," said Signora Paola, and looking at Constanza, she added, "Tell me what is so important that you wanted me to know?"

Constanza was embarrassed, and she started by explaining. "I noticed that Eileen and Vicenza are more than just friends, and I didn't know what to do. I hadn't told my husband, so I wanted to come to you for counsel," she said to Signora Paola.

"What do you mean by more than just friends," asked Signora Paola.

"I don't know what to say, it's embarrassing, but we thought that, perhaps, they are lovers," Constanza said as tears formed.

"And you Vicenza," said Signora Paola looking at her. "What do you want to tell me."

"I want to tell you that it's true, that we are more than friends, and I also want you to know that my husband knew it and always blessed our relationship."

The silence in the room was absolute, and only the Rodella longcase clock in the hallway next to the kitchen could be heard.

"Well," said Signora Paola. "There are two things that I know for sure. The first is that my son loved women," she smiled. "In his charming way, he used to blame me by saying that his love for me made him chase any skirt he saw. I'm sure this is not a surprise to anyone inside this room."

Signora Paola then looked at Vicenza. "Sorry, my son was a

great man, but he was not perfect." She paused. "The second thing that I know for sure is that my son loved, respected, and was always grateful to Vincenza. And by the way," she said, looking at Vicenza. "He also used to blame you for his love of women, saying that you never disappointed him."

Vicenza and Eileen relaxed. All others had their eyes fixed on Signora Paola, who continued. "Now my Pippo is dead, and life moves on. I'm sure that our Vincenza would honor his memory, and I'm thankful for that, but it's up to her to decide her future, and I respect her and support her decisions."

Everybody was astonished, and nobody dared say a word. Adriana was no longer crying, Constanza was visibly shocked, and Adelaide could not hide her fury.

They talked a little bit further, and among other things, Vicenza mentioned her intention to travel to Caltanissetta. "Don Curcio was a close friend of Pippo, and I want to visit him before the Commissione meets."

When they left Signora Paola's house, Eileen asked, "Has your mother-in-law always been such an open-minded woman?"

"No way, she is not. I was so surprised, and I could only think of one possible explanation, but it is not up to us to second guess her, and I prefer not to talk about it now. Our local storm is over, but that's only part of our problems; let's keep focused on our Odyssey and get to Ithaca as soon as possible."

. . .

The following morning, Vicenza left for Caltannisseta, and Eileen with her.

"Let's see when can we have the Commissione meeting?" Vicenza asked Carlo before traveling. "It's in everyone's interest to do it as soon as possible. If we can do it during the weekend, even better. If not, I will go to *Catania* to meet Don Palutto and show Caltagirone to Eileen. But meeting him is not essential. After talking to Don Curcio, I will be ready to meet all capos."

Jimmy was in a terrible mood. Vicenza suggested that eventually, the additional car of Don Rini was not necessary, but Jimmy did not even discuss it. He even switched places with one of the bodyguards. "Today, I will go with the ladies," he said.

Eileen got worried and asked, "Are you concerned with our trip?"

"Too many people are talking about Miss Vicenza, and I don't like it. Let's be very careful."

Vicenza smiled and whispered to Eileen, "As Pippo used to say, 'On security matters, Jimmy's judgments are unquestionable.' Who are we to disagree?"

They were already driving when Vicenza received a phone call from Carlo. "The meeting will be next week. You can go to *Catania* and enjoy the weekend, but please be back Sunday night."

"Do you see?" said Vicenza teasing Jimmy. "Everything is fine, and we can have a nice weekend for us."

Jimmy grumbled a few words that nobody understood.

An hour later, when they were close to Caltanissetta, Vicenza received a second phone call.

"Vicenza, here is Nino from Marsala. Be careful. I don't know where you are, but my people heard something big would happen in Caltanissetta. Wherever you are, look for a safe hideout."

Jimmy immediately told the driver, "Turn as soon as you can. We are going back to Castelvetrano and speed up." Through the radio, he passed the information to the other car. "Change of plans. We are going back to Castelvetrano."

Eileen and Vicenza started to anxiously look through the windows to see if another car was chasing them, and Jimmy unlocked the automatic weapon.

A few minutes later, Jimmy changed his mind and told the driver, "Stop at the next gas station."

Jimmy and the bodyguards left their vehicles, spoke, and Jimmy returned to Vicenza's car and asked the driver to step out. "I will drive now, and you stay here." Jimmy took off at high speed.

Vicenza looked through the rear window and saw some discussion near Don Rini's car, and Jimmy explained. "I asked our man to hold them there and tell Don Rini and Don Carlo that I will be the only one responsible for your safety. There is something quite wrong going on."

As soon as he could, Jimmy left the highway and continued on a secondary road.

"We need to change cars," said Jimmy. "This one has a tracker, and people who work with Don Carlo would know where we are."

"Don't you trust them?" asked Vicenza, surprised.

"I trust them, but there is something wrong, and until I figure it out, let's be extra cautious."

They entered Canicatti, a city where Vicenza had never been to. "First we need to buy some clothes. Do not use credit cards, and give me all the cash you have. Let's not spend much. I don't know how long we will be on the run, and we will need cash for food. All you need to buy is a pair of sandals and a common dress. Buy a scarf to cover your hair. And see if you can remove the makeup you're wearing. I want you to look as simple as possible."

He drove to a nearby discount store, and once the woman returned with their dresses Jimmy told them to get changed in the van and then leave everything there. "And I mean everything. With all these new technologies, they can hide trackers anywhere. Let's take off the cell phone chips, and don't worry, we will get everything back. Don Carlo's people will come to pick up the van."

"I have the other cell phone for those special communications," Vincenza said.

"Give it to me," said Jimmy, and Eileen didn't understand.

They left the car parked on a secondary street, walked to a nearby grocery store. "I will meet you here in half an hour. Please buy enough cheese, bread, and wine for at least one night.

"What is he going to do?" Eileen asked as Jimmy walked off.

"Most likely steal a car," answered Vicenza with a casual expression.

Twenty minutes later, Jimmy came back driving an old and partially wrecked car. "The older it is, the less attention will attract," he said.

They left *Canicatti* driving as fast as they could through provincial roads.

Vicenza asked, "Are we going back to Castelvetrano?"

"No. My instructions are to take you to a safe place until we figure out what is happening."

They drove in silence for more than an hour until Eileen recognized on the signs a name she had heard before. Raffadali. "Signora Paola has a house here," Vincenza said. "Do you know where her house is, Jimmy?"

"Yes."

They passed the city, took a small rural road, and reached an abandoned house, far away from everything. The door was unlocked, and inside there was only a table, a few chairs, with two bedrooms containing only mattresses. Eileen opened the closet in the main room and found a few things: salt, sugar, coffee, olive oil, a pack of pasta, and candles.

"It seems the last one to use this hideout was nice enough to leave behind something for us," said Jimmy.

"Did you call Carlo," asked Vicenza.

"No. He told me not to call anyone."

"Does he know where we are?" asked Vicenza.

"Yes," replied Jimmy.

Eileen didn't understand whom they were talking about, but she chose not to ask. She was confused and overwhelmed and decided to leave for a walk around the house. Everything outside was quiet and isolated.

After a few minutes, Vicenza followed her.

"I know it's too much," Vicenza said, approaching Eileen from behind. "I'm feeling drained too. That's not the life I wanted to share with you."

"It's not your fault," replied Eileen. "It was my choice to be with you, and I do not regret it. I'm just confused and scared, but I have no remorse. When my mother died, my husband left me, and my kids told me they wanted to live by themselves. I was alone without friends. Now it's clear to me that moving to Clairsville was an attempt to have a new life, but I couldn't do it until I met you, and for the first time I have someone and something to look forward to. Someone to share my life with." She embraced Vicenza. "Whatever I have to confront, I will do it. I will overcome my fears, and as I bring my life close to yours, I hope you will bring yours to mine too."

When they got back into the house, Jimmy was near the table tampering with a few weapons. "I believe we are safe here, but we never know. I will keep the m-16. I will give my pistol, the Glock, to Miss Vicenza, and the small one that I keep concealed in my leg to Miss Eileen. It's a Beretta Tomcat 3032, weighs just a pound, and is very easy to handle. It looks harmless, but has seven rounds. Did you ever shoot a gun before?" he asked.

"My father was a hunter, and I killed my first deer in Iowa when I was nine," Eileen said. "I also shoot pistols in the shooting range, mostly a Beretta 92, my father's favorite pistol."

"So, you will not have problems. The Tomcat is the same as a 92, only smaller."

They ate, rested a little, and later when it was dark, a car parked in front of the house.

Vicenza went to the window and saw a man walking towards the door. She looked at Eileen and said, smiling, "Our secret ends here. Now you will know what I was hiding from you."

The door opened, and Pippo entered.

34.

"**Wise and alive.** I knew it, I knew it, I knew it," said Eileen. "But I never dared to ask. Vicenza was so downhearted when you died. You did everything so well that I started to believe you were really dead."

"Eileen, we owe you a lot of explanations," said Pippo." But now there is something much more important to do." Looking at Vicenza he asked. "What in the hell is going on? After you met with DIA, I thought everything was fine."

"It was not," said Jimmy. "I felt that there was something wrong."

"How could you know," asked Vicenza.

"Instinct," replied Jimmy. "Don't ask me how, but I've been feeling it since yesterday."

"And what exactly happened with you today," asked Pippo.

"I received a phone call from Nino, and we aborted the trip. We ditched the van we were in, changed clothes, and left behind the bodyguards assigned to protect us. Jimmy brought us here to hide. He was edgy and suspicious the whole morning."

"Yes," Jimmy said. "Too many people, in too many places talking about Miss Vicenza. That is not good."

"Let's calm down," said Vicenza. "We don't even know if there was a real threat."

"There was," assured Pippo. "I talked to Carlo, and he confirmed. Some agents and a few vans were waiting for you near Don Curcio's villa, but when Don Curcio's guards approached them, they left, and that's all we know."

"Does it mean that Carlo knows where we are?" asked Jimmy, worried that he had not called his new boss.

"He knows, but I told him that you guys drove to Piazza Armerina. He already knows that they found your van in Canicatti, and he is sending some guys to retrieve it, but let's not tell anyone where we are. We need time to figure out many things, and the first is to get Eileen out of Sicily."

"Why?" Eileen protested.

"First, I must explain everything to her," said Vicenza looking at Pippo, "Meanwhile, please, eat a little food we have, and drink a good glass of wine."

Vicenza started. "Pippo wanted to change his life, and the families would never let him go. He had to die, and that was the only way out. But it had to be perfectly done and in total secrecy. Only Jimmy and I knew it. It was sad to burn *Marinella*, but we did it, and we did it flawlessly. The FBI and Don Rini's guys thoroughly investigated, and they could not find anything wrong. Pippo was officially dead, but this was only the beginning. We knew their attention would turn to me, and we had to be very careful."

"And nobody else knows it," asked Eileen.

"My brother Carlo knew," said Pippo.

"And your mother," interrupted Vicenza.

"Yes, I told my mother. I met her in Agrigento the same day you talked with Don Rini."

"I knew it," said Vicenza. "The way she reacted when Constanza told her that Eileen and I were lovers was a clear sign that she had talked to you."

"I always trusted her, and I felt bad that she thought I was dead," said Pippo. "And by the way, if we have a place to sleep tonight is thanks to her."

"Do you know that your mom let Saveria Provenzano hide in this house when the cops were chasing her?" said Vicenza with a smile. "Saveria told me?"

"I didn't know, but I trust she did it. For my mom, widows always come first, no matter which side of the battle they are, and, tell me, how was your meeting with Ninetta?"

"Could you please stop with this chitchat and keep explaining to me what is going on," said Eileen angrily.

"Ok, but the rest, you know. I'm going to meet the Commissione, and after that, we will live our lives," said Vicenza.

"And the special friend that you met at Ortigia was Pippo?" Eileen asked.

"You are right," said Vicenza.

"And the letter I gave you in *Castelvetrano* was from Pippo too?"

"Again, you are right. The letter was a joke from Pippo, and he put Vizzini as an address, referring to the book *Conversazione in Sicilia*."

"Now the explanations are over, we must decide our next steps," interrupted Pippo. "I think the first one is to get Eileen out of Sicily. We are by ourselves, and we don't know people in Sicily anymore. We can't protect her here."

"No way," replied Eileen. "If Vicenza stays, I stay."

"Eileen," said Vicenza, "you must understand that it's not a game. If they came today for me, they might come for you too, and if anyone, friend or enemy, discovers that Pippo is alive, we are all screwed."

"I understand, but I'm not leaving. Done! Let's now try to understand what is going on, and the first question is, who was trying to ambush Vicenza today?"

"And how do they know that we were going to Caltanissetta?" added Jimmy.

"This was not a secret," answered Eileen. "We talked about that yesterday when we were at Signora Paola's house."

"Not a secret inside the family," said Jimmy, "but nobody outside was supposed to know it."

"Don Rini guys knew it," said Vicenza.

"Don Rini is our close ally," said Pippo. Why would he hurt Vicenza if she is the only one who knows the codes."

"It's not from within the families," said Jimmy. "Don Rini sent his men to protect Miss Vicenza. Nino is the one who discovered the ambush, and even Don Petruzzello yesterday was offering people to protect her. We don't know who they are, but we know that someone told them about Caltanissetta, which is very strange. Even Rini's guys and I were only informed about the trip this morning, and whoever prepared the ambush surely knew it since yesterday."

"Is it possible that someone inside your family is leaking the information," Eileen asked Pippo.

If you are asking me this, it's because you suspect someone is. Tell me, Miss Writer, who is our murderer?"

"Well, writers, look for murderers who nobody could guess. But the reality is that the real ones are usually the most obvious choice. And this leads us to the question. Who in the family wants to screw Vicenza? Who feels most threatened by her? Who disapproves of her most?"

"Don't tell me that you suspect Constanza," interrupted Vicenza.

"No, she would not have the guts for this, but what about Adelaide?"

"Please do not tell this to my mother," said Pippo, laughing.

"Why," asked Eileen.

"Because she hates Adelaide, and she always believed that she was infiltrated on our family by the Napolitan *Camorra* working together with the *Milieu*, a Marseillaise criminal organization."

"Maybe Signora Paola is right," said Eileen.

"Carlo already carefully checked. My brother Gino knows how many olives each of our trees could produce, but he is oblivious regarding what happens around him. It's true Adelaide had cousins in the Milieu, and some of them were in contact with the Camorra. We always knew it, but there was nothing concrete that we could suspect, and from what we know, she is not in contact with her family anymore."

"I don't trust her," said Jimmy, surprising Pippo.

"Why?"

"She is a *puttana*."

"Why are you saying that my sister-in-law is a whore?"

"Because I know," insisted Jimmy. "She is a puttana that loves to fuck those young gym-academy guys."

"Did you tell it to Carlo?"

"No."

"Why?"

"Because it's not my job to tell him whom your sister-in-law is fucking."

"Did it happen many times?" asked Pippo.

"I told you already," repeated Jimmy. "She is a fucking puttana! I heard people talking when I arrived and checked, and I even took some pictures of her with her boyfriend going into a hotel."

"And what about Carlo's wife?" asked Pippo.

"She is an honorable woman. *Un po sciocca, ma honesta.*" Vicenza laughed.

"What did he say?" asked Eileen.

"That she is honest but a little stupid."

"Wait. This gossiping could destroy my brother's marriage," admonished Pippo. with these

"I would not be worried about him," replied Jimmy. "He is an honorable man and enjoys screwing young *campesinas.*"

"Oh, I love that," interrupted Eileen, outraged. "She is a puttana because she fucks young guys, and he is an honorable man when he screws his workers."

"I understand," said Vicenza. "You are right, but that is not the point here. Adelaide might be a slut, Constanza is a little silly, and we can all live with this, but why would they do something to kill me?"

"She might not be trying to kill you," replied Eileen. "Adelaide has no idea about the key codes and doesn't know how vital you are for the families. She and Constanza are mad because you attracted Signora Paola's attention. You know women," Eileen added, smiling. "Sometimes, we don't need ulterior motives."

Pippo's cell phone rang. It was Carlo who said that the ambush was prepared by DIA and included drones. "They wanted to have pictures of Vicenza visiting Don Curcio, to prove that she is meeting with the capi. But I'm intrigued," Carlo added. "How did they know that Vicenza was going to Caltanissetta today?"

"There is a leak on our side," said Pippo. "Rini's guys and Jimmy were only informed about the trip this morning, and Don Curcio would not prepare an ambush in his own villa. You will have to recheck Adelaide's connections, and Jimmy will show you some pictures."

Carlo was surprised and furious.

"Okay," said Pippo after ending the call. "It was the DIA, and they have an informant inside the family. I doubt that Camorra or anyone else is involved. Eileen is probably right. Maybe it was an innocent leak. The good thing is that we know who our enemies are. Carlo will check Adelaide, and Vicenza should return to Castelvetrano."

"I agree, "Vicenza replied. "It's better to stay inside the compound until the meeting. Nobody will touch me there. And the sooner we go, the safer it is. Jimmy, would you drive us home now, or are you too tired?"

"I can, and travel by night will be safer."

They agreed to leave, and while walking to the car, Eileen asked Pippo, "Does Veronica know that you are alive?"

"Not yet. I rather have everything settled in Sicily before telling her, but we already contacted an older painter who will host her in Florence."

"Are you going back to Ortigia?" Vicenza asked. "How is work on the new boat coming along?" Realizing that Eileen would not understand, Vicenza explained. "Pippo found a twin sister of *Chiaro de Luna*, our old boat. It looks like *Marinella*, but it's smaller."

"It's beautiful, said Pippo, "but it was in terrible shape, and I am slowly bringing her back to life. She is in a boatyard, and they have already fixed the hull. All sails are already ordered, and the next step will be to finish the work inside the cabin. Once Vicenza transfers the codes and they give you a free pass out, I will tell Veronica, and the four of us will sail to celebrate."

"I don't think so," said Vicenza. "If DIA is following me, it's better that we don't see each other for a long time. And tell me one more thing, are you planning to have the whole boat varnished like *Marinella*?"

"No. Everything will be varnished inside the cabin, but I will have something more discreet outside. I don't want to attract people's attention, and please," Pippo said, looking to Jimmy, "before you return to the owner the car you stole, could you please fix it as a token of gratitude."

35.

The Commissione meets. The gathering was initially scheduled for Tuesday near Palermo, but Don Rini called Carlo and insisted. "It should be at your house. We know that DIA is trying to get your sister-in-law, and it's too risky to make her travel. It's better to have the meeting at your house and let's anticipate it for Monday. Very few people know about the codes, but who knows what can happen? I would prefer if she transferred them to us as soon as possible."

All other capos supported Don Rini's proposal, and Carlo accepted to host.

Sunday, his whole family worked frantically preparing the meeting. Gaetana came Saturday night from Agrigento, and Vicenza also called her sister Simona to help her. It would be the first meeting in the story of the *Cosa Nostra* attended by a woman, and all family should be involved to make it unforgettable.

The only one missing was Adelaide. She had to travel to Marseille, "Apparently an emergency in the family," explained Carlo, who was the last person to see her before she went to the airport. Not even Gino knew what had happened, and Constanza was so busy coordinating the work she could not pay attention when Carlo told her.

Later, Carlo explained to Vicenza. "I spoke with Adelaide, and I showed the pictures taken by Jimmy. She tried to deny it, but in the end, she gave up and confessed that she had met that man a few times. She swore that she didn't know he worked for the police."

"And how did you find out he was a cop?" asked Vicenza.

"I asked an expert to enlarge Jimmy's photos and take Adelaide out of them. We made copies and showed them around. The guy she was screwing works for DIA, and probably, in between fucks, she naively leaked information about our family. But I told her that I would not let her betray my brother anymore. She agreed to go back to Marseille, and we would tell Gino that her father is sick and her mother needs her. She will stay at least six months far from us. After that, she will decide: either she will come back and never, ever fuck anyone again, or she should stay in Marseille and divorces. I spoke to Gino and explained that she had to go. He didn't seem too upset. But I didn't tell him about her escapades. Let's give the two of them a chance."

The preparation was moving fast thanks to Constanza's coordination. She was on top of everything, from the parking to the wines, including the bathroom for the guards and many air coolers. The summer was just starting, but the temperature was very high. For each activity, there was someone responsible, but Constanza was in permanent contact with all of them, and the whole family was thrilled to help.

Vicenza was not sure about what to wear for the meeting. More than be elegant, she wanted to be appropriate, and she asked for *Signora* Paola's help. "We are not like those men who soberly dress. You are a woman, and we should find something that perfectly combines dignity, beauty, and power." The two of them spent hours trying on dresses inside Signora Paola's closet. Not even Eileen and Camilla were allowed to watch, and the result was astonishing. Vicenza was charmingly and adequately dressed in black and had a little violet bougainvillea from her own house gently tied on the left side of her chest. The show was on.

The first guest to get there was Don Palutto from Catania, who landed with his wife on a helicopter. After him, Don Curcio from Caltanissetta, arrived with his wife, daughters, and the son Pietro Curcio.

Fifteen minutes later, Don Rini proudly entered the compound with his daughter Signora Andrea, followed by Don Maltese and his wife from Trapani, and Don Petruzello from Corleone, who brought as part of his entourage Signora Ninetta and Signora Saveria. The two ladies were not part of the Commissione but special guests from Signora Paola, who hosted a parallel lunch for the women at her house. Later, Don Brancato, who, like Don Rini, was from *Palermo*, arrived with his son, Signore Guido, and, right after him, Don Galiano from Agrigento. The Commissione members assembled at the pergola where Constanza served granitas and brioches, and they all applauded when Don Carlos's bodyguards shot down two drones, probably belonging to DIA, trying to take aerial pictures of the gathering.

The last guests to arrive were Don Rugirello and Don Nino, who came together from Marsala. Don Rugirello was the representative of the families of that region, and Don Nino, a special guest of Don Carlo.

As soon as they were all there, they walked inside the house and sat around the dining room table, elegantly decorated for the meeting. There were fifteen chairs for fifteen honorable persons, and for the first time in history, three of them were women: Vicenza, Andrea, and Michaela.

The wives, daughters, and Signore Ninetta and Saveria went to Signora Paola's home to enjoy a Sicilian lunch with Busiate al Pesto and Gamberi Rosso. Other men, including sons and bodyguards, followed Gino and Onofrio to the soccer field inside the compound to play a game, the *Palermitani* against all others, and share beers, wine, and barbecue.

Despite all open windows and fans placed around the meeting table, it was hot, but not a single capo dared to consider taking off the jackets. The Commissione meeting always respected a traditional protocol on the form and the substance.

Don Carlo, the host, opened the meeting, thanking all for being there and explaining. "As you know, we agreed that our beloved friend

Signor Guido Brancato will now have the responsibility to replace my brother in managing our international financial operations. He will be supported on this challenging task by Signora Michaela Galliano and *Signor* Pietro Curcio, who are also here with us and will work under his command."

All members commended the choice, waving their hands, and Don Carlo continued. "At least for the next twelve months, this task will require Signor Guido's full attention. For this reason, he chose to take a one-year leave from the bank, and Signora Andrea Rini, who is also here with us, will be the new chairman." And again, all members commended and saluted Signora Andrea.

"I also have a pleasure to inform," continued Don Carlo, "that as one of her main responsibilities, Signora Andrea will help Don Curcio and Don Palutto open a new bank for the east coast of the island. With this new bank, our families will be delivering more financial services to all Sicilians, with the same efficiency that our construction companies do today." This time, in addition to the saluting, all capos applauded for a full minute.

Don Carlo took a sip of wine to wet his throat and continued. "I would also like to explain why I invited Don Nino, which I did, of course, with Don Rugirello's authorization."

Don Carlo continued. "Don Nino made a mistake that he deeply regrets. He already apologized personally to each of us, and recently he achieved something significant that he and Signora Vicenza want to share with us, and I will ask my sister-in-law to explain."

Vicenza was comfortable and confident and started by saying. "As you know, we all had in the last year some problems with the new director of the DIA, who most recently chose me as his favorite target."

All capo showed their solidarity and concern with her words, and Vicenza continued. "He is an arrogant man, determined to cause us problems. Some of you even saw him on TV, explaining that he is forced to travel to Calabria when he needs a rest since his life is in permanent danger here. Well, thanks to the information Don Nino gathered with his prostitution operations, we discovered the real reason the Directore feels more comfortable in Reggio Calabria."

Vicenza then used the remote control to show on the TV screens placed on both sides of the room some photos of the DIA Directore with a young woman.

"My husband used to say," continued Vicenza with a friendly and sarcastic look, "that every powerful man keeps a secret under the sheets."

All capos shook their heads with a smile, denying Vicenza's words, and Vicenza went on. "The Directore's secret is that he likes young women, and although he thought this young lady was eighteen years old, we know for sure she is only sixteen since her sister works on a Reggio Calabria nightclub controlled by Don Nino."

The capi rejoiced with the news, and Vicenza continued. "Now that we know his weakest spot, he is harmless, and instead of praying for him to be replaced, we should all do our best to keep him as our directore as long as we can."

All Commissione members applauded and congratulated Don Nino.

"Don Nino is young and is not afraid to risk new activities," Vicenza continued. "He is following an idea that was very fond to my husband, the hacking business. Hacking corporations and government agencies look like a profitable business, and we cannot let Russians, Koreans, or Chinese beat us on that," and she added. "My husband was one of the first to use cryptocurrencies when most people were scared. Thanks to it, your accountants will find out that the amount of money I am transferring back to you is larger than you expected.

"My husband got into cryptocurrencies very early, when they were underpriced. Now with a more volatile market, we reduced our exposure, but I can assure you that you will be happy with the numbers." And the capi enthusiastically applauded again.

Vicenza concluded by saying, "Now that I will transfer the codes to Signor Guido, I want to congratulate you, in my name and in my husband's name, who I'm sure would be as happy as I am to see women and young energy on the Commissione. It makes us comfortable that even without my Giuseppe, our families and the Cosa Nostra will have a bright future."

When they finished, Vicenza asked permission to leave the meeting. "My work is concluded, and I will join the other women."

Mission accomplished. And while she walked to Signora Paola's house, she saw the men yelling around the soccer field. The game was interrupted, and both sides were furious with the referee. That is how we will always be, she thought.

When she got inside Signora Paola's, she got the feeling that the main room was even noisier than the soccer field. Eileen was overwhelmed, trying to follow the conversation.

"They all speak at the same time, and what is even more amazing, they seem to understand everything."

The formality of the Commissione meeting was entirely absent among the women, and they were joyfully talking. As it was too hot to be outside, they brought chairs and squeezed them into Signora Paola's living room. When Vicenza sat, Signora Ninetta, who was in a charming mood, was standing up, making an impersonation of Silvio Berlusconi.

Later, Andrea Rini joined the women and sat next to Vicenza. "Everything went very well," she said. "And after you left, they agreed to make a deposit in your account that will allow you to live like a movie star, wherever in the world you chose."

In the evening, one after the other, the guests left. The soccer game ended with a victory for the Palermitani, fiercely questioned by all others. "Another game like this," commented Don Pazzuello's son with a good spirit, "and we will have a bloody war among our families."

Don Carlo's family gathered later at the pergola. Constanza was radiant with all compliments received, particularly when Signora Paola mentioned that her husband, Don Giacomo, if alive, would be proud of what Constanza did.

Vicenza told the others that soon she would leave Castelvetrano and that she and Eileen planned to drive through Italy to Venice. "It might take weeks or even months, and we don't care. We still must decide if we will go back to the US or where else we would like to live."

"You are always welcome here with us," said Signora Paola. "I'm proud of you, and I am surprised to say that Eileen seems to be a lovely woman. As you all know, I do not like foreigners because they do not seem to be able to understand us." And then she looked kindly to Eileen. "But it was a pleasure to have you with us, and one day, maybe, I might even like you," she teased.

36.

Finally in Venice. Eileen and Vicenza were walking at Campo Santa Margherita. The plan was to quickly buy vegetables at the grocery boat docked at San Barnaba. They had important things to do in the evening. It was windy, and they were walking with their colorful scarves waving in the air, green for Eileen and blue for Vicenza.

So many things happened since that first encounter, and Clairsville seemed to be a distant memory. They had traveled for ten weeks from Castelvetrano to Venice, visiting large cities but mostly enjoying little villages. No plans, no concerns. Just the two of them together doing what they wanted, whenever they wanted, and having the best days.

First, they drove to Messina, and from there to Calabria. They were in Troppea enjoying the beach when Carlo called them, saying that Guido Brancato and the accountants had accessed all accounts and confirmed there was more money than expected. All capos were informed, and they were extremely thankful to Vicenza and Pippo. They even asked Carlo to tell Vicenza that she will always be welcomed if she wanted to work for the Commissione again.

From there, they went to Cosenza and crossed the south of Italy to visit *Puglia*. Eileen was amazed that there was an acquaintance of a Vicenza's friend in almost every city waiting for them. The only problem was too much food, and Eileen insisted on a two-hour walk every day to compensate for the feast meals to which they were invited.

In Polignano a Mare, they decided to stay for an entire week; for the first time since she met Vicenza, Eileen wanted to write; her life seemed to be getting back on a more peaceful track.

After Polignano, they traveled within the Basilicata towards Napoli. Vicenza loved Pisticci, and Eileen was fascinated by Matera. It was there they received a phone call from Jimmy gushing with good news. He confirmed the bosses were happy and mentioned that Don Rimi even suggested to propose Vicenza's name for the permanent general consigliere position, but Carlo convinced him to wait until their Italian trip ended.

Jimmy also said he was moving to Palermo to become the chairman of a new security company. According to him, it was Don Carlo's idea. He convinced other bosses to invest in a joint venture that would provide security services to the Sicilian government and the banks. Jimmy would be a partner tasked with creating a department of cyber security, which would include a hacker group comprised of young Russians who were tired of San Petersburg winters and charmed by the Sicilian sun. Jimmy told Vicenza that one of his first meetings would be with the DIA's directore, who was now very friendly to the Commissione. He also confided, in absolute secrecy, that he had met Don Rini's young sister, who was a widow, and they seemed to like each other.

After leaving Napoli, they had to stay four nights in Sant'Agata de Gotti and then to Rome. While there, they met Eileen's younger son, returning from Greece with his girlfriend, a Chinese American born in San Francisco who was also studying at California Polytechnic in San Luis Obispo. For three days, they visited Roman ruins and museums together, and enjoyed cozy trattorias. Eileen felt so relaxed that she called her older son in Los Angeles, inviting him to join them in Firenze, where the two sons, together with Eileen and Vicenza, would be able to meet their father.

It was the *Ferragosto*, the summer peak, and Florence was crowded and shining under the summer sun. The meeting with her former husband was limited to a single dinner. He was bitter, his husband, the fashion designer, was jealous of Eileen, and there was absolutely no chemistry between him and the kids. To square up the trip, they met Veronica, who completely bewitched Eileen's sons.

Veronica couldn't stop smiling. She had just received a phone call from Pippo explaining everything that happened and inviting her to join him at Rimini, where he was sailing with his new boat. Veronica also said that Pippo was planning to live in Austria since, according to what he had explained to her, Austria would be a safer place for him. Pippo had bought a house on a lake in a city called Klagenfurt, which was only a two-hour drive from Trieste, Italy, where he would keep his boat.

After three days of visiting the Uffizi and other galleries, and having Eileen's sons continuously begging Vicenza to tell Mafia stories, Eileen's sons flew to Paris, Veronica went to Rimini, and Eileen and Vicenza drove around Tuscany for almost two weeks.

From there, they drove towards Venice. The idea was to meet Veronica and Pippo, who would sail there. On their way, while in Ferrara, Vicenza had two phone conversations. The first was with Miss Dillan, who called her asking if she should forward her the letters that Vicenza was receiving from her Sicilian friends. Vicenza told her that it would not be necessary because they had decided to return to Clairsville and live in Eileen's house. But first, they had rented an apartment for two weeks in Venice.

Vicenza also received a call from Pippo cautioning her. "I feel the DIA is still following us, and we have to be extra careful." Their visit together would have to be short and discreet.

"But at least, we will get see them on the boat, and maybe soon, maybe in Austria, we could get together," Vicenza said.

That morning they shopped at San Barnaba, had lunch, and took a water taxi. It was time for the meeting.

"We are going to Riva degli Schiavoni, but we are not going to stop," said Vicenza to the driver. We just want to see boats sailing there, and later you will bring us back."

They had agreed to meet before sunset, and the weather was precious; a slight breeze, a gorgeous sun, and Venice was splendidly shining under a blue sky.

"You know what I'm thinking?" said Vicenza while they were navigating under the Ponte de la Academia. "Hemingway's leopard that you once mentioned. Do you remember? The one who died, climbing higher and higher towards the top of the mountain. I feel lucky that instead of searching for an unattainable goal, we stopped to enjoy what we have. And I'm thankful to Pippo for that. He was brave to leave. And by leaving he freed me, too."

"It's a pity that we will not be able to talk to them," said Eileen. "Veronica proudly told me on the phone that she is now a sailor. They have been together on the boat for two weeks."

A few boats were sailing in front of the Duomo, but they knew they had no problem finding the white yawl with her two masts, and there it was; Pippo's boat sailing from west to east.

"Approach that, boat," said Vicenza to the driver, "but not too close. We just want to see them passing." And when they were getting closer, Vicenza added, "Please turn off the engine. I want to listen to their hull breaking the waves."

It was truly a copy of *Marinella*, more regal than any other boat sailing that afternoon in Venice.

Pippo and Veronica saw the water taxi but didn't realize Eileen and Vicenza were onboard. They passed, and Vicenza kept blissfully looking at their wake until Eileen called, "Why *Zina*?"

"What, *Zina*," said Vicenza coming back to reality.

"The boat's name is *Zina*."

Vicenza smiled and explained. "Once, there was a girl in Marinella di Selinunte, who everybody called Vincenzina. But her boyfriend wanted to make a point that she was a woman and not a girl and called her Zina."

"Are you telling me that Pippo named his new boat in your honor?"

"Get used to it, my friend," said Vicenza, teasing. "Not even ex-lovers can forget me."

Vicenza was ready to tell the driver to get closer to *Zina* when Eileen noticed another water taxi behind with a man on the deck taking pictures of Pippo's boat with a zoom lens.

"Wait," she said, grabbing Vicenza's arm, and they both looked at the photographer. The moment he lowered the camera they could see his face.

"It's Pezzini," they exclaimed at the same time.

"*Figlio di una puttana.* Nico lied to us. Pezzini is not dead and is taking pictures of Pippo and Veronica. *Semo fottuti!*" exclaimed Vicenza. "If anyone in Sicily sees those pictures, everything we achieved will fall apart, and they will kill us."

"Calm down Vicenza," said Eileen. "I know it's huge, but let's talk to him."

"To say what?" replied Vicenza. "What can we say? He knows that Pippo is alive and cheated all Sicilian bosses."

"We might offer him money. A lot of money. I don't know. We could threaten that Jimmy will kill him. There must be something that we can do!"

While they were talking, the water taxi with Pezzini changed his route towards the shore.

"He probably finished," said Vicenza. "Now he already has the photos he needs,"

"We don't know what he has," said Eileen. "Let's not panic and follow him."

Instead of taking the Grand Canal, Pezzini's water taxi navigated toward the east in the direction of one of the small canals. Il Canal del Arsenale, according to their driver.

"Follow him," said Eileen to the driver, determined.

It was already getting dark when Pezzini's boat docked near the Arsenale.

They docked not so far behind him. Pezzini was wearing a

photographer's jacket, shorts, and a large bag holding his camera.

"Perhaps, we can steal it?" said Eileen.

Vicenza was perplexed and blabbering. "If they see that Pippo is alive, they will also blame Carlo, and they will never forgive us. They will chase Pippo, us, and our whole family will be discredited. Can you imagine that? It's worse than hell."

"Let's follow him," said Eileen. "We must try to do something. This area has fewer tourists, and probably his hotel is here. Let's find out where he is staying."

Pezzini walked through a few alleys until he reached a narrow canal with a few docked boats and nobody around. Eileen and Vicenza tried to hide, but Pezzini saw them following him and stopped.

"Oh, you are also here," he said to Vicenza after recognizing her. "If I knew, I would have taken pictures of you with Mister Giuseppe and Miss Veronica."

"Why do you want those pictures?" asked Vicenza with a shivering voice.

Pezzini answered confidently. "I wanted to take them to *Marsala* and prove to those who wanted to kill me that Mr. Giuseppe is alive and that I am not the one who should die."

The canal was dark by the sunset and was maybe the most beautiful spot that Eileen had seen in Venice, but the only thing she could see was Vicenza and Pezzini talking near an old boat tied to the dock with some frayed ropes.

"When I sent the Russian ambassadors' pictures to the CIA, I was following Don Nico's instructions, but later, he changed his mind, became Don Carlo's friend, and chose to discard me. I'm only alive because the mother of the man he instructed to kill me told my mom out of compassion, and I ran away. That's how you bosses work. You play with us, your pawns, at your convenience, but now it's different. I am running the show."

Pezzini removed a pistol from his bag and pointed to Vicenza. "I don't know what you have in mind, Miss Vicenza, but don't dare threaten me. I have the photos, and I have a pistol. When I show these pictures I have in Sicily, even your killer Jimmy will be dead. I know what you did."

Eileen was behind him, listening motionless as Pezzini continued. "Many times, Jimmy and I drank together, imagining how we could help Mr. Giuseppe disappear. We knew that the bosses would never accept Miss Veronica, and Jimmy said that burning *Marinella* would make everyone believe the death was not fake. I knew Mr. Giuseppe was alive, but I had to prove it. I wanted to follow Jimmy, but it was impossible. Jimmy was in Sicily, and I couldn't stay there. The only alternative was to follow Miss Veronica.

"If Mr. Giuseppe were alive, he would certainly look for her, and I followed her in Florence, stole her cell phone, put a tracker on it, and returned the cell to her. She didn't know, and I waited. When she went to Rimini, and I saw her cell phone slowly moving north by the coast on my computer, I was sure that she was on a boat with him, so I came to Venice. I knew they would come here. I monitored her cell, but I could not find where the boat was anchored. I believe they were in Burano, but today I spotted them. I saw the boat with a binocular, and I paid the water taxi to take me closer to take the pictures."

"I can buy them," said Vicenza. "Tell me, how much do you want?"

"Why would I want your money?" Pezzini replied. "Without the photos, I would not be able to return to Marsala, and I would have to keep wandering around the world. That's not what I want. I dream every day with Marsala, and the photos will make me welcome there as a hero. Even Don Nico would have to recognize that he was wrong and embrace me as part of his family. No, Miss Vicenza, I don't want your money, and you cannot threaten me anymore because, with these photos, you will also be dead."

At that exact moment, Vicenza heard two shots, and Pezzini fell. Behind him, Eileen was standing up and looking at her with the little Beretta that Jimmy had given her.

Vicenza understood and quickly looked around. It was dark; just the canal, the empty walking bank, and a few boats anchored. She rapidly told Eileen, "Take his wallet, cell phone, and jewelry. I will take his bag." It didn't take a minute for Eileen to empty Pezzini's pockets. Vicenza took the pistol out of Eileen's hand, shot him one more time on the back of his head, and rolled the body to the water.

Nobody saw them running away, and they only stopped when they reached Piazza San Marco, which was full of tourists. "Now let's get rid of the pistol," Vicenza said after recovering her breath. When they began to walk again, she stopped looking at Eileen.

"*Sei pazza*! Do you understand that you had killed him?"

"Of course, I did. What else could we do?"